TRINITY: ASCENSION SAGA - BOOKS 1-3

INTERSTELLAR BRIDES® PROGRAM:
ASCENSION SAGA

GRACE GOODWIN

GET A FREE BOOK!

JOIN MY MAILING LIST TO BE THE FIRST TO KNOW OF NEW RELEASES, FREE BOOKS, SPECIAL PRICES AND OTHER AUTHOR GIVEAWAYS.

http://freescifiromance.com

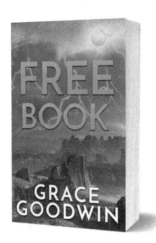

INTERSTELLAR BRIDES® PROGRAM

YOUR mate is out there. Take the test today and discover your perfect match. Are you ready for a sexy alien mate (or two)?

VOLUNTEER NOW!

interstellarbridesprogram.com

PREQUEL

Twenty-seven years ago Queen Celene was forced to flee Alera with her unborn child. Read the story of her escape to Earth in The Ascension Saga prequel — for free!

Click now to find out how the adventure began...
www.ascensionsaga.com

BOOK 1

1

Trinity Jones, Interstellar Brides Processing Center, Miami

"It's just like getting your ears pierced, my ass," my sister, Destiny, grumbled, her hand covering her neck where the NPU had just been inserted by the biggest needle I'd ever seen go into a conscious person. "That *hurt*."

She paced the room, as if the pain would go away by walking it off. Her shoulder-length purple hair swayed as she moved.

"Stop whining. I went first." I wasn't about to let my sisters see exactly how nervous I was. As the oldest, I had to keep my shit together. No matter how terrifying the last twenty-four hours had been, I had a feeling the next twenty-four were going to be far worse. "With all those tattoos up and down your spine"—the markings were elaborate, feminine, and very beautiful, but I'd never admit that to her—"you should be used to the tiny little poke of a needle."

Destiny rolled her eyes, still rubbing the area behind her ear. "That wasn't a normal needle. That's a knitting needle shooting tiny bullets into our brains."

Warden Egara, the official representative of the Coalition Fleet at the bride processing center, was from Earth herself, but didn't appear to have much of a sense of humor today. "The NPU doesn't go into your brain, ladies. The nanotech burrows into the temporal bone surrounding the cochlea and transmits modified sounds directly to the cochlear nerve. And you'll all be very thankful when you can understand anyone you come across." She was efficiency personified. Crisp uniform, sleek dark hair, easy-going, yet serious demeanor. And all that science talk? Not my thing, but Faith was nodding with a fascinated look on her face.

Science geek. Faith had been bringing hurt animals and even insects home since she could walk. For all that, she had a gentle spirit that neither Destiny nor I could claim. I liked order. The rule of law. Tradition. Faith never made plans. And Destiny? Well, my baby sister pretty much walked around beating up bullies and making sure shit got done. Together, we were strong. I just hoped we were strong enough to survive the next few weeks. Hell, years. We were going home to a planet none of us had ever seen. And we were hunting for enemies we didn't know.

The whole thing was a giant cluster-fuck, and I wished I'd listened to Mother two years ago when she suggested we return to Alera. But I'd been in law school. Too busy. Always too busy.

Now she was gone, and it was my fault.

"Stop being a baby or you'll scare Faith," I said. The injection *had* hurt, but since I'd gone first, I'd bit my lip and stifled my gasp at the sharp pain. Really, there should be a numbing solution, or some kind of drug for this.

"Just because I like to dress like a girl doesn't mean I'm not tougher than both of you." My middle sister, Faith, was eight minutes older than her twin. Both of them were almost three years younger than my twenty-seven. They were my half-sisters, but their human father wasn't the reason we were all here—getting ready to transport to another world sight unseen.

Faith took a deep breath, let it out, as Warden Egara prepared the wicked looking tool for her turn. It *was* like an ear-piercing gun, but with a needle meant for an amniocentesis or alien probing instead of adding studs to a little girl's earlobes at the local mall's jewelry kiosk.

"Don't faint. I'm in too much pain to catch you," Destiny taunted.

"Spare me the drama," Faith said to Destiny, who still held her hand over the spot where the NPU had been placed. As Warden Egara stepped closer, Faith swung her long, brown hair up over her opposite shoulder to bare the spot needed for the injection. "Mother taught us the Aleran language, Warden. I'm not sure why this is necessary."

The whistle of pressurized air moving through the needle made me wince right along with Faith as the NPU pierced her skin. "There are over two hundred and sixty worlds out there with thousands of languages. Most worlds are not like Earth; they are much more advanced and welcome travelers from other planets."

In other words, Earth was a primitive, unenlightened and unimportant place in the grand scheme of things. Mother had told us she wanted to hide on a planet so far removed from the politics and bullshit of the Interstellar Coalition that she'd chosen Earth for those very reasons. No one in almost thirty years had thought to look for her here. Until I'd screwed up and called Warden Egara a few days ago. Asked for some information on Alera and the ridiculous Aleran Ardor mother had insisted I was coming down with.

My body was going haywire and I got desperate. Stupid lack of discipline and a mistake I wouldn't make again. One stupid phone call, and they'd come for our mother within two days.

Mother. Shit. She was out there somewhere. The small

space ship that had been in our front yard gave me hope that she was still alive. They'd broken into our home in broad daylight while my sisters and I were at work. Dad had been asleep on the couch. And later, watching the surveillance video from our home security system, my sisters and I learned they'd pointed some kind of stun gun at him to keep him asleep. The aliens had landed, put the drop on Dad, shot Mother with some sort of light blast, and carried her unconscious body out to their ship.

She'd been limp when they took her. No blood that we could see on the video, but that didn't mean she was still alive.

In fact, if what Mother told us about the light of the sacred spires on Alera was true, I had a feeling whoever took her might *want* her dead.

Alera. The planet was one our mother had spoken of for as long as we could remember. But we all grew up just like normal kids. Dad had officially adopted me when I was two. Mother had married him and then had my twin sisters. We all went to school. Typical stuff like science fair projects, prom. Graduated. I went on to law school, like our dad. Faith was a biologist with a strange title working for the forest service. And Destiny? Well, Destiny was our battle specialist. We'd all been trained in basic martial arts from a young age, but for Destiny, fighting was like breathing. She loved it. And she was damn good at it. She managed a dojo and taught classes six days a week. She was so toned that watching her move was like watching a wild tiger, light on her feet but scary as hell.

Unless our house had been part of a sci-fi movie set we didn't know about, the Alerans had finally come for our mother. Bad guy Alerans. After years of listening to Mother talk about her home planet—*our* planet—I knew we were the good guys.

And now they had her. Why? I had no clue, but I wasn't going to sit on Earth and twiddle my thumbs. We were her daughters. We *had* to find her.

I knew what she'd say. I was heir apparent. It was my *duty* to go to Alera and take my rightful place. Period. No searching for her. No trying to save her. She'd scold us all and insist that the future of Alera was most important.

Yeah, no. Not to me. And not to my sisters.

Dad was staying here, on Earth, until we contacted him with news. The Alerans didn't know my sisters and I existed. I'd never understood Mother's insistence that we have no family photos on the walls, no school pictures. Our rooms had always looked like guest rooms. Pretty, but not personal. We didn't leave our clothes out. Or our shoes. There weren't toothbrushes or makeup on the counters in the bathroom.

Our house looked like a guest house. A vacation rental. Always.

I'd hated it growing up. Capital H. But now I understood. They'd taken her and hadn't even looked for anyone else. Had no idea she had children. Daughters.

Heirs.

But if she had been taken by Alerans, and we all agreed she had—me and my sisters, plus Warden Egara and even Prime Nial, the ruler of Prillon Prime and The Colony—we had to find her *on* Alera. Why would they stay on Earth? They knew nothing of the planet. Staying on Earth did them no good. Even if they killed her, they'd go back to Alera and reap their reward.

"Does this work on animals? Think of how amazing that would be. The symbiosis of the universe would be... complete," Faith said, angling her head to the side to give the warden better access so she could wipe the spot with some rubbing alcohol.

Destiny was still pacing, a bundle of raw nerves. "Symbiosis? Really? They could be torturing our mother right now and you're thinking about communing with animals? Do you imagine the bad guys even consider symbiosis? Hell, would they even know what it means?"

"No." Faith grinned, completely unrepentant. "But Trinity

certainly does." Faith glanced at me, her hand going to the side of her head. She'd switched into speaking Aleran. "With her super-sexy *Ardor* coming on, she'll want some serious *symbiosis* with a hot alien hunk as soon as we get to Alera."

I rolled my eyes as Destiny waggled her brows and grinned. "Oh, yeah. Hot, sweaty, symbiosis. Probably more than once."

"I can understand you," Warden Egara added. "And I've shared the details of Trinity's oncoming Aleran Ardor with Prime Nial—"

I groaned, blushing. I didn't need everyone in the universe to know my pussy was wet all the time and aching for a huge cock. That I was becoming a horny slut, eager for a male to take me for a wild ride. Earth guys wouldn't do. I'd tried that. Ten minutes of making out like high schoolers and my poor date had collapsed, unconscious, on his couch. I was like a freaking sexual vampire. Afraid I'd killed him, I stayed for a bit just watching him breathe. That had scared the hell out of me and I'd called the Interstellar Brides processing center first thing the next morning.

And given away mother's location. Got her kidnapped. Tortured. Shit, maybe dead.

"Don't, Trin. I can see it all over your face. This isn't your fault." Faith shook her head, giving me her very best motherly impression.

"It kinda is, Faith."

"Bullshit, Trin. Biology. That's all this is. Maybe we should just get you taken care of here. There's got to be a few hunky aliens around who wouldn't mind a quickie."

"I don't need a quickie. Thanks though." No. Nothing quick would do. I needed a big Aleran male to shove me up against the wall and do me. Hard. *Really hard.* For *hours.*

God, I clenched my inner walls, aching and eager to be filled. This mating urge was getting out of control, but I clenched my teeth—and other places—and ignored it. *Again.*

"—and Prime Nial has assured me he will have an official

Aleran consort waiting for you in the transport center," the warden continued. "I don't know much about Alera, but I've been assured your Ardor will be soothed by the consort." She offered me a small smile.

"You're kidding," Destiny said, looking at me. "Did you know about this? It sounds like a male prostitute."

Warden Egara shook her head. "More like an escort, although there really isn't an equivalent on Earth."

I was sure they could hear my sigh in the next room. "Yes. Mother told me. They are very rare and extremely expensive." Having sex immediately upon arrival with a complete stranger? Not my thing, but my body was telling me otherwise. I was so amped up, I wasn't going to have a choice.

"Hey, wait," Destiny said, holding up her hand, the big needle all but forgotten. "You're speaking Aleran, Warden. How can you do that? How can you understand us? I mean, you're from Earth. You're *on* Earth."

Warden Egara turned and put the NPU gun away. "I was tested as a bride, given an NPU and matched to Prillon Prime. I had two mates who died in the war. When I chose not to mate again, I came back to Earth to help new brides find their mates." She turned around, glanced at each of us, put her fingers to the spot behind her ear. "And you three? I admit, you're definitely a surprise."

"I'm sorry." Always the peacemaker, but I had to say it. How sad. Two mates who died must be devastating for her.

Her smile was resigned. "It was a long time ago. And now, you three need to get moving."

"Yeah, a secret Aleran princess, hiding away on Earth, waiting to ascend the throne," Faith replied, noticing the way the warden had switched topics and clearly didn't want pity or additional conversation about her dead mates. "Trin, your life is like a romance movie."

"Except Mother's been taken and I can't control my own freaking body," I countered. "It's more like an action-adventure-horror." My stomach twisted, remembering the way the blood had drained from my head when we watched the surveillance video, heard her scream of rage right before they'd shot her. Her instant collapse onto the kitchen floor. The way she'd slumped like a wet spaghetti noodle.

She'd hit her head on the corner of the cabinet on her way down. And I didn't know if it was the twisted version of heat I was in or just my natural rage, but someone was going to pay for that. I wasn't normally violent, but I had my moments. And this Aleran Ardor was not only inconvenient, it was flat out pissing me off. *Forced* to fuck or go insane?

What kind of messed up biology did these stupid aliens have, anyway?

"Prime Nial won't be there to meet you himself as he's on Prillon, three sectors away from Alera, but he will have a contingent of guards as well as the Aleran consort waiting to greet you."

"It's hard to think about this Ardor thing when my mother's missing," I said. I rubbed my hands on my jeans, realized I'd thrown clothes on this morning and hadn't even brushed my hair in our mad dash to get to the Brides center. There was no way a consort was going to want to get it on with me looking like this. I tugged at the hem of my t-shirt and realized it was inside out. *Fuck.*

"Your Ardor started a few weeks ago. It was coming on whether Mom was taken or not," Destiny replied. "Just think, if you'd been on Alera, this *heat* thing wouldn't have been delayed until you were twenty-flipping-seven." She waved her hand around in reference to the *heat* thing. It was easy for her to be blasé about it since she hadn't come into her Ardor. She didn't have a complete stranger waiting to fuck her brains out so she could *stop going crazy.* "I mean, if it had come on when you were twenty-two, like mother said it should, then you wouldn't have slept with Aiden Dugen."

Aiden Dugen. I had to laugh. Hindsight was definitely

twenty-twenty. My college boyfriend should have been avoided. As for his cock, yeah, he would never be mistaken for a hot alien hunk. Hell, a *hunky* anything.

"Yeah, but that hot Atlan at the gate is probably hung like a horse," Faith added, fanning herself with her hand. "If I'd known the aliens were that hot, I might have volunteered to be an Interstellar Bride."

"If we stay on Alera, you'll end up married to an alien," Destiny said. "I think that qualifies."

"Well, being only half Aleran, we don't know if you two are going to have to deal with this stupid Ardor. I hope you don't. I almost killed my coworker last week just *kissing* him," I reminded them.

"That Atlan at the gate can go beast," the warden added. "While that might sound hot and sexy, I can't allow you to mindlessly seduce an honorable warrior and then head off to Alera. He'll demand much more than you want to give. He's not just a big cock to ride. You'd get mating cuffs and a hulking beast obsessed with you for the rest of your life. Not fair to either one of you if you just need that Ardor eased."

I stared at the warden for a second, totally surprised she'd used the phrase *big cock to ride* in a sentence. And *mindlessly seduce an honorable warrior?* "I would never be that dishonest, with any male. Alien or not."

"Good." The warden's brows were up and her lips were tight. Clearly, she had not appreciated Faith's joke.

"Yeah, talk about bossy. That Atlan looked like a total alpha male. Probably *way* too bossy," Faith added with a sigh that sounded suspiciously like longing. She tucked her dark hair behind her ear, then gave a little wince when she bumped the NPU injection site. "Even with a big cock to ride."

She glanced to Warden Egara, who smiled in return.

"I'm not going to have a quickie with the Atlan guard just because my girl parts are craving what he's got in his pants," I said on a little laugh, squirming as I thought of *exactly* what he had in those uniform pants. The bulge couldn't have been missed by any woman within thirty feet.

"Fine. The Aleran consort then. While you're getting it on with Mr. Studly, we'll do some investigating." Destiny swung her arm over Faith's shoulders and they both nodded.

"Right," Faith added with a grin. "I don't want to listen to your screams of pleasure. I might get jealous."

I had no intention of going off with an Aleran version of a gigolo who was paid to give me a bunch of orgasms—all while my sisters searched for our mother. That was ridiculous. I'd been horny and eager for sex for weeks. I'd just... ignore it. Like I had been. Or I could just make myself come. It wasn't like I didn't have a vibrator in my bedside table. There had to be a place to pick one up on Alera, along with a whole bunch of batteries.

Taking matters into my own hands had helped... for a while. Lately, it would take the edge off, but seemed to only make my need, my craving, grow worse.

"Warden." A woman in a matching gray and burgundy uniform to Warden Egara's came into the room. "Coordinates are set for Alera; the transport room is ready."

I glanced at my sisters. This was it. We were leaving Earth and going into outer space. To *another planet.*

Oh my god. It was one thing to have my mother talk about Alera. To speak Aleran. We'd used it as our secret language at school and no one knew a thing we were saying. Everything our mother had told us had all seemed like just stories. A game. Fun.

But now it was real. Really, *really* real.

"Holy shit," Destiny said.

"Yeah, holy shit," Faith added as we followed Warden Egara down a long hallway.

The transport room was similar to a *Star Trek* episode. A woman in uniform stood behind a table covered in various controls. Before her was a raised dais with steps leading up to it. Nothing else was in the room.

There was a hum in the air, a vibration beneath our feet. I looked down at my old sneakers, Faith's sandals and Destiny's black shit-kicking boots. I wondered if I should bother fixing my inside-out shirt.

Shit. Why bother? According to Warden Egara, the second we got there some alien *consort* was just going to strip me out of my clothes anyway. Ugh. Just... shit. I knew I couldn't say no and stay sane. Hell, I was pretty damn sure I wouldn't want to.

Destiny took my hand. Faith, the other. We looked to each other, then climbed the steps, turned around.

We were on the transport pad, the portal to another planet. To *Alera*.

"Good luck on your search for your mother," Warden Egara said. She stood tall, hands folded in front of her, and didn't speak about our heritage, or the fact that our mother was the queen. There were only two people who knew the truth—the warden and Prime Nial. And that's the way we intended to keep it. At least for now. "Please, be safe and let me know how things go. I will be rooting for you."

"Thank you," I replied, my sisters nodding.

She looked to the transport tech person and nodded. The hum got louder, the vibrations intensifying. The hair on the back of my neck stood on end. I felt the tight squeeze of my sisters' hands in mine. We were doing this. Together. Now. We would find our mother... alive, and beat the crap out of those who'd taken her. Make things right. Put Queen Celene back where she belonged, on the throne of Alera.

The Jones sisters were headed to Alera. Those alien kidnappers had no idea what they were in for.

"Your transport will begin in three, two, one..."

The warden's voice faded. Piercing cold felt like a thousand frozen needles pressing into my flesh. My last thought was that the NPU injection hadn't been that bad after all.

aptain Leoron Turaya, Planet Alera, Outskirts of the Capital City of Mytikas

THE SKY WAS black but for the stars as I stood watch on the outermost tower protecting the capital. No moonlight tonight, the darkness feeling like an omen.

"It's late, Captain. The watch is mine now." Gadiel was young, barely out of training, but he stood at attention ready to assume my position on watch. His gaze was full of honor and excitement, a look I well-remembered seeing in the mirror. That was before I joined the Coalition Fleet and spent nearly a decade fighting a horror worse than any I could have imagined. I'd seen the Hive, knew what they would do if they ever reached the peaceful planets within the protective arms of the Interstellar Coalition's Fleet of battleships.

After ten years, my father had called me home. I could continue to serve on Alera, he argued. I would have fought for ten more, but my parents still hoped I would awaken to a woman's Ardor, that I would choose a mate—or my cock would —and give them grandchildren to spoil.

I'd met countless women in my lifetime, all across the galaxy, and nothing had stirred within me. My body remained mine alone. And to be perfectly honest, I did not hold much interest in changing that. To be so obsessed with a single female? I'd seen mighty Aleran warriors fall, become nothing more than besotted fools. All because their cocks rose—finally —for The One. To be led around by the balls by a female was not what I desired. To be driven by something other than the honor to defend my planet? No, thank you.

I would remain a soldier, a guard, a fighter for life. An Aleran bachelor. Unaffected by the whims of a female.

"Sir?" Gadiel shifted uncomfortably, and I realized I had been staring into the distance, at nothing. No. Not nothing. The spire. That damn queen's spire and how it glowed bright, the only thing illuminating the darkness.

"Very well," I replied, turning to him. "May the light keep you."

"And you as well."

I nodded in acceptance of his words and left him to attend his duties. The city was at peace, at the moment. The last incursion by an outlying family had ended in bloodshed just weeks before. The tenuous peace would not last. The royal bloodline was weak, with no living members strong enough to carry one of the gifts. Ever since the queen's disappearance over two decades ago, the capital had been under consistent attack by one grasping family after another. These families believed their wealth and armies would grant them the loyalty of the people.

They were wrong. So long as the queen's spire burned bright, the royal guard would defend her throne so that one day she might return to reclaim her place among her people. I had lost hope, for I barely remembered a time before she disappeared, but I would fight until the light of the spire died. When that happened, I would fight for the people in my city, choose a family to rule I found worthy. The battles would be bloody, but currently three families held the wealth and power to potentially ascend to the throne. The day the light of the spire went out would be the first day of a very long, very brutal war.

The tower stairs were dark, but I had no trouble seeing my way as I paced through the shadows. There was no need to count the twisting steps, for I'd been this way hundreds of times since my return from space, from the Hive wars.

It seemed my entire life would be dedicated to battle and blood.

So be it. Gods, I was a broody fucker. I needed an Aleran ale, an hour with the hottest setting on my shower tube and my bed. In that order.

Exiting the base of the watchtower, I slowed my pace, in no hurry to return to my quarters. Below me, surrounded by the twisting alleyways and dense tapestry of stone homes, the royal citadel glowed in the center of the city. The strange tower had been there longer than our people had kept records, built by an ancient race of space explorers who left our primitive planet with two gifts—the citadel itself and those who carried their alien bloodline.

The citadel was both a beacon of hope to all of Alera and a bitter reminder that our people had been abandoned when I was a child. I barely remembered the day the king was found dead, the queen missing. My father, now a retired captain of the city guard, still clung to his faith that the royal bloodline lived on, that his beloved queen would return to free us from the chaos of endless civil conflict.

The light shined, so Queen Celene was alive.

But where?

And why had she yet to return?

The younger generation had given up hope. War was coming, no matter how valiantly the clerics fought to keep the peace. I wanted no part in it. The rich fools would fight over something they could never hold. There would be no ascension ceremony, no new queen, not while the light of the spire shined over Mytikas. Queen Celene's city.

As if the thought had garnered the attention of Fate herself, the NPU implanted behind my ear buzzed with an incoming message.

"Prime Nial of Prillon Prime." The voice ringing in my ear was clipped and professional, not asking permission to send the communication through so much as warning me that the comm was coming.

I stilled. "Prime Nial?"

The night was not cold, but a shiver of dread raced over my skin as I waited for the most powerful male in the galaxy to talk to me. Gods, why was he calling me? Now?

Prime Nial ruled not just Prillon Prime, but the entire Interstellar Coalition and its fleet of warships. The Coalition military, made up of at least two hundred fifty planets, was his to command in our war with the Hive.

Epic responsibility and power, and he was wishing to speak with me.

I owed him a life debt. My blood turned to ice in my veins. What was so wrong that he would need to call in that mark? What did he need, a man with so much power? How could he need the assistance of a lowly soldier? I was nothing more than a pawn on Alera. In the grand scheme, I was as small as an insect.

"Prime Nial? This is Captain Leoron Turaya. How may I assist you?" My voice cut through the night.

"Leo? Can you hear me?" The Prime's voice was deeper than I remembered, and the faint sound of a female in the background drifted to me across the vast expanse of space.

"Tell him to hurry. I don't trust those people," she said. Didn't trust who? What was going on?

"Yes, sir. What can I do for you?" How the hell was he placing a direct call to my NPU? The neural processing unit was standard issue for everyone in the Coalition Fleet, and most diplomats from the individual planets chose to have them inserted as well. Universal translators, they made communication across all the races easy, but I'd had no idea the Fleet could transmit directly to me from halfway across the galaxy. From the ground to a ship? Yes. But from Prillon Prime into my skull?

"I have a very important, extremely delicate task for you, Leo. Are you alone?"

I spun in a slow circle, checking my surroundings. I was on the side of a mountain in the middle of the night at the base of a watchtower. Every sane person on this side of the planet was asleep right now. Besides Gadiel far above me, but he was too distant to overhear. "Yes, Prime Nial. I am completely alone. How may I be of service?"

He cleared his throat and I clenched my teeth. I knew Nial well from my fighting days. He'd saved my life, and I'd sworn to answer his call if he needed me. "Don't call me Prime, Leo."

I couldn't help the way the corner of my mouth tipped up. He might be Prime, but he always said he was just a Prillon warrior saving the Coalition from the Hive, just like any other.

"Fine, *Nial*," I replied, ensuring deference could still be heard. "I have not forgotten the life debt I owe. Ask for anything. It will be yours."

His sigh made my head hurt. "I am transporting three women to Mytikas within the hour. I'm sending you the location of the specific transport station now."

The coordinates were recited in my ear by the transport computer and I recognized the location. "That's on the opposite side of the city."

"Can you arrive in time?"

I looked out over the quiet city streets. Mytikas was a sprawling metropolis that filled the valley between two mountain ranges. "Yes. It will be close, but I can be there in an hour." I'd need to run down the mountain and break a few laws when I reached my EMV, but the vehicle was fast. I'd make it.

"Thank the gods." I could hear the relief in his voice.

"He can get there? They're going to need help. And I don't like the idea of them transporting to a strange planet without someone there we trust." The woman's voice was louder now, and soft, but not tender. Hers was a voice accustomed to giving orders.

"Yes, love," Nial said. "Leo will be able to meet them." *That* tone was one I'd never heard from him before, and I almost didn't recognize his voice. He sounded... gentle. Which, when I thought of the giant Prillon warrior, was not a word I had ever associated with him before.

"Thank god," the female continued. "Especially with Trinity's little *problem.*"

"Congratulations on your mating, Nial," I said. He'd called her *love,* which let me know exactly who the new Prime was talking to. Lady Jessica Deston, his mate. I assumed his second was nearby. And what problem?

"Thank you," he replied. "How did you hear the news? Alera is far from Prillon Prime."

I laughed, the sound bursting out of me. "Everyone in the galaxy heard about it, you lucky bastard. If you didn't want everyone to know, you and Ander shouldn't have claimed the beautiful lady in the fighting arena during a live, interplanetary broadcast." I'd watched the entire event of the two Prillon males claiming their female. Sacred and erotic, there was no doubt Jessica belonged to Nial and Ander. I was happy for my friend, but had felt nothing as I watched the ceremony. The female he'd been matched to via the Interstellar Brides Program, a woman from Earth, was striking, and very responsive to her mates as they'd claimed her. I'd been pleased that Nial had found happiness, but my body remained as it had always been, dormant.

While a Prillon was connected to his mate and his second by collars that shared feelings, emotions and even sensations, an Aleran male had no such connection. Finding a mate was not easy, especially when an awakening only occurred for The One. And *only* for her. My cock would not rise until she was before me. Oh, I could feel a shadow of desire, stroke my length in anticipation of sinking into my mate's tight pussy, but there would be no completion, no satisfaction, until I was buried deep between her thighs. Only then would I come for the first time.

I knew how to fuck a female—in theory—I just hadn't done it yet. Besides witnessing other claiming ceremonies like Prime Nial's, all males on Alera had attended classes for such things. For while it might take decades for our cocks to awaken to The One, it was crucial we could satisfy our female when the time came. Once a cock was awakened, it would rule a male, drive him to fuck his mate hard and often. Failing to bring a mate her pleasure was a great dishonor, and every male's greatest fear.

Until my body awakened, I was solely a vessel for work, not pleasure.

"Yes," Nial replied. "Well, how could I resist?" His own laughter made me smile, his obvious happiness with his mate coming through loud and clear. Being Prillon, he wouldn't have had a dormant cock like an unmated Aleran male, but I had no doubt the first sight of his matched mate had made his cock rise and, most likely, had yet to go down.

"Not to distract, Nial, but who is Trinity? And what problem?"

"Yes. That." He cleared his throat. "As I said, I am sending three women to Alera. They are to be protected with your life. Do you understand? Every resource you can bring to bear, every friend, every weapon and loyalty you owe me is to be given to these females from Earth. They must be guarded at all costs."

My mind raced. Women from Earth? Coming to Alera? With Prime Nial's personal protection?

"It will be my honor," I told him. "I give you my word. But I don't understand. Who are they? And why are females from Earth coming here?"

Earth was a primitive planet, not yet a full member of the Interstellar Coalition. They were probationary members, and wouldn't have been contacted for another century, at least, if not for the Hive threat so close to them. I had not even heard of an Earth female being matched through the Interstellar Brides Program to a male from Alera.

Nial's mate must have been listening, because she answered my question. "They're from Earth, Leo, which means they're mine. My people. They need to be protected. Okay?"

I answered in her strange Earth slang. "Okay. I give you my word as well. I will protect them with my life."

"Thank god." There she went again, thanking a male deity while all in divinity knew the creator was feminine. Strange creatures, Earthlings. "Now, about Trin's problem, she's got some kind of mating fever, like an Atlan, but not exactly. She almost killed some poor guy back home, sucked him dry, you know?"

What the fuck was this female talking about? How did a small, soft, gentle female *suck* a man to death? Did Jessica mean this Trinity female sucked an Earth male's cock too hard? Were Earth males so weak that they'd die from something I'd heard was extremely pleasurable? Was this Earth female *too good* at the task? I palmed my cock through my pants, wondering what it would feel like to have a hot, wet mouth taking me deep.

"No. I do not," I answered, for I was completely confused. My cock didn't stir at the thought, but I was curious.

Nial interrupted. "Trinity's got Aleran Ardor. Don't ask me to explain how a female from Earth has this condition, because I'm not able. The human males don't have enough energy to sate her body's growing lust without dying, so I've asked Lord Jax to send a few guards as well as a—what did he call it?"

"A consort," his mate answered. "Someone she can have hot sex with so she can calm down. He better be really good, Nial.

This consort better have the moves of a Chippendale dancer and the cock of a stallion because I can't just hand her over like a prize to some freakshow alien who's not worthy."

My brows raised in shock. I had no idea what a Chippendale was, nor whether a stallion had a big cock or not. I had to assume it was large. Mine was, running down my thigh, snug in my uniform pants. And that wasn't even hard. Would an Earth female require more to be satisfied? Their soldiers in the ReCon teams were not overly large. Perhaps their females' anatomy was strange, made to accommodate extremely well-endowed males.

But no. I had seen Earth members of ReCon in the cleansing units—and for the most part—been less than impressed with the sizes of their cocks. Alerans were much, much larger.

The use of a consort was not an uncommon practice. Older males who had lost a mate did not lose their physical ability to lay with females of our species. In young, wealthy families in particular, when a female's Ardor began, and she did not want to interview males for a mate, she would utilize the services of a consort.

They were not cheap, yet I had heard the females were well-satisfied. In fact, the consort's value to the royal families was so high that widowed males often petitioned one of the noble houses for comfort and protection in exchange for their services.

Consorts were rare. Expensive. And not normally on formal standby for alien females to fuck on demand.

Who *were* these three females?

"Leo? You there?"

"Yes."

"Can you get to the transport center? Lord Thordis Jax is sending the consort and five of his personal guards to meet them. Their arrival is to be kept a secret. No one can know who they are or where they came from."

While I knew they came from Earth, I had no idea *who* they were. It would be an easy task to fulfill. "Understood. Does Lord Jax know you have contacted me?"

Nial laughed again, and if I'd been close enough, I would have punched him in the shoulder as I'd done in years past. "Of course not. I know him, but I don't know his family. I don't know his guards. I don't trust them, not the way I do you. I don't trust anyone fully in this, no one but you. Keep the women safe. Make sure Trinity gets her Ardor under control, and then help the females do whatever they need to do on Alera. Help them. No questions."

"I give you my word."

"Keep them alive."

"Is someone trying to kill them?"

"Yes. And I do not want them to be found. That is all you need to know."

Strange. But I was a soldier, well-used to taking orders. I was not going to argue or ask questions, especially not with the leader of the galaxy asking me for a personal favor. "I'll be at the transport center in an hour."

"Hey, Leo?" Jessica's voice had changed, gone deeper, sultry. "When you run into them, they won't trust you, so we're using Trinity's favorite food as a code word. Strawberry ice-cream. Got it? You say that and she'll know I sent you."

"Yes, my lady."

"Good," Nial said. "One more thing, Leo. If Lord Jax betrays me, kill him."

Fuck. The Jax family was extremely wealthy and powerful, and the Prime of Prillon had just given me permission to murder their prodigal son. Who *were* these humans? And who was going to come looking for them here? On Alera?

Who was irrelevant. They were mine to protect, so I would. "Understood."

"Thank you. One hour." The strange buzzing in my head ceased, leaving me with nothing but the quiet songs of the night insects and the pounding of my own pulse in my ears. Three females from Earth, one who needed to be fucked, and soon. Not my usual guard duty, but I was up for the task. I shifted my cock in my uniform pants. No, *I* wasn't up for it, but the consort would be.

3

*T*rinity, *Planet Alera, Mytikas City, Transport Room*

I STAGGERED on the transport pad as the cold faded from my bones, the pinprick pain of dead limbs coming back to life making me want to curl up in a ball and cry. Glancing at Faith and Destiny, I could tell they were having the same miserable sensations.

"Okay?" I asked.

They nodded, wiggled their arms, rolled their heads in circles to loosen their neck muscles.

The transport room looked just like the one on Earth, but like Dorothy in *The Wizard of Oz,* we weren't in Kansas anymore. Yet the Aleran males in front of us were definitely not Munchkins. They were big. Not Atlan big like the guard on Earth, but they gave lumberjacks a run for their money.

Grim gazes of six Aleran males stared at us.

"Welcome to Alera," one of them said.

God, Alera. We really were here. I looked behind me. A wall. Yeah, not Earth. There was no going back now since we were light years away. Not time zones, but a galaxy stood between us and the only life we'd ever known. We were in our own sci-fi movie, and I wasn't Princess Leia. I bit my lip, a little freaked out.

Alera.

It must have been the transport that had muddled my emotions because I was strangely on the verge of tears. What a damn mess. This morning, I was heading off to work and now we were on Alera trying to find our kidnapped mother. And that wasn't all. Everyone in this room expected me to fuck a stranger tonight. Now. An alien. A male I'd never met and might never see again.

Talk about romantic... not. I wasn't a virgin, but I didn't fuck strangers either. I'd never had a one-night stand, never was into casual. No friends with benefits. If my body wasn't such a screaming mess, I'd send the gigolo—no, consort—on his way and focus on finding my mother.

And this consort? The guy I was supposed to get naked and horizontal with as soon as humanly possible? It was pretty obvious who he was. The other five wore identical uniforms and stood a step behind him. The consort was attractive, muscular, and at least twenty years older than me. He looked like he was about fifty with dark hair and streaks of gray at the temples. He wore a nice suit of some kind. Navy blue. His shoulders were broad and his eyes were kind. That would help. Thank god this whole Ardor thing only happened once. Like losing my virginity with an alien bang. Once the Ardor was over, I could go about my business. Settle down later. I'd be fine. If I survived this without dying of embarrassment.

"Ladies, I am Cassander of the Jax family. It is my pleasure to serve." The consort bowed low at the waist and swept his arms out to include the guards. "These fine warriors are loyal servants of Jax. We are at your service."

His voice was deep. Assured. Calm.

Maybe fucking him would be more like a gyno visit. Efficient. Gentle. Fast.

Over.

If I'd met the consort on the street, I would have thought he looked great for his age. He was huge, just like the guards surrounding him, but markedly older. A silver fox, my mother would have said.

The guards however, were younger. Dressed for duty, their dark uniforms fit to every curve and bulge of muscle and... other things. I looked away quickly and found Destiny watching me.

"Too bad you can't get it on with one of the guards. Holy hotness."

"Shut up." As a comeback, it was pathetic. As in second grade pathetic. But it was all I had at the moment.

"Leave her alone. Let's get Trin's sexy times done so we can do what we came here to do." Faith crossed her arms as she stepped down off the transport and walked up to the guard closest to her. "I assume we aren't expected to stay in this transport station."

"Of course not. We have secured accommodations for the night. We are to remain on guard until Consort Cassander is no longer needed." The guard bowed slightly, but more a bow of respect to a lady than respect to a superior. My shoulders relaxed and a bit of the tension left my spine. Good. These guys were here, following orders, but they had absolutely no idea who we were. Prime Nial had kept his word.

I doubted we looked like royalty. Hell, my shirt was on inside out. I had to wonder if Cassander even found me appealing. Would he *want* to have sex with me? When was the last time I'd shaved my legs?

But wait. What? "Until he's no longer needed?"

I looked at the consort, who was watching me, his gaze roaming my body. The professional interest I'd read in his eyes before had changed to something more. Something I didn't care for at the moment. Lust. Eagerness. I had become a random piece of ass and it was his job to tap it.

Great. Just great.

"It depends on the female, my lady," Cassander replied. "Some require two days of my attention. Some as many as four. Only you will know when all your needs have been met. I promise I will meet every one of them."

Gag. My need was to get away from this guy and fast.

"Jesus, Trin. Four days? We don't have time for that," Destiny said, always blunt. Unfortunately, she was right. Or fortunately, because if I had to get it on with this guy, I wanted it to be one and done. Like in one hour. Not four fricking *days*.

"What happens if I leave after one day, even if I don't feel— satisfied? What happens?"

He looked shocked, as if he'd never been asked that before. What? Obviously, everyone else wanted to just lounge in bed having sex for days on end. Not me.

Shit. When I thought of it that way, it did sound insane. What woman in their right mind didn't want to do nothing but fuck... again and again? This consort's entire job was to make sure I was satisfied in every possible way. That meant this would be me time. Anything and everything I wanted.

I'd just have to keep my eyes closed and pretend I actually wanted him to be... touching me. As if he could read my mind —and was insulted—he straightened and puffed out his chest. Great. Even consorts had easily wounded male egos. "If you leave before you are fully sated, your relief will only be tempo- rary. You will quickly return to your former state," he said, his voice full of reassurance.

"How quickly?" If I had a few weeks, we could find Mother and move on. Maybe I could even find a man I *liked* and *wanted* to get naked with to finish the job.

"Within hours, or so I've been told." He tilted his head and I suddenly felt as if I was being pandered to. Obviously, he'd never left a female unsatisfied. Permanently. "I will take very good care of you. You have my word."

Damn. I'd just have to hope I was a one-day kind of girl. But

I suspected I was more likely the four-day variety. "Let's go, then."

I must not have looked overly excited about it—which was pretty much how I felt—because Faith put her hand out to stop me. "Wait."

"What?" I asked, wanting to get this over with so we could get on with finding Mother.

"You don't have to go with him. God, this is ridiculous. Why would you go off with a guy you don't like and have sex? It's just... weird. Wrong. There's five other guys. The second one's cute."

The guards glanced at each other, most likely trying to figure out which one of them was the 'second one.'

"She's right, Trin," Destiny added. "It's like getting your v-card punched. Don't just do it to get it over with."

I rolled my eyes, then leaned toward Faith. Destiny stepped closer so we were in a huddle. "Imagine using your vibrator and you're close, really, really, close to coming. Riding the edge... and the batteries die."

Destiny made a funny whimper sound. We might all still live at home, but we were full-grown adults. We had vibrators and boyfriends and sex and real lives.

"That's what I feel like. All. The. Time."

Faith bit her lip and gave me a look of pity. "Then pick one. There are six guys. One of them's got to be appealing to your hysterical Va-Jay-Jay."

I couldn't help but laugh. I stroked my hand down Faith's long hair and we turned as a unit to stare at the men. All six of them. The consort was appealing, but not appealing enough. Destiny was right, the second guard was really hot.

The consort looked irritated now, as if we were not only insulting him, but were idiots as well. "With all due respect, ladies, the guards will not be able to service you as you need. Only a male who has met The One, whose cock has been awakened by his true mate, can be of service to a female. Even then, we consorts have lost our mates. My mate died two years ago in a tragic accident. I am the only one here whose body is awake and fully functional. None of the guards are mated. And Aleran males do not have sex with other females while their mates still live. I will not allow you to ask another male to dishonor his mate in this way. I am but a lowly consort, but my purpose is sacred and valued on all of Alera."

Great. We're here for all of two minutes and we already insulted every Aleran we'd met.

"My apologies, Cassander. We did not intend to insult you or the guards. I would never ask a warrior to dishonor his mate. Never." I glanced at the guards. So did Faith and Destiny. Those big, hot guys, who had to be similar in age to the three of us, hadn't had sex? Hadn't had their cock *awakened?* Mother had mentioned it, explained it, but I hadn't believed her. I mean, every guy on Earth from like fourteen on was as horny as hell. They thought only of sex, of getting into a girl's pants from the moment they woke up until going to sleep.

And these five guards had never felt lust? Or had sex? Never had an orgasm?

"Holy shit," Destiny whispered. "A planet of hot virgin males. Every woman's fantasy."

"It's the consort then, Trin," Faith whispered. "Just close your eyes and think of Justin Timberlake."

I laughed. Faith had always been obsessed with the pop star. Determined to make the best of an awkward situation for all of us, I walked toward Cassander, who bowed and kissed my palm. It was warm. Pleasant. No great rush of lust fired me up at the simple touch, but I didn't need a great lust. Or true love. I just needed to get this alien Ardor taken care of—as quickly as possible—so we could go track down the kidnappers and save Mother.

Besides, we weren't going to get naked right here in the transport room, so at least I had a little time to have a chat with my vagina. She'd have to make peace with the plan. Because I didn't have time to search this planet for a mate. Every minute that passed was one more that Mother was in mortal danger.

Leo

I ARRIVED at the transport center with ten minutes to spare, but stopped short when I saw five guards with Lord Jax's insignia on their shoulders enter the center via a side door. Walking with them was a consort I recognized. Cassander of Jax was well-loved by the ladies. In fact, I had heard tell of males becoming frustrated when their new mates complained that Cassander was a better lover.

Of course, he'd had more than twenty years with his mate before she died. I could only imagine the skill and knowledge he held in regards to a female's body and her desires. He would know exactly how to touch her to make her surrender to his every demand, every need.

I had no doubt that should I ever find The One, I would make sure to satisfy every single one of her needs. Her cries of pleasure would become my obsession. I would play her body like a master, watch every move and every breath until I was her master, until she begged for my touch. Craved it. Couldn't come without it.

In my pants, my cock stirred as a strange scent teased my senses.

My cock stirred. All on its own. What the fuck?

All because of a delicate fragrance, like the translucent petals of the Aleran flower that grew in abundance in the citadel gardens I'd played in as a boy. Crazy.

It had been years since I'd been to the citadel and should not be stirred by simply inhaling the soft scent. Even longer since I'd been fool enough to bury my nose in the center of the silken petals and breathe in their scent. When the queen lived and ruled, I'd played in the gardens while my father went to meetings with the other guards. But the citadel, while in the same city, was far from here and I'd not passed by those sacred gardens on my journey from my guard post. Perhaps the wind brought the scent to me, cloaked in darkness, a taunting ghost of happier days.

Strange. I hadn't thought of those long, bright days for years. But the smell of the flowers lingered, as if clinging to my body with a mind of its own. And to stir my cock? A *scent,* not a female. Perhaps it was time to see a doctor.

"Stop daydreaming and get moving, soldier." I whispered the order to myself. There were three females inside that building and I'd promised Prime Nial to protect them with my life. I had no idea who they were, or why they'd traveled all the way from Earth. But those facts were irrelevant to me. I didn't need to know their names to die for them. That was a warrior's vow. To die for innocents he or she had never met. To protect them simply because they needed someone stronger, more skilled, to defend them from any threat.

Prepared to step out of the shadows and enter the building, I stopped cold as three dark shadows caught my eye as they moved along the roof.

Assassins.

Within moments they'd vanished again, blending into the shadows as if they'd never existed. Phantoms. But I'd seen them. Knew they were real.

Knew they were hunting.

Fuck, there was no question as to why they were here. Why they were stealth and silent.

The Earth women.

Who *were* they? And where had the assassins come from? Surely not Lord Thordis Jax? From all I had heard, he was a decent and honorable male. But perhaps someone in his family was not. Or had assassins followed these females all the way from Earth? From Prillon Prime? Nial's mate, Lady Deston, had spoken as if the females were of great import to her personally. Perhaps whoever hunted these ladies wanted to get to Prime Nial, his second, and their mate. Then why were the females on Alera, not Prillon?

"Where did you go, evil bastards?" My voice was so quiet I barely heard the words as I scanned the rooftops and buildings for movement. I was not a trained assassin, but I was very, very good at killing. And watching. Waiting. I was hunting now.

The door opened as a vehicle pulled up to the side entrance. A large EMV slowed to a stop, and I watched as two guards exited the transport center, checked the vehicle and driver before leading the three females, the consort and the rest of the guards inside. The shuttle was large, but fast, moving past me in a blur as I threw my tracker into the air. The small, autonomous drone would fly just out of sight above them and allow me to follow their every stop and destination through the computer, displaying coordinates I could follow easily.

Racing to my own EMV, I quickly followed, frowned when I spotted a second drone tracking the shuttle. Lord Jax's vehicle was much faster than mine. Much more expensive. My soldier's wages didn't allow for such luxuries, nor did I care for them as long as the EMV took me where I needed to go. I was not frivolous. Depending on how far they traveled, I could remain right behind them, or be twenty minutes delayed.

The assassins, however, would surely have the very best EMV money could buy. They needed to monitor their prey, know exactly where they were headed. Follow. Attack. Kill.

Fuck. I tapped my comm and placed a call to Thordis Jax. His bleary-eyed assistant answered the call.

"What is it? It's the middle of the night, sir. Who are you and why are you calling me?"

"I need to speak directly with Lord Thordis Jax. It's an emergency." I flicked a gaze from the drones to the rear of the Earth females' EMV.

"Hummph. No, it is not. Lord Jax is asleep, and I assure you, whatever your emergency, it can wait for a decent hour."

"Listen to me," I countered, tipping my tone low. "Wake him. Tell him his special guests have assassins following them."

"Who are you?" he asked instead of taking my command seriously.

"It doesn't matter. Wake him the fuck up and give him the message."

The older gentleman snorted again, rubbing his eyes, and I slammed my hand on the comm to end the call. Idiot. I didn't have time to argue, and I wasn't about to tell him who I was. Especially when I didn't know if this seemingly innocent old servant was, in fact, feeding information to Prime Nial's enemies. Prime Nial himself had said to trust no one.

I was on my own.

The assassins would beat me to their destination. Already, the EMV carrying the Earth females was ten minutes out of range. I watched as they grew farther from me on my EMV's display. Fuck.

The assassins would not delay. They would complete their task, swiftly and without mercy, and disappear into the night. I could only hope I got there before all of the ladies' guards were dead.

4

rinity, The Grande Penthouse, The Mytikas Summit Housing Complex

BESIDES BEING A GIGOLO, Cassander was also a tour guide. On our ride, he shared details about Mytikas, the large city we were in. It reminded me of New York or Hong Kong. Sprawling. Crowded. If it weren't for the fact the vehicle we were in was more *Buck Rogers* than Buick, it would seem like we were on Earth.

The same went for the hotel we'd entered. Swanky, like the Ritz. It even had a penthouse level. It seemed social status wasn't reserved just for Earth. We were in a suite, with Vegas-worthy views. Lights and tall buildings were all that could be seen. I had no idea what time it was, but it was dark out. I didn't feel the least bit tired, although I was sure it had more to do with adrenaline than anything else. That and the constant, aching hunger I had to be touched. I felt like an addict who desperately needed a hit. Sex was practically all I could think about. My body actually *hurt.*

Maybe after a few orgasms, I'd feel better and conk right out.

"There are three bedrooms to your guest quarters, thanks to your host, Lord Jax," Cassander said, pointing to the doors off of the suite's central room. Decorated in soft colors, creams and tans, the suite was elegant and screamed wealth. Yeah, Lord Jax was definitely working it. Artwork graced the walls; abstracts I assumed were of Aleran landscapes, but it could have been the Grand Canyon for all I knew. If it weren't for the doors that swished open and closed automatically like in *Star Trek,* it felt familiar and... normal. As if Alera wasn't as culturally different from Earth as I'd assumed. "The guards will remain in the central room, assuring our safety while we are... occupied. There is a bedroom for each of you, my ladies. You and I, Trinity, will take this one."

Cassander was bold enough to take my hand in his and lead me in the direction he spoke. The touch was gentle, warm, but it didn't reassure me, only made me nervous. Yeah, a gigolo to ease my Aleran Ardor. Soooo different from Earth.

Faith came over to me from the window where she'd been taking in the view. "I'll pull one of these comfy chairs up here. Right by your door. If you need anything, I'll be... well, listening."

She blushed, and so did I. Like she wanted to listen to her sister having sex with a stranger. I winced, and apparently, Cassander saw my less than excited expression.

"You have nothing to fear with me. I promise you, my lady. You will feel only pleasure." His fingertips grazed the inside of my wrist in an act meant to be seductive. Instead, I felt annoyed. My body liked it, humming to life with sudden interest. But me? The battle going on inside my head? Angry, upset, *I hate this* me was definitely winning.

I glanced at Faith who bit her lip. I wasn't sure if she was trying to stifle a smile or keep from vomiting.

"Does that thing have real bullets or lasers or what? And

where can I get one?" Destiny asked. Faith and I turned to see our curious—and ruthless sister—tugging a space-age weapon from one of the guards' hip holsters.

"Um... be careful with that," the guard warned. He was the second guard, the hot one. Or, the hottest one, because none of them were bad-looking.

Destiny narrowed her eyes and tossed her purple hair back. She waved the gun around as if she were an idiot who'd never touched a weapon before. "What, you mean someone might get hurt?"

The guard blanched and reached for the weapon.

Destiny dropped the act and aimed the gun at the floor. "Easy, soldier. I was just playing with you." Her deft hands fiddled with it. "Stun mode. Fascinating."

Faith rolled her eyes. "She'll be entertained for hours." Faith's gaze traveled over the guards' uniforms, taking in the array of weapons, knives, blasters, and odd attachments that Destiny would, undoubtedly, dissect like a scientist. If there was a PhD in weapons, she'd have a plaque on her bedroom wall. Shiny and silver, I could just see it surrounded by the blast of purple bedding and purple paint on the walls.

"Yeah, giving the guards heart attacks," I countered.

"So forget about her. About us. What's going on out here. Just... do your thing." Faith pulled me away from Cassander, into a tight hug. Her lips were next to my ear, and her voice so low I was sure no one else could hear her. "I know you hate this. I'm sorry. But we need to find Mom, and we need you to survive long enough to help us do that. Okay. We're right here. We got your back. You know that. We got you."

Tears. Great. That was soooo not what I needed right now. "Thanks."

Faith nodded and stepped away, taking up her new position in the chair, guarding the hallway that led to the fuck-den. Sheesh. Was I really going to do this? Did I have a choice? Every moment since we'd arrived on the planet had made my

Ardor worse. I didn't know if it was the alien men, the air, or what, but my Ardor had gone from the low simmer it had been on Earth to a full blown assault on my senses. I couldn't think. Could barely breathe. I wasn't a child. I could control myself, but I was miserable. Uncomfortable. Needy. My skin so sensitive that Faith's hug had made my skin burn with heat.

Damn.

I looked at Cassander and held out my hand with all the enthusiasm of a criminal facing down a firing squad.

"We'll be right here, Trin. Right here." Faith assured me once more with a nod.

"Okay."

Cassander said nothing but took my hand with a gentle tug. I gave up, let him lead me into the bedroom. Oh, there was a big bed all right. Huge. White blankets and fluffy pillows all turned down, ready for entry. I felt like I was a virgin sacrifice as he closed the door behind us. Locked it.

"Wine, my lady?" he asked, going to a table and pouring a dark liquid into two glasses.

"Can't hurt," I said on a sigh, holding my hand out. I took a sip. Fruity wine burst on my tongue. It wasn't grapes that had been fermented, but something else. Still, it tasted good and I needed some liquid courage. And to loosen up.

I took another gulp as Cassander shrugged out of his jacket. Beneath, he wore a white shirt that was trim to his body. As if it was the most natural thing in the world, he unbuttoned the shirt and slid it down his shoulders and back. He was pure muscle. Step one in his seduction plan, wine. Step two, strip tease.

And I still didn't want him. Shit. I didn't feel all too teased, so I had to hope he had toys in his arsenal, maybe in the bedside table, or a really wicked tongue. I took another gulp of wine, stared at the defined masses of muscle moving under his skin. He was built. Nice arms. Really nice backside. The way my pussy was pulsing and my breasts ached, I should have been all over him. I should just take off my clothes, lay down on the bed, close my eyes and let this man work some kind of magic on me.

He turned, his wine in hand and a sympathetic look on his face. Sympathy, and lust. So, I was what? I new notch on his belt? Oh, look at the famous consort who got to fuck the future queen? He didn't know that, but I did. And I was not feeling this.

I glanced at the bed again and tried to imagine him pounding into me as I held onto the headboard. Or... put my head under a pillow? Kept my eyes closed? Turned off the lights?

I set the wine glass down on the bedside table, shaking my head. No, this wasn't going to work. There was no way in hell I'd let this guy go down on me, no matter how skilled his tongue. It would take four days of foreplay to get my mind as ready as my body for sex. And even then, the idea of him grunting and sweating and pumping into me just made me want to gag. No. Casual sex wasn't my thing. Never had been. So, this stupid alien body was just going to have to shut up and deal for a while.

Yeah, my girl parts were eager for a big cock. But, they didn't rule me and they were going to have to be a little more discriminate than an alien prostitute. They'd just have to chill the fuck out.

"Look, Cassander, I'm sure you're really great at your job. Total stud and all, but I can't do this. I'll be sure to give you a great review, but sometimes a girl's just got to say no."

He looked appalled. Shocked. Like I'd hit him with a stun gun kind of amazed. Had no one turned him down before? God, his ego must be huge.

"But, my lady—"

His wrist chimed. Glancing at it, he stiffened impossibly further.

"What's the matter?" I asked, looking from his wary eyes to his wrist.

"There's, um… a threat. A warning has been sent."

I stilled, my heart leaping into my throat. He might want to bang me, but right now he was the guy who knew his way around Alera. He had a wrist thingie that sent him stuff like those fancy mini-computer watches on Earth. If he said there was a threat, I believed him. I was the visitor here and had to trust him, at least in this.

"Let's go in the other room with the guards." He held his arm out signaling me to precede him. "I need to give them this update." I walked toward the door, but didn't make it two steps before the room's window shattered. I scrunched my shoulders up and ducked down near the door, my hands instinctively going to my head. A dark figure swung in. Covered heat to toe in black, he hung from a wire *Mission Impossible* style.

Holy shit.

"Run, my la—" A blast hit Cassander in the chest and he crumpled mid-word as I scrambled to open the door. His second blast hit the door above my head and I crawled on all fours into the hallway as Cassander bellowed behind me. I heard a scuffle. Another shot. I slammed the door, screaming for my sisters.

"We're under attack! Run!"

That's when I saw Faith crouched down behind her chair, a dead guard on the ground next to her. Destiny was screaming obscenities around the corner, out of sight.

"Faith? What are you doing?"

Faith turned to me, her eyes round with fear. "You know I don't kill things."

I closed the distance as the sound of several shots were fired in the living room area. The explosion of glass made Faith cringe and she peeked around the corner. "Ouch. That was a nice table."

"Seriously?" I pulled her back, out of my way, and took a quick glance around the corner. One guard was still alive. One. But he was hurt. Bad. Blood was pooling under his head on the nice, thick cream-colored carpet, but he was still breathing. And my sister, Destiny, was bleeding, circling, looking for an opportunity to get in a killing blow to one of the bad guys. It wasn't the guy who came through the window after me, so that meant there was more than one. She leapt forward, locked in hand-to-hand combat, moving so fast I couldn't keep track of her motions.

Faith peeked up over the chair next to me. "Jesus, our sister is scary."

"Shut up and get in there." I hadn't forgotten about the attacker in the bedroom. And I had no idea if Cassander was dead or alive.

"What? No way."

"There's another one coming from the bedroom," I hissed. Pushing to get her moving, I scrambled around the dead guard on the floor and took his weapon as we positioned ourselves on the other side of the chair. "You keep track of Destiny. I'll watch the hall."

Inspecting the weapon in my hands, I frowned. I knew the basics about handguns—Destiny had made us at least go to the firing range with her a few times—but this wasn't a weapon like anything I'd ever seen before. Shit.

The bedroom door opened and I pushed Faith. Hard.

"Trin!"

"Move!"

The mask had been ripped from my attacker's head and I could see his face. His hair was dark, his eyes a brilliant green I'd never seen before. His forehead was bleeding from a deep cut—one point to Cassander—but I wished he was still covered up because now I could see his eyes, the grim turn of his curled lips, and all I saw on his face was death. If I saw his face, that meant he had no intention of keeping us alive to identify him. I'd seen enough crime scene shows on TV to know that.

I lifted the gun and pointed it at the assassin. His eyes narrowed, but he kept walking. I squeezed the trigger, or whatever it was. Nothing. Crap. How did this thing work?

"Shoot him!" That was Destiny. How the hell she knew I was facing down a killer, I had no idea. She was a freak with eyes in the back of her head.

"I can't get the gun to work!"

Destiny took a punch to the gut, distracted by my situation. She punched back, hard, swinging and connecting with her opponent's jaw. "Safety on top, not the side. Orange light."

I followed her swift instructions, or tried to, pressing on the orange glowing area. The light turned a pale, pale green. I lifted the gun again, but it was too late. He was on top of us, pulling a very big, very long knife free from the sheath strapped to his thigh. I screamed.

"Shoot him!" Faith yelled, kicking the nearest chair into him to buy us some time.

I fired. A blast of light, or laser, or whatever, shot from the gun. Direct hit in the chest. He just smiled.

I fired again. Again.

He looked amused now. Either there was some weird setting on the gun or he was wearing an alien version of Kevlar.

Shit.

The door exploded inward with a boom that made my ears scream in pain. I squeezed my eyes shut, but knew the bad guy was right in front of me. I couldn't avoid him. Faith dropped to her knees, covering her head.

The assassin looked away from me, toward the door, and all amusement faded from his eyes. I might not be a threat to him, but whomever destroyed the suite's entry door sure was.

5

Leo

"SHOOT HIM!" A woman shouted on the other side of the door, followed by the sound of repeated blaster fire.

I didn't wait, setting a charge on the locked door for three seconds. Moving to the side, I closed my eyes, weapon drawn, and counted.

Three. Two. One. Long fucking seconds.

The explosion rocked the hallway, the lights above me flickering off then back on as I burst into the room.

I took it all in with a sweeping glance.

A female—with strangely colored hair—was fighting one of the assassins.

A second assassin was dead on the ground, surrounded by four dead guards. The difference between good and bad was easy to distinguish; the guards wore identical, and familiar, uniforms, the assassins all black. Their faces were covered.

Another guard, the lone surviving one it seemed, was crumpled on the ground, trying to reach for his blaster, the blood under his head meant he'd most likely black out before he got it.

The other two females were on the far side of the room from him, crouched behind a chair, one firing a weapon on a third assassin.

He whipped his head around toward me at the sound of the blast and my entry, clearly confident the female's blaster shots would do him no arm. Our eyes locked.

I knew that face. I narrowed my eyes at him, and he all but dared me to attack. Bastard. Prime Nial had been right to call me. I doubted either of us expected danger to come upon the females so swiftly after their arrival, nor from this band of evil. It hadn't been more than an hour since their transport. These females held some kind of power, something very powerful people were willing to kill to contain.

"Get down!" I yelled at the females, hoping they would listen. Raising my own weapon. He wore protective armor, but that would not stop me from killing him with a precise shot to his head. I frowned when the assassin turned and ran, disappearing down the hallway where I assumed there was a bedroom.

I had no doubt the consort would be found there, dead. Had the female's Ardor been slaked first? I doubted it based on the timeline of events. There hadn't even been time to disrobe, let alone fuck an Ardor away.

The two females near the chair ignored my order the moment their attacker was gone and stood, turning to the third female, still locked in combat.

Fuck. Two were seemingly safe, but the third was in trouble.

"Kick him away from you!" I yelled as I dashed toward her. The assassin was much bigger than she and I was surprised she'd held him off so long.

She heard me, delivering a hard, swift kick to the assassin's abdomen and stepped back, out of range. Purposely giving me the shot. I lifted my weapon, aimed.

"Don't kill him!" A female near the chair screamed the order, but I ignored her command. This particular band of assassins was too dangerous to remain alive. He had to die. One of them had already escaped. I wouldn't lose two.

He was armored, as I knew he would be. I fired at his chest anyway, momentarily halting his movement. That was all I needed to take the head shot.

He dropped like a rock. Remained still. The female he'd been fighting stepped forward, bent arms raised, hands fisted tightly as if she were ready to keep fighting, and kicked him in the side with heavy black boots, just to make sure I'd gotten the job done.

"He's dead. I assure you," I said, coming up to stand beside her.

She turned to me, glanced up, her purple hair flying. Her eyes were a bright blue, and completely without fear. Her pupils were dilated, but it seemed more from the rush of fighting than fear. She was small. Her odd clothes couldn't hide the curves of her gender. And she'd just fought off one of our planet's deadliest assassins.

It seemed Earth females were brave. Bold. Fierce. But why were they here? Now? And why did someone want them dead?

"Who are you, and what do you want?" The voice washed over me like the burning heat of a fire and my cock stirred. Again. Just as I'd felt earlier. No, not just stirred, but thickened. Lengthened.

Shocked, I turned swiftly back to the females near the chair. One had long brown hair and large, dark eyes. She looked warm. Soft. Too gentle to be the female who'd spoken in such a commanding tone.

My gaze shifted to the other.

Holy. Fuck.

Instantly, I bowed low to the most magnificent female I'd ever seen, but I kept my eyes on her. I couldn't look away if I wanted. Golden hair surrounded her head and shoulders in a silken wave I couldn't wait to touch. Her eyes were a deep, intense blue, and staring me down, analyzing my every move. Her lips were a soft pink I longed to taste, to feel wrapped around my cock.

My fingers twitched at my side and I cleared my throat to disguise the groan of need I felt building like an explosion within my body as my cock came fully erect. Pressed against my uniform pants, which had suddenly become ridiculously too small. I was rock hard, long and thick, but now? Gods, now it was as if I had a pipe growing larger and larger down the inside of my thigh. I'd had no idea how erect I would get.

For the first time in my life, I ached. I wanted, no *needed,* to get closer to her. To get her naked and needy and screaming my name.

Just one sentence from her and I knew. She was mine. The magnificent creature staring me down over the top of a blaster was *The One*. My mate.

Fuck.

My earlier thoughts of remaining a bachelor soldier were all but forgotten. I inwardly laughed at my ignorant self. I would never be alone again because I'd never let this female out of my sight. Or away from my touch.

The clothing she wore did nothing to hide her form. Trim pants that were blue, worn and faded as if she didn't have an S-Gen unit available and wore this pair again and again. A shirt that bared her arms. While tall and lean, she had ample curves. Round and soft in all the right places. I could nuzzle and lick, grip and even spank.

And she'd almost been killed by fucking assassins. I saw red, wished I could kill the one all over again, race after the one who'd escaped.

My protective instincts roared like a caged monster, the remnants of the attack, the bodies on the floor, the blood, the *threat to my mate* taking on colors and intensity I'd not felt moments ago.

Mine.

Trembling with equal parts rage and need, I dropped to one knee and bowed to the female I would devote myself to for the rest of my life. "I am Captain Leoron Turaya. Prime Nial asked me to protect you and assist you in any way I can. I am sorry I arrived so late to the battle. Are you well?"

"Prime Nial sent you? What's the code word?" my mate asked, one pale eyebrow raised. She didn't lower her weapon. I didn't blame her, for she was smart to be cautious. She should trust no one. No one but me, but she hadn't learned that yet.

I lifted my head, gazed up at her. Confused. Code word? I searched my mind and found what she sought. Prime Nial's mate, Jessica, had said something strange about Trinity's favorite food being code. Now, I understood. "Strawberry ice cream."

I had absolutely no idea what I'd just said, some strange Earth term, but all three females relaxed. My mate put the weapon down and I noticed her hands trembled. That would not do. She shouldn't feel anything but happiness. Peace. I longed to take her into my arms and offer comfort, but she wasn't safe here. None of them were. The assassin had fled, but he'd be back for her. His kind didn't leave a job unfinished. If these three were as valuable dead as I assumed, the next attack would be more cunning. And brutal.

Over my fucking dead body. I was at war with myself. The need to protect and defend battled with the need to stand, walk to The One and pick her up, keep on going until she was pressed against the nearest wall. My mouth on hers, my fingers working open her strange pants, seeking her center, finding it hot and wet for me. Sinking into her. Finally.

My cock didn't understand danger, my body demanded action even knowing my mate could be harmed. My need would not lessen, and neither would the size of my hard cock, until I'd spent in her. Made her scream my name. Not once, not twice, but many, *many* times.

The warrior in me pushed through, wrested control from the primal, rutting instincts fighting to rule me. For now. "You are not safe here."

"No shit." The purple-haired female kicked the corpse at her feet again before reaching down and divesting him of his gear. She was efficient, systematically checking every pocket and pack, everywhere the assassin had hidden anything of use to him. She looked up from her work at the other two.

"Help the guard while I get weapons and intel. Get busy." She waved the weapon she held as if dismissing them to do she commanded.

The dark-haired female moved to the injured guard and pulled a small blanket and pillow from one of the chairs. I thought she would cover him, but instead took a knife from his gear and cut the blanket into bandages. Dropping to her knees, she tied them around his head wound to stem the flow of blood. She deftly wrapped his wounds completely and placed his head on the pillow before looking up at me. "Do you have 9-1-1? You know, paramedics or someone who can take care of him? Someone to call? A doctor? Hello?"

While I heard her words, I didn't immediately process she was talking to me. I was too stuck on The One, the curve of her cheek, the color of her lips, the upturn of her nose. I shook myself out of my cock-induced trance and nodded, pulling a ReGen wand from my belt, pushed the button so the blue, healing light glowed. It was too small to correct all of the damage to the wounded man, but it would stop the bleeding until he could get to a ReGen Pod. It was better than nothing— and all I had. "Yes, we do. But wave this over his head for a minute, and it will keep him alive until they arrive."

She frowned and stared at the device as if she'd never seen one before, then began to move it a few inches over the guard's injured head as I'd instructed.

"We should leave quickly. The assassin who escaped will not run and hide. He is a killer. It is not safe for you here."

"Obviously," the dark-haired one grumbled. "We need a place to hide until daylight."

"I know. I will take you somewhere safe. But no more public places. I don't want anyone else to know you're on Alera."

"Amen to that." The purple-haired woman moved on to her third body, stuffing weapons into a blanket she'd tied into a carry pouch. She stripped Lord Jax's guards and assassins alike, missing nothing. One-track-mind, that one.

I came to my full height, eager to be closer to my mate. I took one step before our gazes locked. Held. It was as if there weren't bodies littered on the floor. No hint of danger, or a deadly assassin who might return to finish what he started.

For the briefest of moments, it was just me. Her. *Us.*

My cock pulsed, heavy. My balls tightened and I felt a spurt of pre-cum seep from the tip. Yes, I was truly awakened. My cock wanted this female and it wanted her now.

I had to get her away from here. Away from any danger, then I could allow the eager brute to do the thinking for me.

She tilted her head to the side and licked her lips, looking me over as if her desire was as strong as mine. Bright color flagged her cheeks, her eyes wide, searching. Roving. Perhaps I would be blessed with a lusty mate, one as eager to claim me as I was her. I didn't care who she was or what planet she was from. She was mine.

"Who are you?" she asked, her voice losing the commanding tone, replaced now with something akin to wonder.

I knew just how she felt.

"Leo," the purple-haired female replied before I could. "He knows the code word. We should go. You guys can... whatever, later."

That female began to annoy me with her impatience. Didn't she know I'd been waiting my entire life for this moment? For my cock to stir for The One? That my life had changed irrevocably?

I didn't look away from my mate, yet I knew the logic was sound.

"I am Leo, captain in the royal guard, servant of Alera. I fought with Prime Nial in the Hive wars. I am here to serve you."

Serve you in so many ways. Gods, I wanted to kiss her, lick her and know the flavor of her skin, breathe in her scent, taste her pussy, make her come and then sink into her. Mark her as mine. So I would be completely and truly *hers.*

I thought of the assassin still at large. Of the continued threat to her. This was no longer just a life debt owed to Prime Nial. This was my mate. The One. She was in danger, and I would stop the fucking rotation of the planet to keep her safe.

The brown-haired female smiled up at me from where she continued to treat the guard, with blood covering her delicate hands. She, too, wore odd, worn clothing. All three of them were. They had on pants in blue or black, simple shirts, my mate with strangely short sleeves. Who kept their arms bare this high in the mountain regions? Was it extremely hot on Earth? Was it a style to bare her body for others to see?

The purple-haired one had on sturdy dark boots, the calm one shoes with straps that barely covered her feet. My mate wore white cloth shoes with laces. Simple, worn, a bit dirty and smudged along the edges, as if she weren't one for extravagance. I didn't need expensive garments or jewels to decorate my mate. I wanted her bare, every perfect inch of her pale skin visible, only to me. To see the life flow through the pale veins beneath the skin, to run my fingers along them.

"So, Prime Nial saved your life?" the quiet one asked. "And now you're saving ours?"

I nodded. I would die for my mate. Kill for her. Stop at nothing to protect her, claim her. But they didn't need to know that. Not yet. "Something like that. We must leave." I held out my hand to my mate, hoping and praying to the goddess that she'd touch me. She did not.

She did look at me, though, and my cock wept some more at having those beautiful eyes on me. "I'm Trinity." She angled her head toward the dark-haired one with the funny, strappy shoes. "This is my sister, Faith. And that's her ass-kicking twin over there, Destiny. We just need a safe place to stay tonight. Okay?"

"And some food," Destiny added. "Kicking ass made me hungry."

I glanced her way, said, "Are you sure you don't need more weapons?"

The comment was meant to be sarcastic, but Destiny looked up from the unconscious guard she was separating from all of his battle implements. I noted that she was careful not to jostle his head or the pillow Faith had placed so carefully beneath him.

"Seriously?" she asked, looking up at me. "Hell, yeah. What do you have?"

"He's kidding, Destiny," Trinity told her. A beautiful name for my beautiful mate. She shook her head and rolled her eyes. "If the guard is stable, let's go."

Destiny scrambled around to the guard's other side, but my mate was not amused. And apparently, she was in charge, even though the purple-haired one was so bossy. Fascinating.

"Now, Destiny," Trinity added, her tone going quite commanding. Fuck, that was hot. "Come on, Faith.

"Let's go before more ninja assassins show up," Trinity added as Faith stood and handed me my ReGen wand.

What was a ninja? Was that a special band of assassins on Earth? Had they faced such danger before? The thought made me shudder with relief that they were here, with me, under my protection. I didn't think the assassin would show his face again tonight, but I would not lower my guard until we were somewhere safe, somewhere only I knew. And I would employ every tactic I'd ever learned to make sure the threat couldn't follow us tonight.

"Fine," Destiny countered. "I got enough stuff for all of us." She stood and held out a blaster.

"I don't want it," Faith said, holding her blood-stained hands up in front of her.

"Tough." Destiny shoved the blaster into Faith's chest and held it until her sister slowly, reluctantly wrapped her fingers around it.

"I hate you sometimes," Faith said.

"Only when you know I'm right." Destiny slung the blanket full of gear over her shoulder, raised a questioning brow at Trinity—who held up the blaster she'd been using when I took out the entry door—and stepped up beside me. "Let's go, Leonardo."

"It's Leoron."

My mate sighed and tucked her weapon into the pocket of her strange pants. They, along with her shirt, fit snugly to her lean frame. They did nothing to hide her figure, the curves I would soon have my hands on. "Let's go. I can't take much more."

We carefully climbed through the twisted metal of the destroyed entry door. I had no idea if there were other guests on this floor, but I had to assume they'd fled after the explosion.

In the hallway, Faith gasped, turning to my mate. "What about Cassander? Did you, you know?"

The consort. Fuck. While it was his job, I couldn't think about that rich bastard touching Trinity's skin. Kissing her. Licking her sweet pussy. Filling her—

"No." She sighed. "But, he's... dead."

I nearly shuddered with relief. Not at his being dead, but at him not touching my mate. I clenched my fists at my sides. Perhaps it was good he was no longer alive, for I'd have killed him myself if he'd laid a finger on her. Consort or not. It was completely irrational. I hadn't known of Trinity's existence hours ago. Now, the thought of another male touching her made my blood boil. But, it also meant that Trinity was the one with Aleran Ardor. Who needed to have her pussy filled, to be soothed with orgasm after orgasm.

Goddess, she would not need a consort. Her mate was here, available and had an eager cock. She would not go unsatisfied. Ever.

"Oh, shit. Now what are we going to do about your little problem?" Destiny asked.

"It's fine." Trinity waved a hand through the air as if it were nothing. Either she was minimizing her condition or 'it's fine' meant something different on Earth. Ardor was not a joke, taken seriously by everyone on Alera. Clearly, these females didn't know what Trinity would be in for if she didn't get it under control.

"I wasn't going to sleep with him anyway. It was too weird." She scrunched up her nose as if something smelled bad. "I told him—"

"What? Told him what?" Faith asked. All three of us waited for Trinity's answer, but me most of all. Did she have a male back on Earth? Was she already mated to someone I could not seek out and kill with my bare hands?

Was she hurting? Needed my cock filling her? My mouth on her skin?

I was shaking now, struggling to breathe as the sweet scent of her drifted to me once more. Aleran flowers. Sweet. Ripe. Mine.

She looked years too old to be suffering from the Ardor. Most females on Alera were well past that stage around their twentieth year. My mate looked at least five years older than that. A woman. Mature. Sexy. Stunning.

Trinity shook her head. "It doesn't matter. I'm fine. I'll be fine," she insisted again in a tone of voice that implied she didn't want to be argued with, although I could see because of her tight blue pants that she rubbed her thighs together. No, she ached, her pussy throbbing with the Ardor heat, but was being brave. My sweet mate. "Anyway, he's dead."

"We're screwed," Destiny added, frowning.

"In more ways than one," Faith said, glaring at me. "I *told you not to kill him.* We needed him alive so we could interrogate him and know why we're being targeted."

I blinked. What? These three were interrogation experts?

"The assassin? Absolutely not. He was going to murder you," I bit out. I had no intention of telling them that I knew the assassin who had escaped. Knew the price he demanded could be paid by very few. Until I knew who these three were, I wasn't going to share. I needed something to exchange with them. Information they wanted for what I wanted. I glanced at Trinity. "All of you."

Destiny actually snorted. "As if. I totally had that guy."

"And the one in the hallway?" I pointed in that direction. "The one who escaped? Did you have him as well? Or would he have killed your sisters while you played soldier?" I'd saved Destiny's life, eliminated the threat to her, as any honorable male would do, and she was chastising me as if I were a child? No.

"Touché."

She grinned up at me as Trinity watched the byplay with a completely unreadable expression. Was she overcome by her Ardor? Overwhelmed by what had just happened? Afraid?

I would reassure her, set her mind at ease. Make her worry for nothing, not even her orgasms. I couldn't wait to make her melt. Burn. Scream my name.

I had no idea what Destiny's response meant, this word, touché, nor did I care. She was cooperating. That was all I needed at the moment.

"Come with me," I told them, finally getting all of us away from danger. My cock was a terrible leader. I had to get my head back in control, at least for the moment. I didn't know what threats were outside this floor, this building. Even down the street. "Keep your heads down. Don't look up. There are vid stations everywhere." I led them farther down the hall. Thankfully, Trinity stepped into place directly behind me, close, where I needed her to be. Destiny brought up the rear, her weapon at the ready, and I was surprised to realize I was reassured with her in that position. She was a warrior and my mate trusted her. A strange female, but a capable fighter. I would take all the help I could get. Anything to get my mate far from here. Safe.

And naked. Very, very naked.

6

Trinity – somewhere in Mytikas City

"Do you have any idea where we are?" Faith asked, looking around.

"As if we know where we are on Alera when we're *not* in danger?" Destiny countered in her usual snarky way. Destiny leaned back, inspecting the windows and frame, knocking on the material in some bizarre ritual I didn't even want to guess at. "I like your ride, Leo. I saw the windows are tinted. Is this bulletproof glass?"

Leo had taken us in his own vehicle, after walking a random route for several blocks to ensure we weren't followed. It wasn't as fancy or large as the one Lord Jax had provided, but I hadn't cared if it were a horse and buggy. As long as we were moving further and further away from danger, at least for the time being, I'd felt better. And having him sitting beside me in a closed area—even with my sisters as chaperones—had been intense.

Leo's hands moved with confidence over the controls. "We do not have metal projectiles in our weapons. But the windows are military grade. Nothing can get through them, not even blaster fire." He looked over at me, his gaze lingering, making me squirm in my seat.

Was he as hot for me as he seemed? Or was I reading something into his expression that wasn't real. Was my Ardor warping my mind?

"This is a standard military issue EMV. Nearly indestructible. No one can see inside. You're safe. I assure you."

"How fast does this thing go?" Faith asked.

"This *thing* obeys all driving laws so that we do not attract unwanted attention." He was so serious. His face set like stone. His jaw tight. Everything about him screamed powerful, alpha male. Warrior.

I'd wanted to crawl over and into his lap, straddle his thick thighs and feel the huge cock that was in his pants rubbing against me. To kiss him, taste him. I'd had to bite my lip to stifle a whimper as I breathed in his scent—a temptation that had filled the vehicle. Dark, rugged. I wondered what the sheets of his bed would smell like. Would that scent wrap around me and make it hard to breathe? Would I drown in him?

Did I want to?

Yes. Right now, god yes. I did. He had to have pheromones pumping off him in waves, for I was so close to coming that I ached. God, I was desperate to rub my clit, to get off, but I knew it wouldn't help.

I needed him. His touch. His mouth. His hands. His energy. His alien cock and all that sweet alien cum. Maybe if I humped him, rubbed our bodies together with our pants the only things between us, that would be enough. Would my body be satisfied with that?

Hell no. That was the answer. I wanted naked. Grunting. Thrusting. I wanted him to shove me up against the wall and take me as hard and fast as he could. I wanted to ask him to do it. Beg him. *Beg.*

Then I realized I was going insane, envisioning dry

humping a guy—an alien—that I'd just met as he drove across a huge city... with my sisters watching. I wasn't sure what disturbed me more, that I wanted to go at it with a complete stranger, or that I didn't care if my sisters watched.

Jeez. This Ardor was serious business. Mother had said it could lead to insanity, even death, if left unsated. I'd laughed at her. Now I realized my mistake. My body wasn't my own. Not right now. And I didn't like that lack of control one little bit.

So I tried to forget my eagerness to fuck Leo and thought of our attackers. It was obvious we'd hit a nerve with someone on Alera, that Mother's kidnapping had definitely been carried out by an Aleran. We weren't supposed to be here. We would cause massive amounts of trouble for whomever had taken her. While I was glad to know our existence would piss someone off, I wasn't really thrilled about being shot at.

From the back seat, Faith leaned forward, squeezing my shoulder. "Look, Trin. Look."

Her slender finger pointed out the window to the brilliant sparkling light that our mother had described to us, but we'd never seen. Shimmering like holographic glitter, the queen's light shot into the dark sky like a beacon. It was bright, brighter than the full moon on a cloudless night, and I had no doubt it could be seen for miles and miles. Maybe even from space.

And the light still burned. Mother was alive. For now.

"She's alive." Destiny whispered from the back seat.

"Of course the queen is alive. Somewhere. But it's been almost thirty years since she's been seen. Most think she was captured and is sitting in a containment cell somewhere, rotting. Most have lost hope that she will ever return." Leo, all but forgotten in the driver's seat, supplied the information. I tore my gaze from the citadel, and that all-important light, to watch the emotion, or lack of, cross his face.

"And you? What do you believe?"

"I don't waste time thinking about these things. I follow orders. I'm a soldier. That is all."

"Bullshit." I couldn't take it, not with my pheromones going crazy. The complete lack of expression on his face was going to make me throw things.

"The queen disappeared when I was very young," he offered. "I remember her, remember her laughter, her beautiful gowns, the way she would tussle my hair when my father attended meetings with the king. But that was a long, long time ago. Decades. If she were alive, she would have returned by now. Saved us all from years of war."

"Years of war? What war?" I didn't want to know. Not really. Mother had tried to talk me into returning years ago. Before law school. But I'd been selfish. Didn't want the responsibility that came with being a queen. And too scared to leave the only life I'd ever known. Perhaps hadn't truly believed Alera really existed.

Oh, I believed now.

Leo's hands gripped the controls, his knuckles white, his hands and muscled forearms crisscrossed with dozens of scars. I wondered if the rest of his body was like that. "What war, Leo?"

He turned to me, allowed the car to shift into some sort of automatic pilot. "I'll tell you anything you want to know. But know this. You're mine. So if you get scared or want to run, want to leave, you can't. I'll fight to the death to keep you safe and happy."

"Leo." God, gorgeous Leo. I didn't know what to say to that. He'd met me a few minutes ago, and already vowed to keep me? Possessive, much? I knew—well, I'd seen—the evidence of his interest come to life in his pants. That huge, meaty cock that I wanted to ride so badly. But I didn't know who or what he was. Was he a consort, like Cassander? Had his mate died or was he really a virgin?

That seemed impossible. No woman in her right mind would be able to keep her hands off him. He looked like Henry Cavill's version of Superman, without the tights. The Aleran uniform he wore did nothing to hide his *Fittest Man in the World* physique. He had to be six-four, with broad shoulders and a narrow waist. With the weapon holster on his hip, he gave off that aura of chivalry, as if he were a space-age version of a knight. He wasn't in shining armor, but when he'd come through the smoking ruins of the suite's entry, I'd been mesmerized.

And my Ardor? It had gone insane. Hot all over, my pussy had literally flooded with arousal. My mind went all *gimme, gimme, gimme.*

Now that we were away from danger—at least temporarily —I didn't have to split my attentions. Faith and Destiny could try and figure out who the assassins were, but they weren't going to get far. Not on their own. Or, at least, not tonight in a strange city.

The vehicle entered a private parking facility and Leo told us all to duck down so the camera attached to the security gate wouldn't record our presence when the window slid down automatically.

After the scanner flashed over his eyes, a computer voice thanked him and the window went back up, and he drove into the lot.

"It's safe now. They don't allow cameras in soldiers' quarters."

"Why not?" Seemed to me, it would be the opposite.

"Code-breakers once infiltrated the vid system and staged a perfectly executed attack. Took out an entire city division of royal guards in one night. Over a hundred guards. Some of the oldest. The best. The code-breakers knew where everyone would be. Where they slept. Where they ate. What time they came out of their rooms. After that, no more vids."

Hackers. On another planet. Things weren't that different after all. How horrible. "How long ago was that?" I asked.

"About five years."

We rode a very plain, dark gray elevator and ran into no one. We hadn't gone to a penthouse this time, only five floors up. Instead of a hotel suite, Leo had taken us to a small apartment. I looked around. Living room, a library, two bedrooms, a kitchen—although it had appliances I'd never seen before. It wasn't fancy, more... comfortable. Was this Leo's home?

My sisters were looking around. Faith staring out at the spire, clearly visible from the largest set of windows, and Destiny scoping out exits and entry points.

Everything was normal.

Except me, and this relentless lust making my brain mush and my body about as useful as a lit match thrown on a bonfire. I looked my sisters over, took in the dried blood that clung to them still, acutely aware of the warm, strong male hovering just a few steps behind me, locking the door. "Are you both sure you're all right?"

Faith nodded and looked at Destiny. "We're fine, but how about you?"

"I wasn't hurt."

Destiny rolled her eyes. "We know you weren't injured, but what about your other problem?"

I squirmed, my desire thrumming. My nipples were hard and sensitive, my padded bra only adding to the irritation. I wanted to rip it off, all of my clothes, my skin irritated by the fabric, by being confined. I wanted to climb Leo like a monkey, but I wasn't going to *admit* that. We were close, too close. They did *not* need that kind of ammunition.

Destiny leaned in, whispered, "I mean, it hasn't been cured or fixed or whatever."

It was as if she were worried Leo could hear us. He was walking around the apartment now, doing a security sweep, even though it appeared safe to me. He wouldn't have brought us here otherwise.

I trusted him. I had no idea why I should trust him over the five guards who'd been sent to protect us, but I did. Obviously, someone on Alera had been tipped off about our arrival. We'd either been followed from the transport center or one of Lord Jax's people was a traitor. Perhaps someone at the Brides Center on Earth? Warden Egara? That idea was crazy, but I was quickly learning we shouldn't trust anyone.

Except Leo. He was safe. I knew it down to my bones. He was the one, the only one who I felt could protect us from whatever evil had taken Mother, and wanted us dead.

But I had no right to ask him to risk his life for me. For us. For a woman who'd run, abandoned Alera almost thirty years ago. He'd said he didn't waste time thinking about it, that he resented my mother for leaving her people, for causing so much death. So much war.

How could I sleep with him, use him, and walk away? I had a job to do. A duty to the people of Alera and to my mother, and that did not involve risking the life of a humble soldier. He was a good one. Honorable. Simple. How could I tell him who I was when he hated my family? My mother? His past. He'd suffered. For years. And it was partially my fault. I could have returned more than five years ago. I could have spared him some of those scars.

"Shit. I don't know what to do." I whispered the words, my hands up to cover my face from a sister who would say far too much.

When I didn't answer her question directly, Destiny continued, "Look, I know we all want to go find Mom and fast, but we need to chill out for a while. I mean, we transported all the way to Alera. Today. We were attacked. Today." She held up her bloody hands. "I'd say we need a little downtime."

Faith nodded. "I need a shower. A bed. *You* need Leo."

Destiny grinned and waggled her eyebrows. "And he needs you. Did you, um, see his cock? It was literally tenting his pants."

Faith giggled. "One look at you and... bam." Faith held up her hand and raised her pointer finger in a 'just a minute' sign. Or, an example of how a guy's cock went from down to up. Very, *very* up.

I hadn't missed it. Not at all. Especially since all that... maleness seemed to be because of me.

Not Faith or Destiny. While he'd interacted with both of them, he'd barely given either much more than a second glance. As for me, he practically devoured me with his eyes.

And back to his cock. God, it was, well... huge. His uniform pants had done nothing to hide the thick, long bulge. Had I said thick and long? Even the outline of the wide crown had been obvious. He'd been aroused. Instantly and thoroughly aroused.

"Cassander said a guy didn't get hard unless he was with a woman who was The One. That the five guards had yet to find their mates, therefore their cocks were... impotent?"

Faith laughed. "That's a weird word. Leo doesn't look impotent at all. Maybe dormant. And Trinity, my dear, it seems you've got what it takes to *awaken* Leo."

I was attractive. I didn't flatter myself to think I was gorgeous, but the fact that I'd supposedly awakened Leo sexually was pretty empowering.

"You know what, guys?" I replied. "My Ardor isn't better and I *really* want all that untapped desire focused on me. He's gorgeous and—"

"A virgin," Destiny added.

God, a virgin hottie who wanted me. Blatantly. I whimpered because I was soooo ready.

"You are safe here," Leo said, coming back in the room. We spun about as a unit, and I felt guilty talking about him. He was more than a virgin. He was a Coalition fighter who'd saved our lives. Brought us to safety. He was honorable and wise. Chivalrous and brave.

All that and a big cock, too.

His eyes immediately met mine, but I couldn't hold his dark gaze. Nope. It dropped to the front of his pants. Yup, a hard-on of epic proportions. I had no idea how he was able to walk comfortably.

I pointed. I couldn't help it. "Um... should, does it, I mean—"

Instead of being embarrassed—like an Earth guy would have been for being caught so blatantly aroused—he stood straighter, rolled his shoulders back, which only made his cock more pronounced. "It's for you."

I'd never seen a man so... intent. His dark hair was mussed from battle, his uniform stained and torn by the shoulder. He looked rugged and fierce. My palms itched to run over him, feel the hard muscles, well-defined beneath his clothing. And to feel that cock, learn every ridge, every bulge. Every long, thick inch.

Seeing it made me feel feminine and powerful. Even in my jeans and sneakers, my hair most likely snarled and wild. Oh, and an inside-out shirt. Yeah, totally sexy.

I heard Faith stifle a laugh, but didn't look away.

"Buster, on Earth a guy doesn't show that much interest until at least the end of the first date." Destiny's words had that punch of abrasiveness I was used to.

"On Alera, a male's cock will only rise for The One." He was so earnest about it. If an Earth guy had said that, it would have been the worst line ever to get in a woman's pants.

But here, he meant it. *All* Aleran males were this way. Just like I had my Ardor, he had his... stirring. But I could fuck anyone, even Cassander, the gigolo. It seemed I really did have the power to *awaken* Leo.

God, that was hot.

"See?" Destiny muttered, in response to his statement. We'd been right. "Are you telling me that you've never had a hard-on before?" Destiny asked, blunt as ever. Thank god she was thinking the same thing. I couldn't dare ask.

"No."

"You've never..." Faith asked, twirling her finger around in circles.

His fists clenched at his sides, his breathing coming deeper, his chest rising and falling as a result. His eyes blazed, focused right on me, his jaw clenched. I could relate. I was practically coming out of my skin holding myself back. Any thought about not jumping his bones was gone. I wanted Leo and I wanted him now. Holding me, pinning me to the wall, pressing me down.

"No."

How hot was that? He'd been waiting for this moment, for me, to come all the way across the universe. To *awaken* him.

"But now?"

"I wish to be alone with my mate. To soothe her Ardor."

Leo took a step toward me, but no further. That was it. I couldn't wait any longer. I needed him. Needed his hands on me. His mouth. His cock.

Now.

I launched myself at him, my arms going about his neck, my mouth meeting his. He opened for me, his tongue finding mine.

His hands went to my bottom squeezed. I jumped and wrapped my legs around his waist.

"Okay, then," I vaguely heard Faith say. "We'll just... um, be... elsewhere."

I didn't notice anything else after that besides Leo. His taste, his scent, the hard feel of him. Everywhere. My pussy was pressed against the hard length of his cock and I rocked my hips into him. His tongue was in my mouth, licking, learning. My hands were tangled in his silky hair, holding him right where I wanted.

He tore his lips from mine. Growled. God, he looked so fierce, possessed even.

"Mine," he uttered, his voice deep and rough, and carried me down the hall to a bedroom, kicking the door shut behind him with enough force that the pictures on the wall rattled.

Oh yeah, I was totally his. For the first time since my Ardor kicked in, my pussy and I were in complete agreement.

rinity

MY BACK BUMPED into the wall and now I was pressed between two very hard things. One cold, one hot. Scorching hot. His hands moved from my butt and over me, my thighs, my waist, my breasts.

"I can't wait, mate," he murmured as his hands molded, weighed and played with my breasts through my t-shirt.

I moaned and arched my back. His hands felt so good. Big. Hot. Gentle, considering how wild this was.

"This first time will be hard and fast."

Ya' think?

Through barely opened eyes, I could see how much control he was using. I needed, but god, Leo *needed*.

I had a momentary thought of the Atlan guard at the Brides center. Was this what his beast was like? Wild and... beasty? No wonder no one ever heard of a divorced Atlan woman.

"Hurry." One word was all it took. He lowered my feet to the floor and made quick work of my pants, opening and tugging them down my legs. His hands went to the front of his pants as

I stepped to try to get my feet out of my crumpled jeans, but only had success getting them off one foot before Leo lifted me up again, this time his big hands on my bare ass. They were so big they cupped me from hip to crease.

I hooked my legs around him once again, felt his cock, hot and hard, nestled along my pussy. Bare and pulsing. Thank god for the birth control injection Warden Egara had given me at the bride center, because I didn't think I could stop. And I didn't want to. I wanted him hot and naked, skin on skin. I *needed* his seed inside me. I needed his energy, his wildness to fill me up.

"Are you wet for me? I will not take you unless you are ready."

I rocked my hips, coated the length of him in my arousal. "So wet," I murmured. Everywhere our skin touched was like a mini inferno. My flesh heated beneath his hands. My body was hungry for him.

His eyes met mine. Fierce desire. Possessiveness. Intense control. Need. I saw it all in that one instant. I wanted this. I wanted him. Deep. Hard. Thrusting so hard my back never left the wall.

Without looking away, I felt his hips pull back, his cock shift so it was notched right at my entrance.

God, I could feel how big he was, the crown parting my lower lips. I held my breath, waiting. Waiting.

With one word, "Mine," he thrust up into me.

I groaned. He growled.

The hand on my butt squeezed, and I knew I'd have little bruises there in the morning. His other hand slapped against the wall by my head as his eyes fell closed. A red flush crept up his square jaw, his lips thinned, the cords of his neck went taut.

But lower. God. His cock filled me. Stretched me. Opened me up like no other. I could feel every hard inch of him. So impossibly deep I sucked in my breath. Squirmed.

My pussy clamped down on him, squeezed, milked, tried to

pull him deeper, which was impossible. My clit pulsed as it rubbed against him. My heels pressed into his ass as I held him to me. And inside, something shifted, something hungry and desperate and primitive roared to life inside me and screamed for more.

"Mine." That was my voice, but one I didn't recognize, as I wrapped my arms and legs around him in a viselike grip. Energy, raw, male, covered me like warm, melted caramel, the heat going straight to my clit. To my pussy.

My core clamped down. Hard. Squeezed his cock like a fist.

He groaned. Pulled out. Thrust deeper. Harder. He held me there, riding his cock, stuffed full. Unable to move. Not wanting to. "Fuck me, mate. Take it. Take it all." He ripped open my shirt and his, pressed our bare skin together. Pressed his lips to my neck, my cheek, tasting my flesh, devouring me like he'd never get enough. And every moment, heat filled me up. Energy. Hot. Erotic. Like a drug I'd never get enough of. Every cell was hungry for him. My entire body a living flame.

This was why I'd come to Alera. *This* was what a human man could never give me. What I needed.

He pulled back. Thrust so hard my breasts bounced. I tilted my head back, giving him better access, unable to resist. Not wanting to. I had no choice now. My body wasn't my own. It was his.

"Oh my god," I gasped. It had never been like this. *Never.* And he wasn't even moving. I was so close to coming I couldn't catch my breath.

His head was buried in the crook of my neck and his hot breath fanned my skin. My fingers ran through his sweaty hair. My nipples were hard, aching for his hands. His mouth. Anything he could give me. And my body was already taking him in, demanding his life force, his strength, and I knew that I would never be the same.

For the first time in my life I felt... alien. *More* than human.

This was raw and dirty. The basest form of fucking, and

he'd only thrust into me a few times. It was as if he'd been dreaming of being inside a pussy. Just that and nothing more. He held himself frozen, as if *this* connection alone was so pleasurable he didn't need more.

Well, I did. I'd been desperate to come for weeks. Ached. I'd been on the brink, close to the edge but with no way to jump off. But now I had it. Now I felt whole, as if Leo's hold was all that was keeping me together, that once I gave over to the feelings, they'd be so intense I needed him to hold me together, ensure I didn't break into a thousand tiny pieces.

With the slightest shift of his hips, I came.

My head went back and I screamed, clawed, clenched. Milked.

I had no doubt Faith and Destiny heard, and probably everyone else in the building.

He pulled back once, then thrust deep and followed me over. A jagged sound, like a beast coming unleashed, ripped from his throat. His entire body went taut and I could have sworn I felt his cock thicken even more before he spent. Filled me with his seed. The warmth of it coated my insides as even more raw heat poured into my flesh, filling me with so much power, so much energy that I came again, the pleasure pushing me over for long minutes. When it was done, the aftershocks continued to rock me as muscles in my core pulsed randomly, out of sync, caressing his cock—almost as if my body itself was thanking him.

"I could die happy, Trinity. Right now. Inside you."

I smiled and held him closer, running my shaking fingers through his hair as my pussy continued to pulse and twitch around his length. Happy that he didn't appear any worse for wear for the energy I'd felt pouring from him. That he'd found pleasure as well. And that for the first time in months, I wasn't about to crawl out of my skin with need.

That was his first orgasm, the first sexual pleasure he'd ever felt. And he'd found it with me. *Inside* me. Because of me. I wondered if we were truly more than just Ardor and a male's awakening, if this intense chemistry would lead us to something more.

If I was ruined for all other men.

Yeah, I totally was.

I had no idea how long we remained locked together, unmoving. Savoring. It had been so incredible, I didn't want him to pull away. Or out of me. Our skin was sweaty, our breaths ragged. Eventually, our muscles relaxed, our grips loosened, but Leo still kept me pinned to the wall. As if we were anchored together and if separated, we might fall.

He lifted his head, looked at me. For the first time, I saw that his dark eyes were no longer plagued. There was a contentment, a softness to them.

"Hi," I whispered.

The corner of his mouth tipped up. "Hello, mate. That was... incredible."

"So good," I agreed.

"If you think that was good, just wait until I have you in a bed. Naked. With hours to test all the forms I learned in training."

"Training?"

His grin made my entire body break out in goose bumps. "Oh, yes, mate. Every male on Alera has weeks of classes on how to pleasure our mate. Centuries of learning handed down from generation to generation. And I cannot wait to test every single one of them on you."

Oh yeah, that sounded like a good idea. My pussy was soooo ready for round two. "Okay."

He smiled fully then and... wow. It was the first time I'd seen him smile, seen the full impact of *him.*

I was devastated by his looks. Eyes that didn't blaze with fury, but with heat and simple satisfaction. A nose that had a slight crook and had been broken and hadn't been healed by one of those wand thingies. A square jaw with dark whiskers. I envisioned him with a beard, but a better thought popped into my head. Him between my thighs, that scruff against my tender skin as he used his wicked, wicked tongue...

"That can be arranged."

Without any effort, he turned and carried me to the bed, lowered me to it.

He stood before me, tall and proud, and I took him in, legs parted, hand gripping the base of his cock. He'd only opened his pants enough to get his cock free to fuck and now the material was bunched around his hips. But his cock... it was huge. And still rock hard. He'd just come not three minutes earlier and he was still ready.

Did I say huge? Like porn star big. No wonder I'd whimpered when he thrust up into me. My inner walls, now empty, clenched with eagerness for more.

But, he'd been a virgin and no doubt had plenty of pent-up need to still be so hard. With his grip about the base, there were inches... *inches* of the shaft above it. Glistening with my arousal, proof I'd been as eager for him as I'd said. It was a ruddy plum color, thick veins bulging along the length, as if it had a vital, never-ending supply of blood to keep it hard. The tip was flared, broad and fluid seeped from the tip as if he'd never stopped coming.

His balls hung large and heavy, a blatant sign of his virility, of all the seed he had to give me. Of the amount of it that slipped from my pussy even now.

"You're in bed, mate. Time to get naked," he said, his tone laced with command.

He expected me to strip for him as he watched, stroked himself.

Totally worked for me. While I'd come—and come hard— my Ardor had been soothed slightly, but not completely. Otherwise, I'd be unconscious right now after an orgasm of that magnitude.

In our haste to fuck, I'd somehow tangled my jeans around

my left sneaker, so I reached down and worked it all off, let them fall to the floor. Coming up onto my knees on the bed, I tugged the remains of my t-shirt off, reached back and removed my bra, tossed it over his shoulder.

I'd never seen such an appreciative gaze from a man before. He looked at me reverently, yet full of sexual heat. Completely lacking in modesty, as if he wanted me to watch him. Needed my attention. His fist stroked him harder, faster and his hips bucked once.

He came with a caveman grunt, a thick spurt of his cum arced and landed on my thighs.

"Goddess save me," he said as he knelt there and rubbed his seed into my skin. It wasn't sticky like a human man's, more like massage oil. The indescribable scent filled my head and I leaned back, arching into his gentle touch, wanting more. Wanting it all over me.

"More, Leo. I need you again." I reached for him, wrapped my hand around his *still hard* cock, grateful he didn't appear to need time to recover. I didn't want to wait.

When he caught his breath and let his hand fall to his side, his cock was *still* hard, still aiming straight for me.

"Obviously, I have little control with you," he said. "You're too lovely. Seeing your breasts, your pussy, my cum coating it. You are very beautiful, mate. Perfect."

I licked my lips, wondering how he'd taste—not only his cock but his chest, the tips of his fingers... every inch of his skin —and I swayed toward him, licking my lips. It was as if he were a drug and I needed another fix.

"No. It is you who needs tending," he said. "To come until your Ardor is soothed."

I did feel better after the orgasm, but not completely sated. I wanted more. I was eager for it. Primed, even. But Leo, in all his newfound prowess, had been a virgin until a few minutes ago. I got a sense of his bossiness, but his cock would be ruling him now. He'd be like a teenage boy.

I was the experienced one here. If I wanted him to do something, I'd have to tell him. Or... I could show him what I liked, for how else would he know. I had no doubt he'd like it, too.

"Get naked and get on the bed," I said, practically repeating his words.

He eyed me for a moment, thinking. Perhaps a female hadn't bossed him around before? Tough. My pussy had needs and I was going to take them—and him—into my own hands.

He stripped at record speed and I settled on the bed, watching as he showed me everything. Muscled shoulders that made me sigh. Tapered waist. Thighs thick as tree trunks. And that cock, pointing straight up at the ceiling.

"How long do you think it will take for you not to spontaneously come when you see me?" I asked, smiling at him. I was teasing, but also serious. We couldn't leave this apartment if he would come in his pants if his cock was out of control.

"If I don't breathe in your flowery scent, see the way your nipples tighten beneath my fingers or the way your pussy opens to my cock, then tomorrow."

"And otherwise..."

His hands gripped the blanket, his eyes roving over me as if he couldn't get enough. "Otherwise, perhaps the day after. Or next week, all depending on how many times I take you. Make you scream with pleasure. Watch your eyes glaze over as you come, as you milk my seed. Make me yours. Take my joining energy. I will come inside you mate, over and over, until you can't hold any more. Until you don't need. While you can have any male of your choosing, as your mate, I will take you until can't think of anything but me."

My pussy clenched at the idea of him coming again and again. And again.

"Well, let's see whose need is sated first," I replied, crawling over to him.

His eyes flared at the position, at the way the tip of his cock nestled against my lips. I licked the flared crown and he groaned, burying his fingers in my hair. Urging me on.

"What are you doing, mate?"

I grinned. "I learned a few things, too."

Lifting up, I hovered over his cock, then lowered my open mouth down, one delicious inch of him filling me at a time.

The bedding ripped in his hold when I swallowed, sucked. Teased.

With one strong tug on my hair he lifted me and I rose up on my knees, finding his mouth with mine for a kiss that went on and on until my pussy was weeping, aching. Throbbing.

"Leo."

"I know what you need." Before I knew what was happening, I was on my hands and knees and he thrust into me from behind.

The new position—his huge cock—filled me even more. Stretched me as he wrapped his hands around my hips and lifted me off the bed so he could kneel behind me. He positioned me, my legs splayed outside of his.

"Put your hands around my neck and don't move them without permission." His order was almost a growl but I complied without thinking. His cock felt so good. His skin pressed to my back. My thighs. So much skin. So much heat. His body was feeding mine once more. Lighting me up on the inside. Making me burn. Want.

I'd do anything he wanted, as long as he didn't stop.

"Leo. God. Please." I lifted my hands back up behind my head and locked them around his neck, tugging on his hair in a silent demand that he hurry. Move. Thrust. *Fuck me.*

He moved one hand to my breast, holding me in place as he pumped up into me, lifting his body and mine. The other hand? I rocked my hips, whimpered as his fingertips found my exposed clit and rubbed. Played. Rolled the small nub between his fingers.

"This was lesson nine, mate. Do you like it?"

"Nine?" Lesson? What was he talking about? I couldn't think. I wiggled my hips, tried to lift and lower myself, anything to make the building tension ease.

His very male, very satisfied chuckle barely registered as he toyed with my nipple and sent his hot breath into my ear. "It was always the most intriguing to me. So much freedom for my hands."

He fucked me. Slowly. His cock moving like a slow-burn engine until the rhythm became the center of my universe. My existence. There was nothing but him. And his hands. His mouth on my shoulder. My neck. His heat and energy filling me up, just like his seed would.

"Come, mate. Take me in. Make me yours."

His order was a whisper, but my body heard him, felt the hard demand of his fingers on my clit. My body arced as if struck by lightning and he held me close as I shattered, lost my mind. Became nothing more than sensation.

He held me together, and I took everything.

His seed was a hot jet inside me, his growl music to my ears. He was mine. Right now, he was mine, and I wasn't finished with him yet.

8

$\mathcal{L}$ _eo_

"I STILL DON'T UNDERSTAND why someone left you something at the citadel," I grumbled, driving down the deserted roads. There were few vehicles this late at night. Everyone was in bed, where I should have been. With Trinity. "It's just an empty relic now. Multiple royals have entered and found nothing. And you won't even be able to get inside."

"Don't worry about it, just get us there alive. Okay? That's all we need." Trinity's voice was crisp, clear. Confident. Strong.

I loved hearing the power in her, knowing I'd helped make her that way.

Naked. Inside her hungry body. Filling her up.

In the two days since her arrival and my awakening, I'd fucked her until my cock was sore and my body completely drained. Every male on Alera knew the stories about the females' Ardor. The need for both seed and energy our females were born with. Now, I was part of her. Would remain part of her forever. Our life force mingled. My energy nourishing her cells, preparing her to be a mother, to have children, to be strong enough to survive.

When I was a younger man, I'd believed the honor of easing a female's Ardor was a violation. The idea of giving part of myself, part of my body, my very life force to a female had sounded like a burden.

How very wrong I'd been. Buried in Trinity, her hot, wet pussy milking my cock, the sweet scent of her skin, the soft silken strands of her hair—the sounds she made as I pleasured her.

Not enough. I'd give her everything. Kill for her. Die for her. Give her every last drop of my blood, my seed and my soul. My cock ached, but remained hard and hungry. I knew her now, knew from the way she squirmed in the seat next to me that she was far from satisfied. She needed more. Wanted more.

From me. Only me.

She'd said we fucked like rabbits, but I had no idea what that meant. I hadn't given her much time to talk—about anything—before I'd had my mouth on hers, quieting her except for her moans of pleasure.

And now I was a tiny bit sorry I hadn't given us more time to talk because I was taking the females to the citadel. To collect *something* that had been left there for them. Why the citadel? Did someone leave a package behind a shrub? That seemed unlikely, for the guards who circled the revered building had little to do but watch for strange people, strange packages. Anything out of the ordinary. In the past twenty-seven years, *nothing* had been out of the ordinary.

The spire still glowed brightly. The queen was alive, but silent.

Would this *thing* they needed to collect still be there? I'd definitely delayed Trinity long enough for their item to be found and confiscated. The three of them seemed confident that it was there. They were adamant, refused to go anywhere else.

"I still don't understand why you're here, on Alera," I added, circling back to the first question I'd had about them since Prime Nial contacted me.

"You complaining?" Trinity asked. She placed her small hand on my thigh, and I had to fight the instinct to pull the vehicle over and fuck her right here in the car. Now.

I glanced at her, saw the curve of her lip and I knew she was in a teasing mood. If her sisters weren't sitting behind us... I'd tug her ankles so she slid down on the seat and I settled over her. It wasn't a big vehicle, I was only a Coalition fighter after all, but the cramped quarters would only be to my advantage as I fucked her. I could push off the side and take her hard and deep. And with her leg over the controls, she'd be wide open. Wet.

"Easy, soldier," she whispered.

"You guys have had two days to work this Ardor and awakening shit out of your systems," Destiny grumbled from the back seat. "Chill."

"You're the one who told me to jump him," Trinity countered, squeezing my thigh.

Jump? She had all but flung herself at me. I couldn't help but grin. "The strongest females on Alera have been known to awaken to Ardors that last up to a week. And Trinity is not yet appeased." But fuck, the last two days had been amazing, touching her for the first time. Tasting her lips, feeling the heat of her pussy against my cock, even through our clothing. The tight peaks of her breasts against my chest. "Thank you, Destiny, sister of my mate, for advising her to, as you say, jump on me."

"You're welcome. But I didn't do it for your blue balls. I did it for Trinity's vagina."

Trinity glanced over her shoulder at me. Grinned. "My vagina thanks you, too."

"What are blue balls?" I asked.

They laughed. All three of them. The NPU wasn't needed since we all spoke Aleran, but every once in a while, they added an Earth term that did not process. In that moment, I realized something and set the vehicle to auto.

"You're speaking Aleran. All three of you."

Trinity frowned and I could see the V in her brow with only the lights from the passing buildings lighting her face.

"Yes," she replied.

"But you're from Earth." The NPU wasn't processing and translating directly to my brain. We were all speaking the same language.

"Yes," Trinity added.

Up to this point, Faith had remained silent. "Wow, Trin, you're a killer in bed if it took him this long to start asking questions."

"We know she's a killer in bed because we heard it all," Destiny added. "It's not like they were quiet."

I should have felt embarrassed. Possessive even, for Trinity's sounds of pleasure belonged to me. Instead, I felt pride that I could make my mate feel so much satisfaction. As expected, Trinity was not a virgin and had shown me what she liked. I'd been all too eager to combine what the male classes had taught me on pleasuring a female, but knowing my mate liked my mouth on her pussy, that flicking the left side of her clit made her come within seconds. That there was this little spot deep in her pussy, when I pressed firmly as I sucked on her clit made her scream, made her so wet she dripped over onto my palm. That she liked it from behind the most out of all the positions we'd fucked. So far.

No, I wasn't embarrassed. I was aroused. My cock was uncomfortable and thick in my pants and ready for more. Ready for Trinity. I was completely at her mercy.

And that was why I was driving them to the citadel in the middle of the night instead of driving into Trinity's pussy. She'd asked if I would bring her—all three of them—to the citadel. It had taken a day for me to agree, and even then I'd agreed on the condition that we visit in the dead of night. I promised to protect them, keep them safe and they wanted to go to the most exposed—and revered—place on the planet.

Only when I was deep inside her did I agree. Oh, she'd used her female wiles to manipulate me. What male could deny his mate anything when she had her fingers pressed to the smooth spot behind my balls? She'd teased me with light touches until I agreed, and then she'd gotten me off.

It was only after my head cleared that I added the requirement that it be done late at night.

"I may be completely at your mercy, mate. I may have these *blue balls* you mention. I may even need to pull over and fuck you once again because I can't control myself. But I am not stupid. I am well aware you are redirecting, keeping me focused on the scent of your pussy, the feel of my cock inside your body, the wet heat of you milking me of cum, instead of answering my questions."

"Holy shit, Trin. He's a dirty talker," Faith commented. "I like it."

Trinity's hand gripped my thigh now. Hard. Yeah, she liked it when I was crude, when I told her exactly what I wanted to do to her.

"Yes," Trinity replied, her eyes on mine. I wasn't sure if she was saying yes because she wanted me to get between her thighs and breathe her in, to get my cock nice and deep so she could all but draw the cum from my balls, or if she was admitting she was intentionally avoiding a response.

"I have been accommodating, mate. To you and your sisters." I spoke the truth. They had been safe and protected. Bathed and fed. They each wore Aleran clothing generated in my quarters, using my S-Gen machine. I had done everything they asked of me...and they'd told me nothing.

"Not us, hot stuff. Just Trinity," Faith added, but I could tell from her tone and the smile on her lips she was playing.

I wasn't. While I couldn't force my cock to go down, especially not with Trinity beside me, I *could* focus on something besides fucking. "We are almost to the citadel. I've done as you've requested. My assignment with Prime Nial is to offer protection and assistance in whatever you need to do. But in order to fulfill that, I must be briefed. Now."

The queen's light could be seen glowing above the buildings. We were only a few blocks away.

"Leo—"

I took Trinity's hand from my thigh, moved it away. "Don't Leo me. I will give my life to keep you safe, but I must know everything."

Trinity eyed me, bit her lip. She glanced at her sisters. "We have something to get at the citadel."

"Yes, you've said that. What is this *something*?"

Trinity turned in her seat to face me, one knee bent. "I don't know. None of us do. That's the truth."

"Then why is it so important, so dangerous, that someone wants you dead?" I thought of the assassins the other night and my grip practically strangled the controls. We'd avoided danger, so far. But taking the three females out into the city, exposing them to the world, made me edgy.

"I don't know."

I clenched my teeth to keep from snapping at my mate, demanding she answer me.

"We don't, Leo," Faith added.

"How do you know where it is? It's not like there are places to hide something around the building. It is all open, with guards."

"Our mother told us where to find it."

"Your mother. On Earth." This was hard to believe.

"Yes," Trinity added.

The road we were on went directly to the citadel. The silver building could be seen in the distance before us, the glowing spire a beacon. We were a hundred feet from the guards, not close enough to raise an alarm, but being such a late hour and without anything to do, their attention was on our vehicle.

My frustration grew and I ran my hand through my hair. I wanted to wake up Prime Nial, force him to tell me more. It would be easier than prying the answer from these three stubborn females. Surely, they could handle the most ruthless of interrogators.

"Mate," I growled, and not in a sexy way. "Where?" I couldn't ask more. It sounded ridiculous. *Where did your Earth mother tell you a secret package was hidden at the heavily guarded and fortified citadel on far-off Alera?*

"Inside."

A bark of laughter erupted and I stopped the vehicle in the middle of the street. There was nowhere else to go.

"Is your mother trying to get you killed?"

Trinity frowned, crossed her arms over her chest. She no longer wore the Earth garments, but an Aleran outfit I'd created using the S-Gen machine in my quarters. She didn't look like she'd come from Earth any longer. She'd blend in perfectly on Alera, which was exactly what I wanted. To blend in so the assassins wouldn't have such an easy target.

"Of course not."

"Are you sure she doesn't want you dead? Because there's no way you can get into the citadel with the protection the ancients left behind. They created an energy field surrounding the inner sanctum. No one but their descendants, those of royal blood, can pass without being destroyed. Instant death, mate. I've seen it happen twice, right after the queen disappeared. Two of her less-blooded, greedy cousins tried to get inside. They wanted the throne, the power for themselves."

"What happened?" Faith asked.

"Cellular disintegration. A heat so hot it's cold. An explosion so fierce it doesn't need oxygen. The body explodes, but implodes. Dust." It had been years since anyone not of royal blood had tried to enter the citadel, and even then, it had only been those who wished to end their life, not ascend to the throne. "The clerics guard it night and day to stop others from attempting to end their own lives."

"Jesus, the citadel is a suicide mecca?" Destiny flopped backward in the back seat and put the weapon she'd been cleaning on her lap. "Didn't see that one coming. That really sucks."

Trinity didn't blanch, didn't even flinch at what would happen to her if she attempted to cross the energy field. "We must go to the citadel, Leo."

"Tell me why?"

"I can't. I made a vow to my mother, to my sisters. I can't tell you, but I'll be back. I promise. I'll find you."

Find me? "What are you talking about?" I stared into sad eyes, eyes filled with regret and cold dread filled me even before I felt the hard end of a blaster pressed to the back of my neck.

"You're getting out here, Leo," Destiny said.

I stilled, looked to Trinity.

"We're going in. That's our mission. That's why we're here." She held my stare for a moment, and I knew true terror. She was serious. Dead serious.

"Are you insane?" I asked, my heartbeat quickening. "You can't go in there. You'll die!"

She shook her head. "We won't. Trust me."

"You will, though," Faith said. "You're a nice guy. We like you in one piece. Especially Trinity. And I think she likes one *piece* in particular."

"Faith," Trinity groaned.

I noticed a few of the guards were slowly walking toward

us. Their weapons were aimed at the ground and their stances indicated they were not at fight readiness. They didn't fear someone could get inside the citadel, the protective energy field left by the ancients took care of that. Their role was part ceremonial, but also to keep the peace, if required.

At this time of night, our vehicle was an oddity and they were most likely bored. Still, they were walking this way and I had an ion blaster aimed at my head.

"Get out of the car, Leo," Trinity said. "Please." She tagged on the last, practically begging. The last time she'd said that word was when I'd teased her with my cock, settling the tip just inside her wet entrance and not going any further.

"I won't leave you," I countered. "You're my mate. I won't let you do this. And as a fighter, as I've vowed to Prime Nial to protect you. I refuse."

I heard the click of the weapon's fire safety being released, the high buzz of sound as the weapon held its charge, ready to fire.

"You'll have to kill me, Destiny."

I felt the sizzle, the heat of the blast as it went through my body.

"Or stun you," she countered.

I went stiff, every muscle in my body going rigid, then relaxing. I couldn't move anything.

"I'm so sorry," Trinity murmured, stroking my hair, my cheek.

"Trin, open his door!" Destiny said quickly, but calmly. "The guards are getting closer."

Even frozen, I could move my eyes, watch as Trinity glanced out the front window. Reaching across me, she pressed the button to open my door. It slid up quietly. The guards stopped, thirty feet away.

Trinity didn't move all the way back to her seat, but stopped, her face right in front of mine. I could see every freckle, every worry, fear, doubt. "I'm doing this to save your life. I'm sorry. I really am, but we have to go. My mother's been kidnapped, and I really don't have time to explain or argue. We have to get inside." She leaned over and placed a warm kiss to my lips. "I'll find you when I can. I'm so sorry."

I tried to speak, but only a strangled groan came out. I tried with all my might to lift my arms, to grab her, to keep from doing this. But nothing worked.

"Trinity!" Destiny shouted.

Trinity pushed me out the door.

I fell to the street on my side, a whoosh of air escaping my lungs.

I was bent at the waist and I could see Destiny's big boot, then the rest of her leg come over the back of the seat. She dropped into the spot I'd vacated.

She looked down at me, her purple hair wild. Trinity was leaning forward, looking at me, her teeth pressed hard into her lower lip.

"You want answers, Leo. You'll get answers. Right now," Destiny's promise was more a challenge, but all I could do was watch as Faith waved good-bye from the back seat, Trinity took out her weapon, and Destiny lowered the door, once more hiding them from view.

I fought to speak. To yell. To tackle my mate to the ground and spank some sense into her. My brain worked and worked, but the stun still had a hold on me.

I could do nothing but lay on the street and watch as my vehicle picked up speed and drove right at the approaching guards. Destiny didn't stop and the fighters jumped out of the way, then fired at the back of my vehicle. The other guards, now realizing there was an incident, were running and settling into their positions, bracing for some kind of attack.

The stun wore off, from one heartbeat to the next, and I was up on my feet and running toward my mate. "Trinity!" I bellowed as the vehicle approached the citadel. Then closer. They were driving straight at the energy field.

I stopped. The guards stopped. Watched. Waited. No one had ever driven a vehicle through the barrier before. Would it be disintegrated along with the occupants?

My heart stopped, I held my breath, watched as Destiny drove straight through, as if she had a death wish—or knew, she wouldn't die.

The vehicle skidded and swerved to a stop directly before the main entrance to the citadel. Tall doors, two stories tall.

Slowly, I walked toward the citadel, the guards beside me. Stunned, as I was, they'd all but forgotten I might be a danger. We watched as the doors to my vehicle—the vehicle that had just... fuck, just driven straight through the ancients' energy barrier—opened and three very *alive* females stepped out.

Destiny and Faith used their clothing to conceal their features and their hair. Only the curve of their hips and breasts gave away their gender. My mate? She did not hide. She stood proudly, her hair down, her stance wide. Hands on her hips. She stared up at the central tower, at the line of royal spires pointing to the stars in a magnificent display at its peak. At the single spire that had burned bright since Queen Celene's time.

Trinity turned and faced me. Only twenty feet separated us now, but she might as well have been on another planet, because I couldn't get to her. The distance was small, yet impossible to breach.

Our eyes met. Held.

"Holy fuck, Trinity."

"You wanted answers," she called. She held up her hands, shrugged. "Now you know."

Destiny and Faith went around the vehicle and to the entrance.

There was only one possibility.

The guards were talking now, whether to commanders off-site or to each other, I had no idea. Nothing like this had happened in twenty-seven years and now it was my mate who'd crossed the barrier and lived. Who stood steps away from the citadel sanctum. From confirming once and for all who and what she was.

Royal.

The daughter of Queen Celene.

Destiny stood before the tall doors—there was no lock— and they swung open automatically, as if recognizing the one who requested entry and welcoming her. Destiny walked forward, disappearing into the dark interior of the sanctum. We all stood, staring. Waiting, knowing what might come next, what would prove them truly worthy. The blood on the sacred stone. The final judgment.

The second spire lit and everyone around me gasped. My heart skipped a beat. The added illumination was almost blinding.

Faith, who must have been holding off for the ultimate proof of Destiny's identity, followed. Just like her sister's had, Faith's face and head remained covered until she slipped inside.

After a minute, another light soared into the sky. Another spire came to life.

Another sign that would cause chaos and celebration. Perhaps ignite the spark of unrest among the noble families into a full-fledged war.

All this time, Trinity stood still, looking at me. Waiting. For what? My reaction? Forgiveness? Why hadn't she trusted me with the truth?

"This mother you spoke of," I called, the facts crystallizing in my mind now. No wonder Prime Nial wanted these females protected. "The one who told you there was something for you to retrieve at the citadel?"

She lifted her chin, took on a regal bearing that was geneti- cally hers. "Queen Celene." She bowed to the guards, who looked as shocked, and numb as I was feeling. This simply was not possible. "My name is Trinity Herakles, daughter of Queen Celene and King Mykel, Princess of Alera."

I watched as my mate, a princess, walked into the citadel. I knew in a few moments my mate would place her blood on the sacred stone, that the citadel would judge Trinity worthy. When another spire shone bright into the night sky, her light all but blinded me, just as she had from the moment I met her.

I was nothing, just a simple Coalition fighter, a guard. I was not worthy of such a female, and yet, my body had awakened for a princess. The eldest daughter of Queen Celene.

My mate was heir to the throne of Alera. She would rule the planet.

If she survived.

And her comment in the EMV? About her mother being kidnapped?

Fuck. She'd been talking about Queen Celene. Her mother. Kidnapped by whom? When? Who would dare? And where would they keep her?

As if a spell had broken with her disappearance, the guards descended, stunned me once again. They weren't as considerate as Destiny had been, using a much stronger setting. Pain sizzled through every nerve and fiber of my being, but it was nothing to the pain of losing my mate.

I would find her. I would protect her.

Princess or not, she was mine. And maybe a hard-hearted ex-Coalition fighter was just the kind of monster she needed to keep her safe. Whether she wanted me to or not.

The world went dark. The four illuminated spires—one for the queen and one for each of her daughters—would alert the entire planet to their existence.

No more hiding. No more secrets.

Those lights, the beacons of hope, were the last things I saw as I lost consciousness and fell to the street.

Ready for more? Read Ascension Saga, book 2 next!

Leoron of Alera has learned the truth about his new mate's identity, but landed in the hands of her enemies. The time for secrets is over...

Click here to get Ascension Saga, book 2 now!

BOOK 2

PROLOGUE

 ueen Celene of Alera, Prison Cell, Location Unknown

I KNEW FROM THE ANGRY, quick slap of my captor's boots on the smooth, metallic floor that something had happened. Something that would make his customary ranting and raving seem pale in comparison.

"Open the door." The bark was louder than usual through the thick metal.

His order was obeyed instantly, but even the speed of the two guards he had chained outside the door wasn't enough, and I watched as he struck them with an electrically charged flogger repeatedly for being too slow.

The two aliens—whose race I could not define—flinched, but didn't make a sound. Like me, both were prisoners. Perhaps more so, for I was not a slave destined to live a life of cruelty and despair.

And this bastard knew it. Thrived on it.

I wasn't a slave. I was a queen. Even in my red and black lumberjack plaid pajamas I'd been wearing when they'd taken me. I sat on the edge of the small cot I'd been provided, my ankles crossed, my hands settled demurely in my lap, my chin up and my eyes shooting as much disdain and disgust as I could manage while cold, hungry, bleeding. I would not give in to this alien's glee at weakening me.

"What do you know of the citadel?" he asked.

My silence was all the answer he would receive, but hope flared in my heart. I'd been taken days ago. Perhaps a week. With no sunrise or sunset to mark the time on this spaceship, I wasn't really sure how much time had passed. I could feel the subtle hum of the engines, note the smooth movement of the ship through some quadrant of space. We were not on Alera, that was for sure, but I had no idea if we were within the planet's orbit or half a galaxy away.

But in the time since they'd stormed the house and yanked me from my bed, they'd never asked me about the citadel itself, only about the royal gemstones. The mark of royalty I'd hidden all those years ago. Inwardly, I was pleased with my forethought to secure their safety, deciding not to take them to Earth with me twenty-seven years ago. If I had taken them, both the gems and I would be in the hands of evil now.

Better me than the power and tradition the royal gemstones represented. The royal bloodline would continue, even if I were to die in this cold, wretched cell. Alera would survive. The ancient bloodline—and their gifts—would survive me. The same could not be said if the gems and their powers fell into the wrong hands.

No usurper would stand a chance of claiming the throne without them. The people simply would not accept their rule, not while I lived. Not while the light of the spire glowed over my home city of Mytikas.

And while my captor wasn't happy about it—he wasn't happy about *anything*—he knew this. Or his master did. And that was why I was still alive.

The only reason.

The gray-skinned giant walked closer but I refused to look away. To let him see anything but my confidence in the line of succession. In my daughters.

"Talk, female," he snarled, spittle flying from his lips. "Tell me what you know, or I will bleed you."

I gave a slight shrug to let him know I'd survived that action once. I could do it again. "We both know your master won't let you kill me."

"There is pain, Celene," he vowed.

Inside, I shook with fear. But outside, I remained calm. This alien monster with his gray skin, black eyes and huge, scaled hands had already beaten me. Starved me. Threatened me. Screamed. Raged. But no more.

He might not know it, but he was a fool. A pawn. I had never seen another of his species, had no idea what dark planet he came from. He was nothing to me.

I remained silent and he dropped to his knees before me, so that our gazes aligned. Black meeting crystal blue. I believed he meant for me to fear him even more, but he was a supplicant now bowing, before me. A worm.

"The citadel. Three more spires light the sky. What do you know of this?"

Unable to contain my joy at this confirmation, I defused the smile with a soft chuckle meant to enrage him. It worked, for the hideous gills in his neck flared.

"I suppose, if the legends are true, there must be three more living royal descendants on Alera." All of this he already knew. "One of them is probably parading around in the royal gemstones and being crowned the new queen as we speak."

If this were true, I would not be held here. I'd be dead.

"Your cousins, the only other royal family members, never had a spire light for them. Not one. And they tried many times."

"Then the Goddess deemed them unworthy," I clarified.

Again, the history of the spires was something he knew. "Perhaps She changed Her mind?"

Not possible, but this male didn't believe in the strength of a female. He didn't understand the divine wisdom—and power—of the Goddess. The idiot.

"The spires would not light for them after all these years," he countered. "Not while you live."

My smile turned malicious and I shrugged once again, as if this conversation, as if *he,* were boring. "It's been a long time. A very long time. Your master waited too long to take over the throne. With the additional spires lit, he's too late."

I hoped he would slip, tell me his master's name, give me some way to track and eliminate my enemies, the threat to my daughters. But I was becoming accustomed to disappointment.

"Bitch queen." He stood and I braced for impact. Even knowing the blow was coming wasn't enough. That monstrous hand struck the side of my head and everything went black.

*aptain Leoron Turaya of Alera, Mate to Princess Trinity,
Cleric Building, Interrogation Room, Sub-Level Three*

THE PUNCHES and kicks that rained down had ceased to hurt
hours ago. I was numb. I felt no pain, could only hear the
sound of flesh on flesh, a hard boot against my already broken
ribs, the hiss of air as I struggled to breathe through what had
to be a punctured lung.

"Where are the females? Where are the queen's daughters?"
The voice did not belong to my tormentor, but to one of Alera's
highest-ranking clerics. "Three females entered. None of them
exited the building. Where are they?"

"Still inside, I guess." I had no idea where they were, was
still reeling with the revelation that the female whose Ardor I
soothed, The One, my mate, was the future queen.

"The citadel is empty. The sanctum was searched by the
royal family."

"There is no royal family on Alera." That was the truth as
far as I was concerned. Or, at least it had been until Trinity and
her sisters arrived. Queen Celene's cousins, those deemed

unworthy by the citadel and unable to light a spire, had not earned the right to call themselves royal. Most people on the planet agreed. If they did not, we would have had a new queen years ago.

"The royal family searched the citadel. It was empty. Where did the females go? How did they escape?"

Trinity and her sisters weren't found inside the citadel? Where were they?

The large male doing the dirty work was a man I'd never seen before, but the inked markings covering his body indicated he belonged to the clerics' private army.

An army they had systematically denied creating the past few years as they jostled for power after the queen's disappearance. No one had claimed the throne in the twenty-seven long years since. And now, no other would, except my mate. Three decades of plotting and scheming brought to an abrupt end by the light of a few spires.

I tried to laugh, but the sound came out as a wheeze. "Worried that your evil... plans to take over Alera... are ruined?"

The cleric was not amused and he nodded at the brute beating me to continue. Still smiling when the first blow landed over my already broken ribs, I clenched my teeth and endured, focused on the hem of the long, elaborate cape wrapped around the body of the cleric sitting a few steps away. The cell was cold, but I knew the soft, black shell and even softer silver lining would keep him warm in much worse conditions.

Beneath, he was dressed as all the clerics were, in a fighter's uniform with a ceremonial dagger at his hip. I knew he had been trained to wield the blade better than any standard Coalition fighter. The uniform cloth was an array of sharp angles in silver and black while an expanse of white crossed his chest and shimmering silver graced his arms. The silver was tradition, a token of their eternal service to and respect for the royal bloodline.

And apparently, a complete lie. At least where this male was concerned. He was a master-level cleric, an expert in hand-to-hand combat—yet he refused to get his hands dirty with me —and I'd seen the links of silver chain around his neck proclaiming his status to the world.

Despite his youthful frame, I estimated he was near sixty years old with deep lines around his eyes and mouth, not from laughing, but scowling... as he was doing now.

More of me was broken than whole. The taste of blood filled my mouth and I had to wonder if I were spitting it up due to internal bleeding, or if my mouth filled with the dark liquid because my lips and cheeks were flayed open.

I didn't focus on any of that, nor the questions they asked. All that filled my mind was her voice. Her scent. Her taste. The feel of her pussy as it had clenched and milked my cock. The soft feel of her hair as it brushed over my chest when she'd kissed her way up from pleasuring my cock with her mouth. *That* had been an experience I'd been waiting a lifetime to have fulfilled.

I thought only of Trinity. My mate. The One.

There was no fucking way I was going to die now at the hands of the clerics. They might be brutal and vicious, but I would survive. For her. My cock had only just awakened and there would be nothing that kept me from returning to Trinity, to sinking between her parted thighs again. To ease her Ardor, which had yet to be resolved.

She would be suffering, aching with a need that returned with a vengeance. I knew she wouldn't seek out a consort. She would need me—my cock—to soothe her.

I would get out of these chains, out of this barren, cold, evil room and satisfy her in any way she needed.

I was no longer a servant to the Coalition. I was a servant to my mate.

The fact that she was an Aleran royal only doubled my loyalty.

Tied to a chair, my ankles bound to the front legs, my arms pulled behind me and cinched behind my back, the punches rained down. There was no way to protect against them.

Another strike had my head flying back.

I didn't bother to lift it. I knew what was next, the indescribable pain of the neurostim devices. The technology was designed to heal, but had been modified to stimulate pain receptors in the body... and nothing else. No bruises. No physical damage. Hours of torture. The practice had been outlawed decades ago for driving people mad.

The cleric cleared his throat and the brute paused his strikes, which was almost worse than the continued assault. It gave me time to feel everything he'd already done to me.

"Princess Trinity announced herself to one and all. But who were the other two? Her sisters? I need their names and descriptions from you, Leoron. One way or another, I will get them."

"Fuck you." I was proud of the sisters, of my mate. They'd thought ahead, Destiny and Faith covering themselves, remaining hidden from the cameras as they'd bolted into the citadel. I'd thought it odd, at the time. But then, I'd assumed they'd come out the way they went in. Through the front door.

Instead, all three of them had vanished into thin air.

Just like their mother had, twenty-seven years ago.

The cleric sighed. "Use the stim."

I cringed before the small device touched my flesh. The moment it did, I bellowed in rage and in pain. The device was impossible to defeat, sending a burst of power through every nerve receptor in my body.

My body arched off the chair as if I were having a seizure and I had no control of the movement. When it was pulled away, I slumped over like a bag filled with sand. Dead weight. My limbs, my head too heavy to hold up for another moment.

Silence. Cool, cold silence.

"He's no longer responding." The big brute said, his voice

bland. It was as if he'd done this before, as if I were just a single person in a long line of many who'd been tortured in this room. And died. As if he were *bored.*

"Stop then. I want him to suffer. He's no good to me dead." The cleric's order was soft, but annoyance was clearly audible in his tone.

"He hasn't given up anything. Not one word about the spires. Who the other two royals are who entered the citadel. He hasn't even said why they were with him." The deep, gravely voice of the one who had beaten me filled my head. "I've seen his kind before. He'll let us kill him, but he won't break."

"He will." My hair was gripped, my head lifted by the cleric. While my eyes were open, I could barely see the male before me beneath the swollen eyelids. "He will. But not today. Tomorrow morning is soon enough. Cut him loose. Water. No food."

The cleric released his hold on me, and I felt my head fall forward. I tried to lift it, but it was as if the stupid thing suddenly weighed a hundred pounds. Perhaps I was in worse shape than I'd realized.

With a grunt, the giant released my restraints. The bindings fell away from my arms and legs, and he kicked the chair out from beneath me. It tipped and I fell with a hard thud to the stone floor.

The cold felt good against my swollen face.

"Do we give him a ReGen wand this time?"

The question made me wince. For several hours now, they'd beaten me to the brink of death before healing me with a ReGen wand just enough to start again. I knew this could go on for days. Weeks.

I didn't care. I would survive. For her. Trinity. My mate.

The cleric's laugh was pure evil and I shuddered, faced with the evidence of my stupidity. For years I'd believed the clerical order when they'd claimed their soldiers were just for protecting the citadel and the queen's future. I'd believed their stated purpose of serving the people and having no ambition to rule Alera themselves.

I'd been wrong. Three families were powerful enough to fight for the throne. Just three. But the clerical order had its own army, spies, a network so vast I wasn't sure they could be beaten if they decided to take the throne. And if they had allied themselves with one of the other power-hungry families?

War. We were on the brink of war. And I was falling hopelessly in love with the female who would be at its epicenter.

The cleric stepped on my hand as he walked away, crushing the already aching digits into the cold, hard floor of the cell. "Let him suffer. Perhaps in the morning he'll be ready to talk."

They were hoping I'd do just that. But I wouldn't. The only other Alerans alive who knew about Trinity, Faith and Destiny were the Jax guard who'd been injured—and, with Faith's help, hopefully recovered—and the assassin who escaped. Everyone else was dead. No consort, no other guards. I doubted these men knew of the injured one. Perhaps were aware of Lord Thordis Jax's involvement, but doubtful. Definitely not of Prime Nial's request for my help.

As for the assassin? I'd recognized him from my time in the Coalition Fleet. He'd worked in their Intelligence Core. He'd killed Hive, mowing them down without remorse. Among other things.

He was very good at killing.

I never knew his name. Had never asked. But I'd been happy to have him at my back or watching over an op through a sniper's scope. And now? Was he working for the clerics? One of the royal cousins? Lord Jax?

If he'd been sent by the asshole leaving me here to rot, I doubted they'd be torturing me for information. They would already know who the sisters were. Where they were from. When they'd arrived.

They appeared to know nothing, only became aware of them once the spires lit. Which meant my mate had more enemies than I knew about. And the assassin was still out there.

The cleric had shown me vids of my EMV, of the females as they exited the vehicle, their faces intentionally hidden. They'd even captured the look of disbelief on my face the moment Destiny stunned me before pushing me out. Luckily, the door of the EMV had obscured the camera's view, the females' faces remaining hidden. But I couldn't lie and tell the cleric I knew nothing. The citadel guards hadn't seen Faith's or Destiny's faces, but they were eyewitnesses to my stunned ass landing on the ground, the door closing, and the females driving through the energy field that surrounded the citadel. Their dash inside. The way the spires illuminated after they entered the sacred building. And worst of all, Trinity, standing proudly facing all of us, giving us her name. Her true name.

Trinity Herakles, royal heir, daughter of Queen Celene. And she was my mate.

I was the only one who could give these brutes answers. Yet, I had none. Or only a few. I realized now that was intentional. Trinity had kept secrets. For my own good? Was the stubborn female trying to protect me?

They were from Earth. Trinity had the Aleran Ardor, which meant she was at least part Aleran.

But the spires? The lights? The females were royalty. Their ages were right for them to be Queen Celene's daughters... but could that be true? Was my Trinity actually Princess Trinity, as she had claimed? She was the eldest, and I'd seen the other two defer to her on more than one occasion. But a princess? *The* royal heir?

Heavy footfalls reverberated through my cheek and ear where I had them pressed to the floor as the giant followed his master out of the room. The cell door slid shut behind them. I was alone.

Earlier in my captivity, I'd checked out the small space for any means of escape. There was nothing of use. No cameras, no knobs. Smooth walls and floor, fortified door. There was nothing but the stark, white light that shined brightly to prevent me from truly resting. How long had I been trapped here? How long had Trinity been alone? I had no idea what day it was, how much time had passed since I'd been captured.

I used my feet to push myself across the floor to the thin mattress in the corner. It wasn't soft, but it would keep the cold from seeping into my bones—my broken bones. I would spend the hours until dawn thinking of Trinity.

Reaching between my thighs, I gripped my cock through my pants, stroked it. It was hard... it would remain that way even beaten and bloody. For her. The slight hint of pleasure, of heat that sparked through me at my shifting grip, was my only sense of relief in all the misery.

"You just can't stop playing with that big cock, can you?"

That voice. So sweet, so sassy. So mine.

"Trinity," I whispered, stroked harder.

"Yeah, if I had that beast between my legs, I'd probably touch it, too."

I blinked, tried to see, but the vision before me was blurry and my eyelids were still swollen. I saw the outline of a female, pale hair. I took a deep breath, even with the pain in my lungs. Flowers. She smelled like flowers.

"Trinity," I repeated. I was dreaming of her now. Was I that close to death? Was the Goddess granting me a dying wish to see my mate before me once again?

"What did they do to you?" she asked, and I felt a gentle touch on my shoulder, down my cheek. I leaned into the heat of it, the softness.

Such a good dream.

"I won't tell them. I promise, mate."

"Oh, Leo. You're so strong. So brave. You can stop now."

I pushed to sit up, winced. "Never! I won't stop until you are safe."

I couldn't see, couldn't do anything but fight back. I would not die.

"Shhh," she crooned to me. "That's it. Lie back down. Yes, Leo, listen to me, your mate's voice. Good. I'm going to put this little transport button on you and we'll be out of here. You might have saved me back at that penthouse, but it's my turn to save you right back."

"Trinity?" I croaked.

"That's it. Time to get out of here."

I felt a hard press on my shoulder, then a soft, small hand in mine.

The familiar sizzle and pull of a transport tugged at me, but I wouldn't believe it. I'd looked for an escape and knew there was none.

I was dreaming. I was dying. Yet my mate was here. My dream had come true.

When the ice-cold twisting of transport came to an end, I was awake. In agony, but more aware. Of her. "Trinity." I reached for her, blindly. Found softness. Held tight.

"He needs help... now!" my mate shouted.

It was no longer cold, but I was still on a hard floor. I could hear the quick footfall of many people, the immediate ease of pain in my face, my leg. Blinking, I could see out of one eye now. The blue glow of a ReGen wand was my first sight, but as it passed back and forth, I saw Trinity. Really saw her.

Blonde hair. Blue eyes dark with worry. Pink lips. So kissable. Her clothes were different than I remembered. She wore a warrior's uniform. Coalition Fleet issue. Armored. An ion blaster in her hand. And she looked beautiful. Perfect. Unharmed.

Fragile. Small. Weak. How dare she risk breaking into the cleric's building?

"What have you done, mate? Why are you dressed as a warrior?"

"Shhh. Don't worry about me. You're the one in trouble here."

"You," I said. My throat was so dry, I was hoarse. "No. Get away from me. You're in danger."

She leaned down and kissed me on the lips, the touch like a sacred blessing. "It's okay, Leo. I got you. We're not on Alera. You're on Battleship Karter, you're safe. *I'm* safe. Jessica—Lady Deston—helped me get you out of there. She used your NPU to track you."

Just like Prime Nial had used the forgotten technology buried in my skull to make contact with me, request my assistance in protecting Trinity and her sisters. I owed Nial a life debt, but he hadn't needed to call in that favor. He was my friend. Protecting innocents was what I did. I would have helped them regardless. But thank fuck, he'd called on me. I never would have met my mate otherwise.

I turned my head slowly, reluctant to look away from her, half afraid she would vanish into thin air. A frowning Prillon warrior dressed in medical green was looming over her. The blue glow came from a ReGen wand in his hand, as well as that of a young assistant in a lighter green uniform, who was trying to heal the broken bones in my hand.

The doctor spoke. "Your majesty, he needs a ReGen pod immediately."

"Yes, of course." I felt the squeeze of her hand as I was lifted onto a gurney, wheeled down a hallway. I held onto her. She was here. She was safe. For now, that was enough.

"Were you really in that cell with me?" I was half convinced I'd been hallucinating. Was *still* hallucinating.

She walked quickly beside me, along with others who were still waving ReGen wands as we moved. The familiar walls of a Coalition battleship zoomed past, the colors changing from blue to cream to green as we neared the medical station. Others talked around us, but their voices blurred. Nothing was clear. Nothing but Trinity.

"Yes. Jessica gave me a miniature transport beacon and had her team send me directly into that prison cell to rescue you."

I tried to sit up then, but big hands held me down. The doctor. Make that Prillon warrior. Huge Prillon warrior. "Lie down. Rest. Or you'll cause additional injury."

"You were transported into the cell to rescue me?" I asked.

"Yes, can you believe it?" A booming voice cut through everyone else's as we continued down the hallway.

"Prime Nial," I replied. The hands were still on me. I couldn't sit up to bow or offer him deference of any kind.

"I'm glad to see you alive, friend. Your injuries are grave but will heal with a few hours in a ReGen pod."

"Trinity," I replied, squeezing her hand.

Prime Nial understood my request. "She will be under my personal protection while you are healing," he vowed.

"As if I'm going to leave his side," Trinity countered.

"You are well. Not injured?" I asked her.

"I'm fine. And I'm so sorry, Leo. If I'd known what they were going to do to you, I never would have—" Her voice cracked and I couldn't bear to see her in pain.

"You were right to leave me," I reassured. "I would never have allowed you to enter the citadel if you had told me your plan. It was reckless. Dangerous. There are better ways. Safer ways. You should have told me the truth."

"I'm sorry. We had a plan, and I tried to keep you out of it. I didn't think they would hurt you."

"You are mine. My mate. When I get out of the ReGen pod, I am going to take you over my knee and spank your ass for lying to me. And for the risk you took to free me. You should have let me be, Trinity. Never risk yourself. Never."

"I agree." Prime Nial sighed. "Jessica has already felt the sting of my palm for her complicity in the rescue operation."

"You were in a meeting! Ander was off killing things," Lady Deston countered. "Like Trinity was going to wait for you big guys to get your butts in gear."

"And *your* butt has paid the price," Nial rejoined.

Trinity's lips thinned, clearly not pleased with the direction the conversation was going. "I don't need a man to save me. Jessica and I handled things."

"You should have come to me," Prime Nial said, gently pulling Lady Deston to his side and wrapping a protective arm around her. "I would have sent in a team of warriors to free him. Not one, small female."

"Small, but mighty," Lady Deston added, winking at my mate, despite Prime Nial's discussion of her recent punishment.

Apparently, Earth females were very difficult to tame.

I might be headed into a ReGen pod, but my mate clearly needed a reminder of who was in charge of her safety. A reminder I would be happy to supply once I could get up off my back.

The medical team pushed the gurney into the medical station, and I took in the long row of ReGen pods, a few currently in use.

I was carefully lifted and settled into one at the Prillon doctor's direction, but I held my hand up to keep the lid from lowering.

"Mate," I said.

Trinity leaned down and her pale eyes met mine. Clear, honest, open. Yes, she was a dream I'd never dared even hope for.

"Yes, Leo?"

"When I wake, I will spank your ass, then I'm going to fuck you from behind until you scream my name." I kept my voice low so none of the technicians could hear. "If you're not in line by then, I'll spank you again as I fuck that tight, perfect pussy of yours over and over until you know who you belong to."

She stared at me, her mouth open, her cheeks flaming pink, a color I'd learned to love. She was mine.

"You are mine, Trinity. I will die to protect you. But no more secrets."

She bit her lip and stood, backing away as the technicians closed the ReGen pod's clear covering over me as if I were dead. But she didn't agree to my demand.

We'd been open and crude in our sex talk with each other, especially when it came to pleasure. But I'd never vowed to punish her before. Never demanded her secrets. Her complete trust and total surrender.

But she wasn't an assignment any longer. A job. A mission.

She was mine. My mate. Mine to love. Mine to protect. Mine to fuck and pleasure and care for.

I grinned then, the first time since we'd been separated.

Prime Nial would keep her safe while the ReGen pod took care of my injuries. Which was good. Because when I was healed, I wanted my mate rested and prepared to scream my name.

2

Trinity, Battleship Karter, Medical Station, 18 Hours Later

I LOOKED DOWN at Leo's face beneath the glass. He appeared to be sleeping, but I knew he wasn't. I had to repeatedly remind myself that this was not a Snow White scenario. He was not in a glass coffin. He was not waiting for me to kiss him and wake him up.

He was comatose in a ReGen pod, just as he had been for more than seventeen hours. Jessica had tried to help me deal. She'd taken me on a tour of Battleship Karter—which blew my mind in a way transporting to Alera hadn't—fed me. I'd slept in a private room in Jessica and her mates' ship quarters.

I was the personal guest of the queen of the entire Coalition of planets. They didn't address her as queen, they just called her Lady Deston. But the fact remained, no one argued with her. She snapped her fingers and she got what she wanted on this ship.

Even Commander Karter, a big, gruff Prillon warrior I'd met briefly at dinner the night before, deferred to her. Even when she teased him about sending him a nice Earth girl to bring him to his knees.

I've never seen a Prillon blush, but Commander Karter practically ran from the table when Jessica brought up the subject.

I might have been a princess, but she was *queen*. With Nial and the scary looking teddy bear, Ander, scowling at anyone and everyone she spoke to, I began to understand the appeal of having a strong warrior at my back.

But I didn't want a Prillon, or even one of the hulking Atlan beasts I'd seen come in from the fighting. I wanted the stubborn male unconscious beneath the glass. Or silicone. Or whatever fucking material this shit was.

I splayed my hands wide above the glass, as if I could reach through it and touch him. I wished the strange gift I could feel blossoming in my mind was stronger. Maybe it would allow me to reach his mind telepathically. Or heal him with a touch. I didn't know. No one did. The citadel itself bestowed the gifts on those of royal blood. I'd placed my hand on the stone, felt the stab of crystal as it bored into my palm taking what it needed to confirm my identity, to judge me, to light the spire.

My sisters would have matching scars in the center of their palms and I wished they were here so I could talk to them. Discover if the lightness in my head was normal. If the strange buzzing energy I felt building inside me was normal. If they, too, saw the flashes of light and dark I was seeing around people since I'd come out of the citadel.

If I was normal.

I rubbed the bloodied mark in my palm, my thoughts making me aware of the ache. It was nothing compared to what Leo had endured. Nothing. I refused to ask for a ReGen wand to heal the small injury when Leo lay bloodied and broken before me.

The Prillon doctor circled the room, apparently unconcerned, his presence providing a release for my tension. "How long does this healing pod take? He's been in there forever."

The doctor lifted his head. He was checking an adjacent pod, one that had already healed—and *released*—two other warriors. "Some wounds require several days of regeneration. Leoron was fortunate there was not more damage to his internal organs or nervous system. Stim torture can cause permanent brain damage."

"What?" The doctor had officially lost his mind. He'd already told me the worst of Leo's injuries, when I threatened him with bodily harm if he refused to detail Leo's condition to me. Fortunately, Prime Nial and Jessica had been with me at the time. I hadn't missed the small nod of Nial's head that passed between the two warriors before the doctor responded.

My brave warrior had cuts and bruises everywhere, seven broken ribs, a punctured lung, bruised organs, his heart was in some kind of electrical shock and not beating correctly and his central nervous system had been nearing shutdown. *That* had made Prime Nial curse and storm out of the room. Something about illegal weapons, but I ignored him and stayed next to Leo's pod until my knees were wobbly and Jessica wrapped her arm around my waist and led me from the room.

I'd been too damn tired to argue. But now? Now I was ready to hurt people if Leo didn't wake up. And soon.

And *no one* had mentioned the prospect of *permanent* brain damage.

"He was indeed, fortunate, Princess." Prime Nial stood across from me, staring down at his friend with almost as much intensity as I. "I do not approve of the risk you took, but Leo was very fortunate that your plan was a success. He would not have survived much longer."

Fury poured into me. Cold. Hot. Both at once. I could barely breathe, but my mind raced with all the ways I was going to make those clerics pay. "I'm going to hunt down the man who did this and make him pay."

The leader of the Coalition and ruler of his own star system didn't even change his expression. "Do you think that is wise? You must think like a queen now. Every action you take will have repercussions. Added meaning and weight."

"I know." And I did. My mother had sent me to law school for a reason. I'd been a state champion in debate, on every leadership council and in every class that had to do with civics, law, and military history. I knew, but there were some lines I would defend. Some people were untouchable. My sisters. My mother.

And him. My Leo. I didn't know about this mate business yet, but I knew Leo had suffered for me. Because of me. And the helpless rage I'd felt when I realized where he'd been taken —and why— I never wanted to feel that again.

"He is mine to protect. I will destroy anyone who threatens him. Anyone who harms him or my sisters." My body shook with rage, my hands trembling on top of the glass, so I removed them, hiding them at my sides.

Here I stood, spewing threats of death and destruction, and Prime Nial actually chuckled. "I suggest you be prepared, your majesty."

"Prepared for what?" We'd been staring down at Leo inside the ReGen pod for the past ten minutes. Even though the countdown on the machine's timer made it clear when the healing would be complete, I had insisted we return to the pod early, just in case.

Leo looked the same now as he had long hours ago when the doctor had sealed him inside. His usually pristine uniform was filthy and torn. Dried blood remained caked to his skin. He looked just as injured now as when this pod put him into some kind of hibernation and the healing mode began.

Prime Nial lifted his gaze to me at the irritated tone in my voice. I was still thinking about hunting. Bounties. Soldiers storming the clerics' building. But then Nial smiled softly, giving me a look similar to the one I'd seen when he looked at

Jessica. As if I were *cute*. A Chihuahua puppy barking like a grown Rottweiler. His hand came out to pat my shoulder, but he stopped just before, as if he'd remembered himself.

Oh right. *Your majesty*. I wasn't just Trinity Jones, Earth girl anymore. I was Her Royal Highness, Princess Trinity Herakles of Alera. It seemed there were rules. Protocols. Even for a Prime, who ruled multiple planets and colonies, as well as acted as commander for the entire Coalition Fleet.

"He will be completely healed, I assure you. That is why I want to prepare you."

I frowned. He made no sense. "I don't understand."

His gaze darted to the timer, then back to me. "In less than a minute, your mate is going to climb from this machine and be very angry with you."

"And horny," Jessica added, the door to the medical bay sliding closed behind her. "Really, really horny." She came up to Prime Nial from behind and wrapped her arms about his waist. Smiled at me. "Just remember, make up sex is really hot."

"My love, there is no making up with us. Ander and I are always right."

Jessica rolled her eyes at me. "As if."

"Who hasn't been able to sit down comfortably for allowing Princess Trinity to risk her life unnecessarily?"

Jessica lifted Nial's hand to her mouth and kissed his palm. "It was hot." Prime Nial truly had spanked Jessica for her help? Based on the way Jessica's cheeks flushed a bright pink, and her eyes turned glassy with interest, I had to assume it was a yes. "*And* the make-up sex after was really great. That was a total win-win for me."

Prime Nial growled but held perfectly still under her attentions. Who was the puppy now? "Just great, mate? Perhaps Ander and I need to do it all again to see if you still feel that way."

I laughed at their banter. Clearly, they were in love. I hadn't had much interaction between Jessica and Ander, her other mate, but I had no doubt that while it seemed Prime Nial was in charge, Jessica gave this mate specifically a run for his money. The way she winked at me, I could see the guy was putty in her hands. She'd turned the entire conversation around on Prime Nial and now he felt the need to go fuck his mate to prove his prowess.

Yeah, he might rule the free universe, but she ruled him... and he *liked* it.

The ReGen pod beeped, turning all of our attention back to it. With a pfft sound of a seal being released, the glass lid pivoted up. Leo's eyes popped open as if he'd been pretending to sleep, then he sat up so abruptly, Prime Nial, Jessica and I all jumped back.

Leo's gaze took in the room, as if remembering where he was, then moved directly to me. Didn't shift away from me, even though Prime Nial was also in the room.

His big hands went to the edges of the pod and he hopped out.

"Mate," he growled. "You are in big trouble."

"Told you," Jessica whispered.

Prime Nial had been right, although he didn't gloat like his mate. Leo wasn't injured. Other than being filthy and covered in dried blood, his eyes held the clarity of someone in perfect health. His spryness indicated his injuries were gone. But Jessica won the prize. Leo's cock tented the front of his uniform pants. He was horny.

So was I. We'd fucked for two days, but my Ardor hadn't been eliminated entirely. I'd felt it creeping back upon me, the hum of arousal building in my blood as time passed. It wasn't as bad as before Leo had taken me the first time up against the bedroom wall, but if I didn't get his cock inside me soon, I'd be right back there.

I also recognized my interest in him wasn't solely driven by the Ardor. I just wanted Leo. As a woman wanting a man. It had been so good, he'd made me crave it. Crave him. I'd somehow forgotten how big he was, but the room was crowded with the long row of pods and he just looked... huge. His shoulders were so broad, his hands like big dinner plates, but I remembered how gentle they could be. The rippling muscles, the way his ragged breathing—and it wasn't because he was in pain—made his chest seem even more expansive.

And now... with all that intensity focused right on me, I licked my lips and said, "Leo."

He held up a hand stopping me from saying anything more. I swallowed.

"I do not care that you are an Aleran princess. You are my mate. You are not to risk your life for me. You are more important. More valuable. I forbid you from pulling such a dangerous stunt ever again."

"I'm royal, Leo. One day I will rule Alera"

"Yes, but you are mine. And I will rule you."

I arched one brow and began tapping my foot on the smooth floor. "Oh yeah?"

"Yeah," he countered, his voice getting quieter, not louder.

"Perhaps it would be best if you took your... discussion to private quarters?" Prime Nial suggested.

Leo grunted his agreement.

"We didn't have a discussion after I helped Trinity," Jessica added with a grumble.

"Mate, would you rather I announce to every doctor and medical technician what they will really be doing?"

"Excellent idea, Nial. Thank you." While Leo was speaking to the leader of Prillon Prime, his eyes were solely on me. Those dark depths held heat and frustration and a primitive... something that needed to be assuaged.

"Upper level, quarters six-four-three," Prime Nial shared. "We will debrief. Later."

"Tomorrow," Leo replied. Before I could even move, he had me tossed over his shoulder and was carrying me out of the room.

"Leo, put me down," I said, pounding at his back. "This is ridiculous. I can walk just fine."

He harrumphed, but didn't stop. "Yes, it is ridiculous that I have to remind my mate that her life is much more valuable than mine."

"I can't help that I'm a flipping princess."

"It has nothing to do with you being an Aleran royal. It has to do with you being my mate. It seems I haven't fucked you well or hard enough for you to realize that. I will be fixing that right now, and I assure you, you will not be walking just fine after."

The threat made me shiver, eager to get on with things. It didn't take long for Leo to reach the quarters Prime Nial had allocated for us. I didn't see much of the main room except what I could around Leo's ass, but the bathroom was large. I doubted most rooms were of this size, but then again not everyone on the ship was a princess. Or Prime Nial's close friend.

Leo pressed buttons on the wall, which turned on the shower. Steam immediately began to swirl in the glass enclosure. He finally settled me on my feet and I stood, staring, as he tugged off his torn and dirty clothes, dropping them to the floor, most likely to be burned, or whatever one did on a battleship. Mother had told us about life on Alera, not outer space. As far as I knew, she'd never seen the inside of a battleship.

I couldn't help but stare as every inch of him was revealed, but the dried blood was a visible and gruesome reminder of what he'd gone through. He stepped into the tube, began washing it all away. I hadn't been in the cell where they'd held him—tortured him—for long, but I remembered.

"Mate, you have five seconds to strip and join me or I will be tugging you in as you are."

From the depth of his tone and the way his eyes were still on me, I knew he was serious. That, and the fact I'd been carried like a sack of potatoes across a battleship.

I made quick work of the outfit and stepped into the warm tube when he opened the door. Without thinking, I took the soap from him, began to wash him. His cock was hard, just as I'd always seen it, the vein up the length pulsing with his life blood. The crown was broad and I remembered how it would stretch my pussy nice and wide for the rest of him.

"I'm sorry," I replied, staring at his chest, his cock bobbing and bumping against my belly.

"For what specifically, mate?"

"For you being hurt."

"That, Trinity, I could endure. What I couldn't survive would be if you had been hurt. Captured. You have no idea what the enemy is like." He stilled my hands with his, and I lifted my chin to look at him. The water beat down on both of us. Here, in this warm cocoon with him, I felt safe, like nothing could ever harm us. But that wasn't the truth, the evidence of that swirling down the drain.

"I couldn't just leave you to them," I countered. "I was able to help and I did."

"Unacceptable."

The shower tube was snug, meant for just one person, or perhaps two normal sized people. But Leo was so big there was nowhere to go, nowhere to look but at him.

"Unacceptable?"

"I will not have you in harm's way."

"Even if you might die?" I asked, completely exasperated.

"Yes."

"Well, that is unacceptable to me," I said.

He took the soap from me, washed us both efficiently and thoroughly. While his touch wasn't meant to be sexual, it was impossible not to be aroused. His hands were on me. Everywhere. My Ardor was making it hard for me not to lick drops of water off his chest. The water shut off and a hot wind turned on.

I let out a strange eep of surprise, but Leo put a steady hand on my shoulder. "You do not wash like this on Earth?"

"With a big, sexy man I can't wait to—"

His jaw clenched and I stopped mid-sentence. I'd never showered with a man before. Never wanted to. With him? I was about to melt into a puddle at his feet. "I do not want to hear about other males. You are mine now."

"No, Leo. I have never taken a shower with a man. And not with a full body dryer. We use cloth towels to dry off."

He gave a slight shrug as the unit shut off. I wasn't completely dry—my hair took fifteen minutes with a hair dryer —but Leo seemed satisfied enough to pull me from the tube and into the other room. He grabbed the corner of the blanket that seemed to have been spread across the bed with military precision and yanked it down. "While I do not expect you to have limited yourself sexually before we met, I am the only male you will shower with now."

He sat, faced me and was still taller. With his knees parted, his balls were big and heavy, hanging down between his thighs, his cock jutting up and out. I could even see a bead of pre-cum slipping from the slit. "I am the only male you will touch. Kiss. Fuck. Do you understand?"

"Of course. I'm not a cheater, Leo. Do you think so little of me?"

He slashed his hand through the air. "The complete opposite. But it appears we need to put some rules in place, for Earth females seem to have notions that their mates are not in charge of their safety and well-being."

I crossed my arms over my chest. Felt slightly ridiculous that we were arguing naked. "You think you're in charge of... me? Of us?" I, too, waved my hand, indicating whatever the hell we were.

"Of course," he repeated. "I am the male, the stronger one. Look at our size difference, our skill differences. I protect you. I cherish you."

"What do I do then, lay in bed all day with my legs spread to service your big cock?"

His eyes narrowed, his jaw clenched and I knew I'd gone a touch too far.

With lightning fast reflexes, he gripped my wrist and tugged me forward so I all but stumbled until I stood right between his knees. "You are itching for a spanking, aren't you?"

"You're a Neanderthal," I growled.

He sighed. "You are mistaken, mate."

"Oh? About what exactly?" I asked, my tone snarky.

"I will make the decisions when it comes to your safety, to your well-being. That is non-negotiable."

"And I can't do that for you? Knowing I had the ability to save you from... from torture? That's your safety and well-being!"

"It is not the same."

"Because I'm a woman? A princess? This was one of the reasons I didn't tell you. I might be a princess, but I'm still me." I placed my hand between my breasts.

3

I GROANED, leaned in and kissed Trinity's skin directly above where her hand rested against her chest. The spot was warm, silky soft and while she smelled of utilitarian battleship soap, I couldn't miss her own flowery scent. The scent that made my heart full, my cock throb. My hands tightened on her round hips.

I had to make her understand. I was not insulting her or her intelligence. Far from it. "Mate. We will talk about the future, protecting your sisters and your throne, with Prime Nial."

"And my mother."

"Yes. I know she was taken. I heard you and I listened. I will help you find her. I give you my word. But between us. You. Me. You are my mate. My mate!" I did not shout. I wasn't mad, but riled. Determined to make her understand the primitive need driving me to protect her. "I am not human. I am not like the males you knew on Earth. I can not allow harm to come to you.

Ever. Prime Nial is the same way with Lady Deston. Every male on Alera is the same. Are Earth males so pathetic to think you are not worthy of such protection? Devotion?"

"You're not talking about protection or devotion. What you're talking about is possession. I'm not a thing, Leo. You can't own me. You can't dictate my life."

"I am not a tyrant, Trinity. I will not take what is not freely given."

I watched as her sharp mind worked this over. "So, what, exactly, do you want me to give you?"

"Trust. Honesty. Tell me what you need, what you want. Tell me what worries you. Trust me, mate. Trust me to take care of you, to ensure your happiness. Accept the gifts I offer to no other, only you."

"You are so not what I was expecting," she said, and I had no idea if that statement worked in my favor or against me. I remained silent and waited for her to work things out. I wanted her hot pussy riding me, milking me. I wanted her to welcome me into her body and her heart. I needed her trust, her surrender. I needed it more than I needed to breathe. I couldn't stand beside her and watch her destroy herself by giving too much, taking risks she should not take, allow others to harm her, insult her, threaten her. No.

She'd seen the way Lady Deston was with Prime Nial. Surely he was more of this... Neanderthal than me. And Ander, the two of them together were doubly intense. Lady Deston loved her mates, how they were dominant over her. Well, most of the time. She wasn't passive. And if she laid in bed naked and with her legs spread as vulgarly as Trinity had put it, it was because her mates were good lovers, not because she was weak.

"I... I can't be subservient to you. I can't obey. I'm not built that way."

My hand came up, brushed her damp hair back over her shoulder. "Don't you see, mate? I am subservient to you. You need, I provide. You are my female, and my princess. You will rule the planet with me standing watch behind you. I will be more than your lover, Trinity. No one will harm you or threaten you during your reign. They will not take more than you are willing to give, not with me there to protect you."

She shook her head. "We will find my mother and she will rule. Not me."

"Someday, you will be queen. But know this, I will kneel before Princess Trinity, but I will not kneel for my mate. When we are alone, you are not royal, you are mine."

"I will not kneel for you either," she countered, her chin tipped up, her tone defiant.

Ah, my princess.

"That's because we are equals," I replied. "That's what I've been trying to tell you."

Her eyes fell closed briefly as she shook her head. "How can we be equals if you forbid me from doing things?"

"Because my heart is completely full of you."

Her eyes flew open, met mine, a second before she climbed into my lap and kissed me. No, not kissed. Devoured. Her tongue was practically down my throat. I could feel the soft press of her breasts against my chest, her pussy coating the base of my cock with her wetness.

For a second, I was lost. Surprised. One second we were arguing, the next she was all over me. I wasn't complaining. I relaxed, the fight being replaced by instant desire. I was already hard—I doubted I would ever go down with her around, let alone in my lap—hard and eager to sink into her.

After Goddess knew how long, she pulled back. "Now."

"Yes, mate. Whatever you say," I replied, gripping the base of my cock as she lifted up on her knees, settled me at her entrance, and lowered herself down. Opening. Stretching. Taking me.

She laughed—such a sweet sound. "You'll do as I say as long as I'm riding your cock?"

I grinned, wrapped an arm about her waist and flipped us.

Her back was on the bed and I stood at the edge. Her legs went around my waist. Fuck, she felt good. Hot, wet, tight. Perfect. The time we'd been apart had been too long.

"I have something for that sassy mouth of yours," I replied, fucking her hard. I couldn't be gentle. Not now, not this time. The wet sounds of our coupling filled the room. I was going to come just watching her responses. The way her eyes fell closed, her back arched, her breasts swayed, her pussy dripped. "But it's busy right now."

"Yes!" she cried.

"That's it, mate. Take your pleasure."

She reached between us, put her fingers over her clit and circled. I watched how she liked to touch herself—and fuck, I was going to come knowing she did so.

"Leo," she groaned as she came. Her inner walls milked my cock as if it wanted it deeper, harder. More.

I gave it to her, just as I would give everything else as she rode out her pleasure. At least as long as I could last, for after a few hard thrusts, I couldn't hold back. My balls drew up and my seed filled her. Pulse after hot pulse. It was so intense, the incredible feel of my mate, I all but collapsed on her, taking my weight on my forearms just before I crushed her.

Our skin was slick and slippery as our middles were touching, our breathing ragged. I lowered my forehead to hers, the aftermath filled with another sensation, of her body drawing my energy in, absorbing me. My life force fed her and I was innately pleased that she would always carry part of me, of my essence, within her. I knew many wealthy young ladies used the services of a consort to avoid this soul-deep connection, but I willed my body to cover hers. Fill hers. In every possible way. She was mine.

"Do you think we'll ever take it slow?" she asked after a time.

I rolled to my back, took her with me so she was tucked on

top of me, my cock still buried inside her. Smiling, I kissed the top of her head, her hair soft against my lips.

"Don't worry, I'll be taking my time spanking your ass."

"What?" She lifted her head up, all but glared at me. Ah, the princess was back.

"For putting yourself in danger."

"I... we said, I mean...it's—"

I cut off her sputtering. "By the way your pussy clenched my cock when I said spanking, you like the idea. If you enjoy the sting of my palm on your pretty bottom, I'm going to have to think of an actual punishment."

She pushed up on her elbow and I couldn't help but stare at her cleavage, eying one of her nipples that her movement exposed.

"I am not a child to be spanked."

I lifted her easily and we both hissed as I pulled her off me. Sitting up so my legs hung off the side of the bed, I easily maneuvered her until she was over my lap, her legs trapped between mine. Her upper body was on the bed beside me.

"Leo!" she cried.

I gave her the lightest of spanks, not even enough to pinken her skin. "You want this," I said.

She glared at me over her shoulder but did not tell me to stop.

My hand slid down and between her thighs, found her pussy hot and swollen, coated in my seed. Her hips began to wiggle and I continued to watch her face.

"Don't you?" I pulled my fingers away.

"Leo!" she cried again, but her voice had lost its edge, was imploring.

"Stop or don't stop?" I asked, my fingers brushing ever so lightly over her eager flesh. I knew with her one orgasm she'd be sensitive and eager for more. It was the same for me. Her Ardor didn't need to be soothed solely by my cock in her pussy —which was incredible—but by orgasms. And touch. Energy.

Heat. Skin on skin. Although orgasms *and* skin would be even better.

And taking the time—finally not lost in a sexual haze—to play with her, to become even more intimate with her, was crucial. Our relationship was too new, too much had happened. We were fragile now, but with every caress, every whimper from her, we grew stronger.

"Don't stop."

I spanked her then, following the swat quickly with a finger sliding deep into her pussy.

She gasped out, then moaned. "God, yes. Don't stop. I love it."

I slipped from her, spanked her, the evidence of her arousal on my fingers smearing across her perfect ass. "See, mate. Being submissive to me isn't all bad."

She stiffened at that, so I spanked her again, then finger fucked her once more.

"Please," she begged. I'd get her to understand. We had until tomorrow. And I wouldn't let her up, wouldn't stop pleasuring her until then.

4

Leo, Battleship Karter, Private Guest Quarters

A MONSTER SAT across from me. Scarred from temple to chin, Prime Nial's second, a warrior named Ander, was the most intimidating Prillon fighter I'd ever seen. Like other Prillons, his skin was golden-hued, eyes a rich brown. Nearly as thick and tall as an Atlan, his shoulders were heavy and muscled, his gaze penetrating and unapologetic. The thick scar that ran from the top of his forehead, down the outside of his eye socket, along his check and down into his neck was hard to miss. It proved his fierce bravery, his time fighting the Hive. He was infamous as the male who stood shoulder-to-shoulder with the most powerful leader in the galaxy. Word was that Ander could not be bought. He could not be bargained with or cajoled. He was Prime Nial's dark side. Quiet. Observant. Direct. The enforcer.

And on his lap? A female, curled up and resting her head on his chest as if he were her favorite chair. While seated, she appeared to be quite tall for a female. Blonde, like my mate, yet so different. My cock didn't stir for this female. Completely relaxed, Lady Deston was petting her mate's chest, so content that her eyelids drifted closed for long moments as he held her, stroking her hair with one of his large, scarred hands. Their connection was palpable, but the red collars proved their mated status to anyone not as observant.

The scene was surreal.

Next to them on the sofa, Prime Nial ignored the byplay, completely focused on the female, *my* female, seated next to me on a couch facing them.

Not in my lap, no matter how many times I tried to pull her there.

And she was far from content.

"I will *not* tell anyone where my sisters are. With all due respect, Prime Nial, we had a plan. I don't want to be a bitch, but after the attack at the penthouse, I don't trust any of your people. You've got a mole. Someone leaked information."

I leaned back until my body rested against the cushions and satisfied myself with running my hand up and down my mate's rigid spine. "She is correct, Nial. If the traitor is not among your people, then he is on Alera, in Lord Jax's household."

Prime Nial closed his eyes with a sigh. Opening them, his gaze—the left eye completely silver from Hive integrations—darted to where his mate and his second were sitting calmly, staring at him. But I watched as something passed between them, something intangible, and Nial lifted his hand, rubbing the red collar there. That collar linked him psychically to his mate, and to Ander. I could only imagine the level of intimacy and found myself wishing I were a warrior of Prillon Prime so I could slap a collar around Trinity's neck and get the truth from her once and for all. Know, without question, exactly what she was feeling. What she needed.

Every single one of her secrets.

But if I *were* Prillon, I would have a second, another male devoted to my mate. Fucking her. Protecting her. And selfish as it was, I didn't want to share her tight pussy with another. Nor her kiss. Her sighs. Her screams. Trinity was mine and mine alone.

She'd screamed my name, *mine,* just as I'd promised she would, the sound making me come so hard I'd nearly blacked out.

My mate awakened something in me that was difficult to control. With the rise of my cock, this unfamiliar *demand* to be with Trinity, inside her, next to her, touching her, talking to her was never-ending. My need was an obsession and I wasn't coping well.

Even now, with Nial and Ander, their mate happy between them, I felt unease at having the males so close to what was mine.

Completely and totally irrational, but all I could do was keep my mouth shut and pretend to be civilized. Perhaps, once the mating had settled in, I wouldn't be so edgy, so territorial and protective. Maybe.

From what Nial had said, we were the only Alerans on the ship. It wasn't as if I could ask someone about the Ardor, or about my awakening. I mentally shrugged. Being ignorant only meant we would fuck more until we discovered the truth.

I wrapped my fingers in Trinity's long, golden hair and tugged gently. Relenting at last, she sat back and leaned into my side. Her floral scent filled my nose. It was enough.

"I know I am nothing more than a lowly soldier, Nial, but I am less concerned with your traitor than the assassin who nearly killed the princesses within hours of their arrival on Alera. I saw his face. I knew him from my days in the Fleet. He was with IC. The Shadow Unit."

Ander lifted his perceptive and intense gaze from his mate's face to mine. "What is this Shadow Unit?"

Prime Nial sighed, his silvery gaze shifting from Ander to me, then back. "They are assassins, Ander. Most of them are

Everian Hunters, but every once in a while, a warrior with a very elite set of skills is invited to join them."

"I have never heard of this unit within the Intelligence Core. Under whose command?" Ander asked.

"Mine. Mine and, soon, Queen Celene's. Alera has always held a seat on the royal council. The Shadow Core answers to the council, maintaining order and stability within the Coalition." Nial ran his golden-hued hand through his hair and Lady Deston moaned softly, slipping off Ander's lap and going to Nial in response to some hidden pain. She wrapped herself around him and he pulled her onto his lap. Ander stood, pacing the small room in agitation. What the fuck were the feelings they shared through the collars?

"I've never heard of such a thing," I said.

Trinity glanced at me, clearly confused as well, but remained silent. While the queen may have shared details—including the Aleran language—with her daughters, I saw now that she hadn't told her daughters *everything*.

"It is a secret organization, Princess. One day, you will sit on that council." In a complete change of tone, Nial chuckled, and sliced his hand through the air. "And you, Leo, a lowly soldier?"

"You move like a killer," Ander muttered.

"You are no ordinary soldier, Leo, and we both know it," Nial finished. "It was no accident I chose you. Who else would be best served to protect the three princesses of Alera?"

"Besides her mate?" I countered.

"Good fortune, indeed, that you are mates. Besides your level of skill and experience to assist you in her protection, claiming Trinity certainly makes it easier. If your instinct to protect is anything like mine, it is intense." He kissed the top of Lady Deston's head.

Beside me, Trinity stirred on the couch cushion. "Leo? If it's all top secret, how do you know about this uber-top-secret guild of assassins? And what one of them looks like?"

I couldn't face her, didn't want to see the look in her eyes when I shared what I was. I took my hand off her body because touching her felt wrong right now, when I was forced to remember what I'd become in the Fleet. The things I'd done to protect my planet. My people. I wasn't just a lowly Aleran guard monitoring a watch tower. As if.

I'd fought in the Coalition Fleet, defended all worlds, but in the end, I'd killed for Alera. No one else. "Because I was one of them."

"Who? One of those shadow people?"

I nodded once. "I was a member of the Shadow Unit. Yes."

"Who was it? What's his name?" Ander asked, clearly not interested in the clandestine group, but solely the assassin who had once been one of us.

When Trinity remained silent, I answered him. She hadn't run away screaming. We both had secrets. We both had a depth, pasts, that affected what we were now. It was Trinity's heritage, her very DNA, that set her course in life. She might have lived on Earth, but it was her purpose to be on Alera. It was my purpose to be her mate. Perhaps my time serving the Fleet, all the horrors I'd seen, the battles I'd faced, the people I'd killed, were to bring me to this moment, to protect her. To be skilled enough to keep her alive.

I'd been groomed to be *hers*.

"We don't have names," I replied. "We called him Nix."

Nial lifted a tablet from the table and began entering data onto a screen I couldn't see. He used voice recognition and a bunch of code numbers and words none of us would remember. After a moment, he sighed and placed it on the table before me, the assassin's familiar face staring up at me next to a complete military dossier. Including his real name. Vennix Blyndar. Nix. Aleran.

Trinity leaned forward to look, a shudder racing through her when she saw the male's face. "Yep. That's the guy who burst through the window, killed the... um, consort, then tried to kill me."

5

I DIDN'T EXPECT the sharp spike of terror that seeing the killer's face evoked and I reached for Leo instinctively. All I could see was the assassin's mocking grin as I shot him over and over with the blaster. I could have been using a pea shooter for all the damage it had caused.

Vennix. Nix. He had a name. A terrible, terrifying name.

Then I was floating for a moment. I landed in Leo's lap, my ear pressed over his heartbeat, his warm hand resting against my other cheek, holding me to him. "I've got you, Trinity. Never again, I promise you. Never again."

Focusing on the steady pulsing sound, I let his heat soothe me, sink into me. It was almost as if he was feeding my Ardor, but there was nothing sexual passing between us. This was gentler. Softer.

I was falling in love. Not falling. Fell. Hard.

This was why Jessica liked to sit in her mates' laps. Why they insisted on putting her there.

Damn it. I knew the signs. There was no denying it, not

after what seeing him hurt and bleeding had done to my insides. Not when simply sitting on his lap banished my demons so quickly. I instinctively knew I was safe with him. He would die to protect me. I'd seen it first hand in that miserable cell.

He was making it all too easy to lean on him, to *need* him, and I wasn't ready for that. It was so intense. So... much.

Pulling away, I climbed from his lap and situated myself on the sofa facing Nial, who still held Jessica. She looked at me like I was crazy for crawling out of Leo's lap. Maybe I was, for I felt cold and lonely, even only a few feet away. But I couldn't think when I was in his arms. Not like I needed to. He was too comfortable. Too sexy and warm and safe.

I couldn't feel any of those things, for once I did, I would forget. My goal, my purpose for leaving Earth. I needed to find my mother. I needed to figure out a way to help my sisters.

I needed to hunt down and kill an elite assassin.

And I couldn't do any of that curled up on Leo's lap like a sleepy kitten.

I was a princess. Heir to the throne. My mother was counting on me. The citadel had chosen me, deemed me worthy. When I'd placed my blood on the stone I'd felt... something changing inside me. Something different. The mythology behind the royal family of Alera stated that those born with royal blood, those strong enough, were born with special gifts.

The truth was different. We weren't born with anything special. We were *changed* by the intelligence that ran the citadel itself. I was different. Seeing shadows that weren't there. Seeing light where there should be none. I had begun to suspect the true nature of my gift, but I was still evolving. Into what, I wasn't sure yet. And I had no idea what my sisters were going through. What their gifts might be.

"We have to find him," I said. "I might be safe here on this battleship, but he'll try to kill my sisters." If I were on Alera, he might try to kill me again as well, but that concerned me far less. In fact—

A thought came to me and I blurted it out. Stood suddenly. "Use me to lure him out."

"What?" Jessica tilted her head. "You want to be the bait?" She was quiet for a moment. Thinking. "It would work. They *really* want you dead."

Prime Nial and Leo spoke at the exact same time. Two baritone voices barking in stereo.

"No."

"Fuck, no."

I met Jessica's gaze and understanding passed between us. No collars were needed. If our mates wouldn't help us, we'd figure this shit out on our own. Earth girls stick together. We'd done it earlier to save Leo, we could do it again.

Ander moved to stand silently behind the couch, directly behind his family. He must have felt something through the collar, or was very talented at reading human expressions, because he actually growled at me.

Yeah, Nial might be Prime, but Ander was scary. Intense.

Leo jumped to his feet, fists clenched, and moved to stand in front of me, blocking Ander's view. "Do not take that tone with my mate."

"Your female seeks to endanger mine. This will not be allowed." Ander's voice was venomous now.

"What the hell are you talking about?" Leo countered.

"Control your female, Leoron," Ander warned, without answering the question. "Or I will lock her in the brig until she sees reason."

"I'm right here, gentlemen," I stated, trying to get around Leo's big body. "And you're not locking me anywhere. And stop talking to each other through those dang collars. It's not fair." I sighed. "I'm heir to the throne of Alera. A fucking princess. I think that somehow outranks all of you. If I want to set a trap for this assassin, I will." I faked to the right, then stepped out from behind Leo to square off with the scarred Prillon scowling down at me. Leo pulled me back against him, wrapped an arm about my waist, but at least he didn't shove me behind him again.

"And if I want to help her, you can't stop me." Jessica was inspecting her fingernails, still lounging in Prime Nial's lap as if she didn't have a care in the world. Had she lost her mind? Finally, she leaned back and tilted her head up at Ander, batting her eyelashes at him without shame. "Or, you cavemen could just stop being stubborn and help a girl out."

We all turned to Prime Nial, Jessica turning to stare at him next with so much love on her face I had to look away. He looked from her to Leo, and finally, his gaze rested on me. Sighed. Even ran a hand over his face. For someone who was half Hive parts, he looked like a guy who was completely pussy-whipped. Prime or not. "It's dangerous."

"Too dangerous," Leo protested, giving me a squeeze that was far from playful.

Prime Nial raised his hand. "It's dangerous, Trinity," he warned. "These are highly skilled warriors. Leo's sworn not to speak of his role, but under the circumstances, sharing a little was understandable. My role allows me a little more lenience. The Shadow Unit." He sighed once again. "They are sent into Hive occupied territory to do reconnaissance. They know a hundred ways to kill with their bare hands and are skilled in the use of every weapon from every star system. Your mate may seem mild, but he's anything but."

I blushed, because while he was talking about his cool demeanor, I was immediately thinking of his wild fucking.

"You are not baiting a wild animal," Nial continued. "But a highly intelligent, trained killer."

Leo. My Leo was one of these warriors? He'd gone into Hive territory alone? Been sent into the most dangerous, deadly, horrifying places in the war and told to fend for himself. To kill, over and over?

The vision of Leo somewhere, tortured and alone, like he'd been in that cage, filled my mind and I turned around in his hold, wrapped my arms around his waist. "I'm so sorry, Leo."

Ander grunted, totally ruining the moment. "Nial tells you a monster is hunting you, and all you can think about is comforting your mate?"

He wasn't my mate, not really. Not yet. We hadn't gotten married, or bonded, or whatever kind of weddings they had on Alera. But he was mine right now. And while I seemed to rule his dick, we were just... going out. Seeing each other. Hell, hooking up. But mated? Not quite. Still, love didn't care about terms, did it?

Ander was right about one thing. "I don't care if this Nix guy kills me. Not if you catch him. Find out who has my mother. Protect my sisters."

"No. Fuck, no." Leo's arms tightened around me until I fought to breathe. "I forbid this. No. You will remain here, on Battleship Karter. I will hunt him down. I will kill him. You will not risk yourself."

Sighing, I wiggled until he loosened his hold a little and I could look up into his eyes. "How long would that take? Weeks? Months? I don't have that kind of time. My mother doesn't have that kind of time. I can't wait. There's too much at stake." Turning to Prime Nial, the most powerful military commander in the galaxy, I begged him to see reason. "The four spires are lit. The entire planet knows my sisters and I exist. Whoever has my mother surely must know by now. They might kill her if they think she is no longer necessary."

He stared at me, his whiskey-colored eyes thoughtful. "Why did they take her after all this time? Why did they travel all the way to Earth and drag her, as you said, from her bed? Why not cut her throat and be done with it? Take the throne? Why are they keeping her alive?"

Leo cleared his throat. "The royal gemstones. Does she have them?" He looked down at me, waiting for the truth.

I didn't lie, but I couldn't tell him everything either. "No. But she hid them."

"Do you know where they are?" he asked.

Swallowing hard, I nodded, but didn't speak.

"Where are they?" Jessica asked. "We should go get them and bring them back to the Karter. If they're that valuable, if someone kidnapped the queen for them, then we can lock them up. They'll be safe until you get this all figured out."

She was watching me, the sharpness in her gaze in complete contrast to her earlier contentment. But then, that was the main reason I'd fled from Leo's lap. It was too easy to feel safe there. Safe and warm and consumed with the need to get him naked. Inside me. To forget about all the bad stuff, the bad guys. How my mother could be hurt or dying. And my sisters. Were they well? Safe?

I sighed. "They have remained safely hidden for nearly thirty years. I don't think they are in any danger of being found."

Leo narrowed his eyes. "And you know, for certain, they remain safe?"

"Yes." I'd seen them. Held them for a moment when I'd gone to the place my mother had told us about. That only she and her three daughters knew of. To prove they were there, that they really were still safe. The gemstones were concealed in a hidden compartment inside the citadel. And beyond that, the secret compartment lay within a hidden room below the sanctum. A puzzle within a puzzle. "Whoever holds her will not learn their whereabouts. My mother will not tell them where they are. She'd die first, to protect us."

She was strong. Strong enough to survive. To flee across an entire galaxy and start a new life while pregnant with me, mourning my father. Brave enough to risk her heart and fall in love again. Have more children. Prepare them for the future we now faced. I couldn't imagine it. "Queen Celene is the strongest woman I know."

They didn't ask again and relief flooded me. I didn't want to fight. Not about this. They had to trust me in this, and fortunately, they were. Perhaps it was because it was the queen, herself, we were referring to. Nial was giving her the respect and deference she deserved in knowing how to rule her planet, to keep it safe from any kind of threat.

"You are determined to do this?" Leo asked. I had to wonder, in this moment, if he saw me as Princess Trinity, and not as Trinity, the one he called mate. I respected him for that, for he'd said he would bow to me as princess. He would defer to my judgment, at least in this.

And my heart grew even more in love with him for it.

"Yes." I looked up into his eyes, held his gaze. "I need your help, Leo. Please. Don't fight me on this. Use me to draw him out. I'm willing to take the chance. I have to protect my sisters."

"It is my job to protect you, but in this, I can't. I will never forgive myself if anything happens to you." And that was the crux of it. But this wasn't just about me. It was about Faith and Destiny and the future of Alera.

"Then kill him first."

Prime Nial met my gaze, unblinking. "We need a plan. As Prime, I can't allow you two off this ship until we have a plan in place."

"I agree. My mate doesn't leave this ship until I know I can protect her. Trinity is everything to me. She is my life."

"We understand. Jessica is ours just as Trinity belongs to you." Ander's deep rumble was not condescending or judgmental but completely honest and without a hint of embarrassment. The way Ander held her, touched her. The way she relaxed in his arms and just let herself *be*. Hell. I was envious.

But maybe I didn't need to be.

Leo's open declaration of absolute and complete devotion to me caught me off guard. The things he said to me in private I took in stride, attributing his words to passion in the heat of the moment. But calmly, coldly stating that I belonged to him, that he would die to protect me, that I was *his everything?* And to Prime Nial and Ander, two of the most powerful males in the galaxy?

He was everything I'd ever dreamed of in a man, and yet, what did I have to offer him? Danger at every turn? An uncertain future and years of war? An assassin hunting me and my sisters? And as much as I wanted to curl up in his lap and let everything go like Jessica had, I didn't have that luxury.

I was a princess. And if my mother were not found, if the light of her spire went out, I would be queen. I would never truly be able to put his needs above the needs of my people. My mother had drilled into me the needs of the many outweighed the needs of the one. Justice. Law. Honor. Duty. I had a duty to my people to consider their wants and needs above my own.

Above Leo's.

And right now, what my people needed was a plan that would help find my mother and keep me—and my sisters—from getting killed.

The discussion was heated and went on for several hours. I learned much about Leo and his skill, about his analytical and merciless mind. He listened to me without interruption. He considered my words carefully before responding. All of these males did. And Jessica? I learned she was ex-military, a journalist who'd been framed and sent to jail. Despite curling up in Ander's lap like a kitten, she was every bit as tough as her two mates. And somehow, they made it work. The three of them.

They gave me hope that, perhaps, Leo and I could figure out a way to make this thing work between us.

Everything he did and said, every movement and tilt of his head, the way he backed down Ander and Prime Nial both when he disagreed with them? Or I did... *everything* made me want him more. Double damn, I was still in heat. My Ardor flaring up like a hungry beast inside me. And there was only one male I wanted touching me, heating me up, making me burn.

The discussion seemed as if it would never end, as my condition worsened and I squirmed on the couch. But after going through the plan—start to finish—one last time, even Ander seemed content.

Ander cleared his throat. "Are you certain, Leo, that you do not wish for us to contact the IC, have them send some additional warriors from the Shadow Unit? They would make this easier for you."

Leo shook his head. "No. Their arrival would only put Nix on alert. I would not risk additional danger to my mate. I promise, I will handle this when we return to Alera." He turned, looked down at me, ran his thumb across my lips. "The plan is sound, but I need some more time with my mate before we go back. Her Ardor has not yet cooled."

Heat rushed through my cheeks and I knew I was blushing, but I was mesmerized by the light touch of his thumb tracing the sensitive curves of my mouth. He was right. Even with talk of luring out an assassin, I needed him still. His energy. His cock filling me up. His body blanketing me with heat.

Him. I needed him.

"On that note—" Jessica laughed and hopped out of Nial's lap. She was smiling as she walked out the door. Both Prillon warriors bowed to me and followed behind.

Blinking, I tried to think, to say something to clear my head. "Jessica, she's a wild one. No wonder she has two mates."

Leo's smile made my heart dissolve into a puddle of melted goo in my chest. "She is nothing compared to you, mate. Nothing. And if anything goes wrong with this plan, anything at all, I will spank you until you can't walk."

I laughed, my pussy clenching at his words, my breath quickening along with my pulse. "Go ahead, Leo. Spank me. Make me burn. It won't stop me. You know I love it. It makes me crazy. Makes me need you more."

"You will be the death of me." His voice was hoarse as he lowered his head to kiss me.

rinity

"Leo," I murmured as he pressed me up against the wall in our guest quarters and nibbled along my neck. Goose bumps rose across my skin and I was instantly eager for him. Well, not instantly. The hours of planning only made my need a slow simmer. Until now. Until his lips touched my skin.

He offered a grunt in response and continued to kiss, lick and explore the line of my neck, the top of my shoulder, even that sensitive spot behind my ear. My hands went into his hair, tangled there and held him in place.

God, he felt incredible. Every hard inch of him that pressed me into the wall, especially the thick feel of his cock against my belly.

His hands lowered to the hem of my shirt, lifted it up as he dropped to his knees and began to kiss every inch of skin he exposed.

"You're so small. So fragile," he breathed.

I gave a laugh, but it was quickly followed by a whimper as he nibbled along the line of my ribs. "I'm not weak."

He lifted his head then, the spots he licked cooling now in the air. His dark eyes met mine. While I could see heat there, his desire for me, it also held... pride? "No, not weak. Never weak. You're one of the strongest females I know. Perhaps that is why you are my mate."

"Oh, Leo." He said the sweetest things, and he wasn't saying that as a line. He meant it. "We argue. You hate when I do crazy things."

"The craziest is yet to come. It will be almost impossible to pretend you are not my mate. My cock will give me away."

He pushed my shirt up higher, over my breasts to bunch up under my arms. I wore a utilitarian space-generated bra—I doubted the S-Gen machine could make Victoria's Secret lingerie—and yet he still looked at my breasts as if he were a horny teen getting his first glimpse. A horny mate who would soon have to pretend otherwise.

It was easy to forget Leo had been a virgin until we'd met. I'd totally deflowered him, turning him into a total man-slut. Yet, now, he was on his knees before me. It was as if he were worshipping me. The idea held appeal—what woman didn't want to be worshipped?—but there was too much at stake, too much danger for feelings like that right now.

While I was starting to feel the same sappy, consuming things for Leo, I couldn't say them, couldn't act on them. Soon enough, I would be the ruling princess of Alera with a ruthless assassin who wanted me dead. It was insanity to lure him out, but there was no choice. The planet needed a royal once again and the assassin couldn't make another attempt with me safely on Battleship Karter.

I had Aleran responsibilities now. I didn't have to get up in the morning, go to work Monday through Friday to earn a paycheck. Do a yoga class, save for retirement. Those were simple Earth encumbrances. My mother had prepared me for Alera. For leading the planet. She'd told me of sacrifice, of crown over person. I *was* Trinity Jones, but I was also Princess

Trinity. To the Alerans, I was the princess, nothing more. To Leo, I was both. He understood my responsibility to lead, to put the planet before everything else, including my own needs, my own wants. His, too.

I wanted Leo. I wanted to call him my mate. To tell him I thought of him that way, as the one I wanted to be with. Unconditionally and forever.

But I couldn't. Not now. It wasn't the right time.

I had to think he knew that because he wasn't pushing, wasn't expecting the words in response. He wanted them, I was sure. It only fed the alpha male in him. But he was loyal to the royal family and had his own responsibility in this.

His job was to keep his princess safe while I did what was best for Alera.

I would use myself as bait, even subtly. If something happened, my mother could still rule—when Faith and Destiny found her—and then my sisters themselves as the next in line.

I was replaceable. The crown was not. Alera needed the crown, needed the royal line to continue, or war and chaos would reign.

I could not let that happen. Not after all my mother sacrificed, was *still* sacrificing.

So not announcing to all of Alera that Leo was my mate was a sacrifice of my own.

That didn't mean I couldn't show him now how much he meant to me, how much I needed him.

Me.

Trinity Jones.

I grabbed my shirt, yanked it up and over my head. Took off the bra.

Alera needed a royal. Now. The spires were lit—it was our own doing—surely confusion was reigning. I needed to step into my mother's shoes until she was found. I would be safe at the palace, yet Leo could not remain at my side. This little window of sexy times would be the last for a while and I was going to make the most of it. I wanted us naked and him inside me. Like, ten minutes ago.

Leo remained motionless as I did that, but after blinking once, then again, he got off my shoes, pants and panties in record speed. I dropped down, straddled him so I was in his lap, his arms instantly wrapping around me.

I felt the rough texture of his clothing against my bare skin, understood the power shift in this moment.

"Do what you want," I said, holding his gaze. I cupped his square jaw, felt the rasp of his whiskers. Breathed him in.

His eyes flared wide at my offer, then the corner of his mouth tipped up.

"I love every way we've fucked. Perhaps you can suggest another position?"

I bit my lip, remembered again our relationship was like a tipping scale. We balanced each other. I wanted him to take control, to be the dominant lover, and yet while he would do that, he needed my guidance on what I wanted.

Having a mate who'd only known sex with me, only known sex in the ways we'd done it made me feel empowered. Yet, I was shy in my suggesting something new. All I had to do was offer the idea, though, and he'd take over. Like he always did. I clenched my inner walls with anticipation.

Sliding off his lap, I crawled away from him, then stopped. Glanced over my shoulder. His gaze was raking over every inch of me, from my swaying breasts to my pussy which was on blatant display for him.

"Like this," I whispered.

His lips parted as he considered.

"Surely your training included the subject of taking a woman on all fours." My words were practically a taunt.

"Touch yourself," he said, instead of answering. "Show me how wet you are. How much you want my cock buried in you from behind."

When his voice took on that deep, authoritarian timbre, I shivered, then shifted my balance so I could do just as he commanded.

A rumble rose from his chest as he watched my fingers slipping through my slick folds, sliding into my pussy, then out. I could hear how wet I was; there was no doubt he could *see* it.

"Good little mate," he replied, tugging open the front of his pants so his cock sprung free. As he moved with easy grace, I realized he had no intention of taking off anything else. No. His cock was out and he would service me. Take from me what he wanted. Dominate, even though it was his first time this way.

I curled my back, thrust my ass out in silent offer.

When he placed a hand beside mine on the gray carpet, the rest of his body curved over me, surrounded me with his heat. And at my core, his cock slid through my folds until he settled at my entrance.

"You want me to fuck you like this?"

"Yes," I breathed, my pussy dripping with anticipation.

"You told me to do what I want. I'm in control?"

"Yes," I said again.

"That's right. While my princess rules Alera, my mate submits to me."

He thrust into me in one hard, deep stroke, nipped the spot where my neck and shoulder met. Claimed me like a wild animal.

I tossed my head back, moaned at how he opened me up. Every time was like the first. He was so big, almost too much for me to take. My inner walls needed time to adjust to the invasion, but I loved it. My body felt claimed and that was part of his dominance. I would mold to him, my pussy, my heart, my mind.

In this, there was no thought. I gave everything to him. Let it go. Gave over.

He shifted back so his hands settled on my hips. Fucked me. In. Out. Hard. Fast. He moved me across the floor, and I grabbed hold of the side of the bed, crawled forward so I leaned over it.

Leo followed, sunk right back into me. We groaned and he fucked me even harder. Pounding me into the bed.

"Leo!" I cried.

"Take it, mate. Take me. Give me your pleasure. It's mine. You'll feel this tomorrow, will remember who you belong to."

I was his. Perhaps I hadn't come yet because he hadn't allowed it. But now, the heat took over and I came on a silent scream. Hot and fierce, my mind sizzled, my body tingled.

"Trinity!" Leo groaned as he held himself deep. Filled me.

My cheek was pressed into the soft blanket as I caught my breath, felt the heat of his seed seeping out of me, coating my thighs and, I was sure, the bed.

"We're not done, mate."

Leo pulled out and easily rolled me onto my back, pushed my thighs wide and to my chest. After an orgasm like that, I was like putty in his hands. Open.

"The sight of my cum slipping from you is something I will never forget. A Neanderthal, you called me? I do not know what that is, but in this moment, I feel like one. I've claimed you. Marked you. No male in the universe will question you are mine if they saw you this way. Some will even be able to scent me on you."

The idea was hot and sexy and I knew why he was going all caveman. We'd have to pretend we weren't mated and it would drive him crazy. No, it already *was* driving him crazy.

"How's your Ardor?" he asked, swirling a thick finger through my swollen folds.

"Better," I murmured, beginning to roll my hips, eager.

"You will not leave this ship until it is soothed completely. I will need my princess sharp and focused on the mission, not on the need of her pussy. I will not have your staff seeking a consort for you. You will know when we transport back to Alera that this pussy is mine. I know what it needs. My cock, my mouth, my fingers. When to give it pleasure, when to make it stay wet and needy to have you begging me for release. Not your Ardor. Me."

The truth of his words was like a shimmering halo around him in the darkened interior of the bedroom. The energy that surrounded him was so beautiful, I had to blink, awed. It was like he was the darkened moon at the center of a solar eclipse, light shooting out from his edges.

Were my eyes playing tricks on me again? Since I'd placed my blood on the sacred stone inside the citadel, strange things had been happening. People looked different, as if I were a psychic gypsy and could see the truth of things. Or lack of. Was this the *gift* my mother had told me about? The special superpower my mother had claimed was given to all of the royal line whom the citadel deemed worthy? Was this a talent designed to help me rule? And what of my sisters? Could they see this strange light as well?

I wondered what I would see if he told me a lie...

"Trinity. Are you listening to me? You are mine."

Oh, yeah. He totally believed that one.

"Yes, Leo," I replied. I would be so eager for him at the palace. Even without the Ardor, I knew I'd still crave him.

His cock glistened and was still rock hard. He didn't wait to take me again, sliding deep, fucking me as our eyes held the entire time, so that when I came again, I knew it was because of him. I belonged to Leo. My body, soul. And my pussy.

⚶

"Besides doing a public broadcast, I wish I could speak with my sisters... privately," I said. We'd napped and showered and fucked again. Now we were both naked in bed, wrapped around each other. My head was on his chest and I could feel the slow, steady beat of his heart. His hand was in my hair, stroking. We couldn't be apart, couldn't not touch. I needed to feel his skin, make the most of every second we had left.

"You miss them."

"Not in the way you think." I shifted so I could look up at him, my chin settled on his pec. "On Earth, we all lived together. We were pretty old to still live at home, but it worked for us. Perhaps it was because we were different—me, all Aleran, them, half—but we never really thought about it."

His hand didn't stop its stroking my hair and I closed my eyes. I had no idea I'd love the simple gesture so much.

"We're close, the bond we share, even though Faith and Destiny are the twins. But we've also always been independent. We went to different colleges. Schooling." I added when he looked confused. "We only saw each other for holidays, over the summers, for six years as we studied far away. While I *miss* them because they're my closest friends, we have jobs to do."

"Mmm," he replied, his chest vibrating with the rumble. "You have yet to tell me what these *jobs* are."

"To find our mother."

"Yes, I assumed that."

"I only know our initial plans, not what has occurred since that night in the citadel. I haven't seen them or spoken to them since then."

"You'll have to explain that disappearing act to me someday as well."

I smiled, glad he wasn't forcing me to explain it all.

"It's been several days. They may have learned something, have information for me... for *us,* that might help our plan, or change it even. It would be great to know what they know."

"I agree with that," he added.

"But we're on a spaceship somewhere in the galaxy and they're on Alera. It's not like even when we return to the planet I can track them down. I won't be free to do anything."

"I can."

I sat up then. "You can?"

He pushed up onto his elbow, a satisfied, sated smile on his face. Oh, he was so handsome. "I can make contact with your sisters. I am more than just my big cock, mate."

I shoved his shoulder and he fell onto his back once again. "You are so much more." Glancing down his body, I watched as his semi-erect cock went fully erect. "But right now..." I reached down, gripped him, stroked him from base to tip.

"Right now, I can be the cock that you ride." His eyes fell closed and his hips bucked at one forceful stroke of my hand. "Climb on, mate."

"We fuck, then we phone my sisters?"

I moved to straddle his waist, hovered over him awaiting his answer.

"I do not know what phone is. But if it means to contact your sisters, then yes. Fuck, then phone."

Sliding down slowly, I took him deep, but I took my time. I sensed that this would be our last time together before returning to Alera, and I was on the verge of tears.

For the first time in my life, I truly wanted something for myself. No, not wanted, needed. Craved. Leo was mine. How or when he'd become my anchor, I didn't know. The thought of not being able to touch him, talk to him, or walk into his arms and know he would wrap me up in safety and heat had me on the edge of panic.

Yes, I was strong. Yes, I'd been groomed my entire life to do what would come next, challenge the old guard on Alera and reclaim my mother's throne.

But she was supposed to be with me. In all of my childhood imaginings, I'd never once envisioned the situation my sisters and I were currently in. My mother missing. Me, nerdy, book-worm, uptight *me* responsible for billions of lives, the future of an entire planet. Without her there to guide me. My sisters out there somewhere, risking their lives in secret while I stepped up to the plate and revealed my identity, and my existence, to the entire population. As I faced an entire planet, and my mother's enemies, alone.

A single tear slipped down my cheek as I took him inside me. His eyes were closed, but somehow, he knew, his eyes opening and finding the telltale sign of my stress and sadness before it had even fallen to his chest.

"Trinity." His cock was inside my body, but *he* was wiggling his way into my soul. One word. Just my name, and I lowered my forehead to his chest, kissing where I knew his heart beat. For me. In all this insanity, he felt like a miracle, too good to be real. I was going to place him in danger. Again. Ask him to risk his life for me, again. It was wrong of me to ask, but I couldn't let him go.

"I need you, Leo."

He sat up and pulled me to his chest, our bodies still connected, his arms locking me to him, and held me close. "I am yours, mate. Anything you need, I am yours."

Lifting my head from his chest, I looked into his eyes and spoke what truth I could. "I need you."

"I'm right here." Leo lowered his head, kissed me. Not hard or fast. There was no dominance or demand in the kiss. It was reverent. Love. It was love. And I'd never felt it before. Not like this.

I shifted my hips, riding him gently, touching his shoulder, wrapping one hand in his hair to hold his lips to mine. And I loved him back with my mouth. My body. And it hurt. God, did it hurt. The pain in my chest foreign, the shaking of my hands, my body, this feeling of weakness, it was all new, and I realized I had never made love before.

We'd fucked. We'd played. He had fed my Ardor with his strength and taken my body places I didn't know I could go. We'd teased and pleasured one another. But this?

This hurt. This twisted my insides in a slow vise. This was going to kill me, and I didn't want to stop.

We rocked together, every movement small. Gentle. But no

less erotic. I hugged him to me as I came and he followed me over. My face pressed to the side of his neck, his name like a prayer on my lips as my pussy milked him of his seed. We were wrapped around each other, clinging, touching everywhere we could. His energy eased into me, the heat of him to finally ease my Ardor and be a balm to my aching heart. I loved him. The emotion was ridiculous and unreasonable. I'd only known him a few days. But I loved him, and I didn't dare tell him. Not when I could die tomorrow.

If something happened to me, if the assassin, Nix, from this elite killing unit, came for me, it would be far better for Leo to mourn a princess he'd helped through her Ardor, a friend and lover, than a woman who'd loved him with her entire heart and soul.

7

*T*rinity

AN HOUR LATER, we were dressed and in Commander Karter's office. Leo and me, Prime Nial, Jessica and Ander. I had to hope the two of us didn't look like we'd spent every available moment wrapped up in each other, but then, Jessica was glowing, too. Looked like Prime Nial and Ander were taking full advantage of their battleship detour as well. Her lips were swollen and her skin was flushed. Unlike me, she seemed to have a constant smile on her face when she was around her mates.

All I could think about was the fact that I was going to get Leo killed. And he wouldn't even hate me for it. But I would hate myself. Then again, I was going to be the ruling regent very soon. Surely, I could protect him *somehow*.

"Thank you for allowing us safe passage on your ship, Commander," Prime Nial said.

The hulking Prillon leader smiled, bowed slightly to Nial. His coloring was similar to Nial's and Ander's. A caramel tone of skin and eyes. His hair was a rich brown. The Prillon warriors didn't look human. There was no mistaking the sharper angles of their cheekbones, of their noses. And their coloring ranged from palest gold, to deep brown to a gorgeous copper. I'd never seen so many gorgeous men in one place in my life.

Commander Karter was one of them. He was, perhaps, a decade older than Prime Nial and had the confident, no bullshit bearing of a military man. "My ship is available to you anytime. It is an honor, Princess Trinity, to have you on board as well."

I reached out to shake his hand.

"Ah, an Earth greeting." He gave it a firm squeeze. "One of my former captains is an Earthling. She is mated to a very large Atlan. I think you two would make fast friends—you and Sarah, not her beast. Warlord Dax took his new mate to Atlan. I'm sure she would be thrilled to have you in her home, once all of this is over."

I smiled, glad he and everyone we'd met—aside from the assassins—were all very nice. "Thanks." I wasn't sure where he was going with this, other than just trying to give me another Earth-female friend out here in space. But Atlan was a long way from Alera, from what I understood. But then again, that's what transport technology was for. And I was going to rule an entire freaking planet... "I'd love to visit her someday. Thank you. Maybe Lady Deston would like to accompany me?"

"Hell yeah. I'd love to do a girl's weekend." Her smile was radiant, especially when Ander's blank face turned to a scowl. "Maybe we could binge on my shows."

For a moment, life felt normal again. Surrounded by alien warriors, on a battleship, talking about binge-watching TV. "What do you watch?"

She rubbed her hands together and recited a list of police procedurals and crime dramas. Me? I wanted dragons, Jedi Knights or hot Tolkien elves. Well, just one elf, anyway. That silver-haired badass and his bow were hot, hot, hot—

"I am grateful for your kind offer to Trinity, but we are here for a reason, Commander Karter. Lady Deston. And that reason has nothing to do with play," Leo stated. "My mate is being hunted by one of the Fleet's deadliest assassins. Now that her Ardor has cooled, I am looking forward to eliminating that threat. With my bare hands."

And that was Leo, practically growling like a riled grizzly bear at two of the most powerful and respected warriors in the galaxy. For me.

Jeez. Why was that so freaking hot? And why had he realized that my Ardor was over before I did? For a fleeting moment, I panicked that Leo wouldn't want me anymore. That I really had been just a job, my problem something his honor had demanded he take care of.

But then I remembered the Aleran men were different. Leo's body woke up for me. That thick, magnificent cock had never been inside another woman. He was mine. As long I as I lived, he was mine.

Commander Karter bowed slightly at the waist, distracting me from my momentary lapse of all reason. "Of course. Your Highness, you can record your message here, in my office, and we will broadcast it all over Alera, as you requested. But first, I understand you wish to speak directly with your sisters?"

"That's correct. From what Leo has told me, direct communication can be made via the NPUs we all got from Warden Egara on Earth."

I glanced at Leo, who nodded and said, "Prime Nial contacted me on Alera to meet and guard you and your sisters."

"A wise move. From what I've been told of the incident following their arrival, your help was quickly needed," Commander Karter said.

I blushed, remembering all the *assistance* Leo had given me over the past few hours.

"He's been very... helpful," I offered, hopefully not blushing too hard.

The older Prillon eyed me and Leo, as if assessing the truth since we didn't wear collars like his kind. I didn't see one about his neck, so I assumed he was unmated. While Jessica and her mates were well-suited, I had to wonder what it would be like for the commander to have a mate, and a second, on a battleship. We'd only been here a short time and I'd heard the battle alerts, the constant hum of warriors coming and going, racing to medical. Training and stomping around. Living here, on a battleship, as I'd heard many Prillon mates did, would be an unusual lifestyle. "Congratulations on your mating. A very serendipitous event."

That was true. I'd been on Earth and Leo on Alera. If Mother hadn't been kidnapped, if Prime Nial hadn't called him, Leo and I never would have met.

"I am the fortunate one," Leo admitted, placing a possessive hand on my shoulder.

"Say the word and I'll ask Warden Egara to fix you up." Jessica looked thrilled at the prospect, but the commander shook his head.

"Thank you, Lady Deston, but I am perfectly content."

"Liar." Her one-word response was spoken softly, with a gentle smile meant to tease, but it landed in the room and shocked the men like an armed grenade right before the explosion.

"Jessica." The warning came from Prime Nial, and not as one mate to another, but as the Prime telling her to back off. I'd never seen this side of him before and it was fascinating.

Leo, apparently, had had enough. "The princess wishes to speak with her sisters, but we do not know their whereabouts on Alera."

"Even I heard the news of the three spires alighting. The news spread through the entire Interstellar Coalition within a few hours," the commander said. "You will be recognized everywhere you go, Princess. Every planet. Every battleship. Your face has been spread far and wide. You are famous, the long-lost princess. But until Prime Nial told me the other two spires were set alight by your sisters, I had no idea who they were. Every agency is reviewing the video feed, looking for a glimpse of them."

"As we wanted," I told him. "They can freely move about the planet continuing their search for our mother. They will search for her while I will take on the role of royal heir until she is found."

Ander cleared his throat. "It will not take them long— whoever wishes them dead—to make their way to Earth for answers."

Prime Nial shook his head. "I have placed a ban on all transport on or off Earth unless it is initiated by the Interstellar Brides Program until this matter is settled."

"Holy shit." Jessica blinked in shock, her eyes going wide. "Can you do that?"

"I can, and I did. No one will be able to get on or off the planet without my permission unless they are a bride."

Wow. He had locked down an entire planet for me and my sisters?

Nial continued, "The stability of the Coalition is of great concern. The planets cannot send warriors to fight the Hive if they are entrenched in civil conflicts."

It made sense, but his words also made the weight on my shoulders that much heavier. Leo had said the planet was on the brink of war. Alera could tear itself apart if my sisters and I didn't find our mother. Or worse, didn't survive.

Ander spoke, "Their arrival has caused unrest. Reports from the planet indicate a large number of people flocking to the capital city to view the spires. To witness their illumination for themselves. The royal guard has recalled warriors from the outlying areas to return to the city at once."

Jessica looked at me, and I saw worry in her eyes. "It's a madhouse down there. I hope you know what you're doing."

"Me, too." I searched for Leo's hand. Found it. Held tight.

Ander held up a small transport disk, just like the one I'd used to rescue Leo. "We will transport her directly into the queen's palace for her safety. With one trusted guard, of course."

I glanced at Leo. My guard. Once we arrived back on Alera, we somehow had to convince the entire planet that he was *just* my guard. Nothing more. Not someone I would kill to protect.

Should have taken that stupid acting class in college.

I didn't like thinking of Alera in turmoil, that the spires alighting would lead to chaos instead of peace. It only made me more determined to find my mother, to put the government back to rights with her at the helm.

"This is why I need to speak to Faith and Destiny," I said. "They will know things we don't."

Commander Karter went around his desk, sat down. "Yes, Prime Nial has kept me updated. I agree, the more information you have, the higher chance for success of your mission."

"We are here seeking your permission, Commander." Prime Nial stood directly before the desk. "To make the transmission from your ship."

Commander Karter folded his hands on his desk, met the Prime's eyes. "Your courtesy is well-appreciated, Prime. Permission granted, of course."

Nial bowed as the commander pressed a few buttons and spoke to someone about coordinates, NPUs and other words that I didn't understand. Not because *my* NPU didn't work, but because the technology was way over my head.

Jessica grinned, clearly satisfied with all of this. It seemed she liked to be in the thick of things. I just silently exhaled. I was learning much from Prime Nial. He held more power, more sway than the commander. Yet, he deferred to the battlegroup leader with deference and courtesy. There was a chain of command to things. But common courtesy went a long way.

"Trinity?"

A woman's voice rang clear and loud in the commander's office.

"Faith?" I said back. It was like she was on speaker phone, but I hadn't even known the call had started.

"I'm here, too. How the hell are you calling me inside my head?" That was Destiny, straight to the point. But Faith wasn't finished, either.

"Where are you, Trin? You were supposed to be queen supreme by now. Instead, it's like a freaking war zone down here. There are people everywhere. Fist fights. Even the animals are freaked." Of course, Faith would talk about the animals. She'd always had a soft spot for any injured thing. "No one on Alera has said you've been seen. But your face is *everywhere*."

Leo looked grim.

"I am glad you contacted me and we removed you from the planet, Princess," Prime Nial murmured. He might be Prime of a planet and in charge of a whole slew of battleships, but I was the never-to-be-heard-of heir to the throne of a planet whose queen had disappeared decades earlier. I was a sensation.

As for what Nial said, I was glad he'd helped me, too. We now had a plan in place, and I had backup.

"I'm on a battleship out in space on Battleship Karter with Leo, Prime Nial, Jessica and her second, Ander," I told Faith and Destiny. "It's like *Buck Rogers* and *Star Trek*. Combined."

Commander Karter nodded, clearly satisfied with the connection. "I'll leave you now. I have a meeting I must attend. Please, take your time."

The door slid closed behind him. The fact that he left us in his office was a blatant sign of respect.

"Where are you two? Are you safe?" I asked.

Faith's voice was filled with disgust. "Regular slave labor over here. But I'm in. They hired me right away. What about you, Destiny? Any trouble getting in?"

"No. Everything is going according to plan. I'm a regular old nun."

"A nun?" Faith said, then laughed. "As if. Did you tell them about Paul Carbano or Sam Wallowitz? Like they'd take you after what you did with those two hotties."

I couldn't help but roll my eyes, remembering Destiny's exploits in high school. Leo, Jessica, Nial and Ander all stared at me, silently listening.

"What is a nun?" Leo asked.

"Well, not a nun, specifically, since these guys are allowed to have sex, but I'm officially an initiate of the clerical order," Destiny said.

Next to me, Leo tensed, his jaw tight. "You play a dangerous game, Princess."

"That *is* you, right, Leo?" Faith asked.

"Yes."

"Hey, Leo, how's it hanging?" Destiny asked.

Leo grinned, but it didn't last long. Jessica slapped a hand over her mouth to stifle a laugh. Nial scratched the back of his head and was actually blushing. Clearly, he'd learned a few Earth slang terms from Jessica.

"Destiny, the clerics are not to be underestimated nor trifled with."

Oh, boy. I could practically see Destiny roll her eyes.

"I got this, Leo. They aren't all that bad. Think the strange Italian vampire court in *Twilight*. Minus the freaky kids and all the superpowers. They just *think* they're all powerful."

The clarification made some sense since we'd seen that movie series too many times to count when we were teens. Not so much for Leo, but he was familiar with these real clerics and I was not.

"And one of them is—God. He makes me so damn mad, Trin. I think I'll have to torture him for fun before I leave this place."

"You wouldn't hurt a fly," Faith argued. Despite Destiny's

penchant for violence, she really was a great big softie at heart. She'd learned a lot of ways to kill, but never actually killed anything. She even caught spiders and let them go outside. In some ways, she was just like her twin.

"Watch me."

"Sounds like he's a hottie, to me. You never could take a sexy man with a sassy mouth." Faith was merciless. It was a twin thing.

"I've got something for that mouth to do, I'll tell you that."

My sisters were talking about oral sex over an interstellar comm with the leader of the entire coalition fleet listening? Holy crap.

Facepalm. "Hey, you two! Knock it off." My sisters weren't prudes. They weren't virgins and their minds were far from innocent. But then, neither was mine, for I was sore in places a nun didn't even know existed.

"Sorry." That was Destiny. I expected that to be the end of it, but she kept talking. "I think when we went into the citadel, something happened."

If she was talking about seeing strange lights around people, I wanted to hear about it, but not now. Not in front of others.

"I think I'm—"

"Guys," I interrupted before Destiny went off on a random tangent about odd abilities.

"It's the Ardor, Trin. I'm screwed."

"Oh, shit. You, too?" Faith asked. "I was hoping I was imagining it."

Great. Both of them in Ardor? This complicated everything.

Faith, as usual, seemed to read my mind. "Don't worry about me, Trin. It's early. I can hold out for a while. Long enough to get things done."

"Yeah, me too. What's the plan?" Destiny asked. "I'm ready to kick some ass."

"Not you, Dest," I countered. "You need to stay where you

are, do whatever it is you're doing. The less you know about my plans, the safer it will be."

"That's right," Faith said. "A three-pronged attack."

"Not attack, Princess Faith," Prime Nial corrected. "You are to remain in hiding as you have been, learning details that may help find the queen, but nothing more. Princess Trinity will be returning to Alera and taking over the throne. She has a number of trusted fighters to help her and will be safe at the palace. You do not have trusted fighters or a secure fortress to live within."

Faith sighed. "If you didn't call to tell me your plans, Trinity, and I doubt you want to share any of the juicy details about Leo with everyone listening in, why did you call?"

"Yeah, you're just teasing me with the thought of kicking ass and taking names," Destiny added.

$\mathcal{T}$rinity

"I WANTED to know you're all right, obviously. But I need to hear from you what's going on down there. We have a plan. I'm going to use myself as bait to lure the assassin to me in the palace. I'm going to be all over the news in a few hours. But if you need to reach me..." I looked at Prime Nial. "Is there some way they can use their NPUs to get ahold of me?"

"I'm afraid not. The communication must be initiated from a central command point."

"Back to plan A," Destiny said. Plan A was a series of designated meeting places and times that we'd set up prior to our transport to Alera. It was risky, and a pain in the ass, but we'd make it work.

"Okay. Plan A. Talk soon. Stay safe, please."

"Midnight?" Faith asked.

"Right," I confirmed. I'd tell Leo the rest later. "Be safe. Don't do anything stupid. Okay?"

"We'll find Mom. You just keep the planet from tearing itself apart. And don't worry about me. I've got an ion blaster in a thigh holster. Being a nun has its perks. Bye!" Destiny said, then disconnected.

"Don't worry about us, Trin. Love you. Stay safe and we'll all be together again soon." Faith dropped off next.

The call ended and the pent-up energy I'd felt talking to my sisters burst like a water balloon, leaving me deflated and tired.

Leo held his arm out as if he somehow knew I was sad to say goodbye. Maybe I did miss them more than I thought. We were all in danger. I wouldn't feel completely content until all of us, including Mother, were safe. I went to him, hugged him.

Everyone was quiet for a moment. Everyone, but Jessica. "You can't make your first big splash wearing *that*."

"There is nothing wrong with her attire," Ander said, the first time he'd spoken since we'd entered the commander's office. Man of few words, that one. He went to the door and called for Commander Karter, who returned promptly.

"Only if she wants them to think she's a battle-ready warrior coming to kill everyone. And that's just for her big-screen debut. When she transports, she needs to be... in the role."

The guys stared at Jessica as if she were speaking another language, even though their NPUs processed English. Just not that kind of movie star slang.

Jessica walked toward me, hand curled under her chin as she inspected the cream and brown uniform I was wearing. It was standard issue for civilians, here on the ship. Or so I'd been told. And to be honest, it was comfortable. Jessica, however, looked appalled. "No. No way. You need a dress with sparkles. You need diamonds and bling. You have to do something with that hair. It's gorgeous, but a ponytail isn't very royal, you know?"

Shit. She was right. I was so used to wearing whatever I wanted, I hadn't given it much thought. Never had been big on playing dress-up when I was a child. It had seemed like a waste of time. Especially when little Destiny would come in and tackle me in her exuberance for defense training. Fighting in a dress and heels was not fun. "She's right. I can't wear this. I need to be seen as a princess, not as some random Earth girl." I looked at the commander. "How do I fix this? I doubt you have ball gowns and tiaras on this ship."

He straightened, his shoulders wide, his voice filled with pride. "We have multiple S-Gen units programmed to provide anything you need." He looked very pleased with himself. And, apparently, he really, really loved this ship.

"The long name is Spontaneous Matter Generators. Like 3-D printing but a thousand times better. They can make anything. Seriously." Jessica looked at my boots. "Even glass slippers, Cinderella. Come on."

She took my hand and tried to tug me out of the room. I turned to look at Leo and made Jessica wait.

He came over. "Go with Jessica. She will not take you far. While you are Trinity Jones, my mate, in here, and for me"—he tapped my forehead and then the center of my chest right over my heart—"you must look and act like Princess Trinity for everyone else."

"But—"

He kissed my forehead. "You are safe and I will be awaiting your return. Go."

I nodded, realizing I was acting silly. I let Jessica pull me from the room then, Ander on our heels. Leo and Prime Nial remained to speak with the commander, clearly trusting Ander to watch over us.

How much trouble could we get into on a battleship? Really?

Turned out, a lot. Turned out every female on the ship wanted to be part of the process. I was stripped and lotioned, my hair twisted and coiled, curled and combed as a parade of women brought me samples of their favorite gowns from their home planets. My make-up was done, with Jessica's oversight. Since she was from Earth, and she looked gorgeous all the time, I trusted her to make sure they didn't turn me into a clown. Seemed that females from all over the universe liked to dress up, when the occasion called for it.

This was... fun. Lighthearted before the chaos I knew was to come.

We'd only been there for an hour when the door slid open and a young woman I'd never seen before entered with a squeal and threw herself at us. She was petite, a couple inches shorter than me, with long, straight black hair and striking green eyes. She was human. More than that, she had commander's bars on her uniform just like Karter's, a Prillon mating collar around her neck, and an adorable toddler girl on her hip. A very human little girl who looked like she was about two years old.

"Oh my God!" The woman hugged Jessica, then me, then Jessica again. Then me. "I'm Chloe. Chloe Phan. Los Angeles! I can't believe there are more Earth girls on this ship!"

She sounded so excited, I hated to disappoint her. "Earth girl, yes. On this ship? Not for much longer. I can't stay. I'm so sorry."

The news didn't faze her. "Oh, I know. It's just good to see someone from home all the way out here in space. And a princess at that." She grinned at both of us and I couldn't help but smile back. Her energy was contagious. "This is Mara. She's just had her birthday a couple weeks ago, didn't you, baby?"

The little girl squealed as her mother tickled her belly, full of joy. Such a normal, beautiful thing on such a strange, stressful day. "She's beautiful."

"I hear her little brother is a handful." Jessica wiggled her eyebrows. "A Prillon brother to watch over her?"

"Torture her is more like it. He follows her everywhere, crawling around at warp speed. I hate to see what happens when he can walk."

Jessica chuckled, but I felt lost. What? "I'm sorry. I don't understand. You're mated to a Prillon?" I looked at Mara, her round, chubby little face looked one hundred percent human to me. "But, isn't Mara human?"

Mara wiggled and squealed to be put down, and Chloe complied, watching as her daughter toddled around on remarkably steady feet for someone so small. But Mara was independent and, apparently, fearless. Or, she had a thing for big, mean-looking Prillon warriors, because she made a beeline for Ander and didn't stop until she was standing between his legs, her hands on him, demanding to be picked up.

Chloe glanced that way, grinned when Ander complied, looking like a giant holding a kitten. Mara, however, had begun talking to the big warrior, her young voice rising and falling as she told him whatever her two-year-old mind found important. Chloe turned her attention back to the selection of shoes on the S-Gen screen in front of her. "Oh, Mara's half human, half Prillon. Her baby brother's got way more Prillon in him. Big and fast, he's my caramel colored cutie." She sighed. "Ander's in trouble. She's in conquest mode. She's already got Dorian and Commander Karter wrapped around her little finger."

I stood still as several ladies tugged and pulled at one of the gowns, trying to make it fit. It wouldn't, but I knew they were enjoying the process. And Ander? Mara had decided to move on, so she crawled up his body—with a small assist from the large warrior—took his face in her little hands and kissed him on the cheek. Done with that, she demanded to be put back on the floor.

Chloe laughed again, our gazes met, and she returned to her search for the perfect pair of shoes.

Ander sat in a chair near the door the entire time, his gaze rarely leaving his mate. And the stark devotion I saw there shocked me to my core. Here, surrounded by laughing females, he let his guard down and seemed to enjoy watching Jessica direct the show. His scarred face and massive body didn't appear to bother any of the other ladies present, nor scare the little girl. They ignored him. All but Jessica, who stopped every couple of minutes to walk past and touch him. Hand on his cheek. His shoulder. His knee. Whatever was in reach. Like she needed the contact.

Or he did. Knowing Jessica as I did, I wondered that such a huge, fierce warrior would be so vulnerable when it came to her.

I wondered what I would discover if I could run around inside Leo's head. And did I want to know?

Yes. Yes I did.

When Jessica was in a rather animated discussion with an Atlan female about one of the gowns, I approached him. "Thanks for watching out for us today."

He inclined his chin, just a bit. "It is my honor, Princess."

So serious. All. The. Time. No softness in him at all, except for Jessica. Well, and for cute little babies. I'd seen Jessica curled up on his lap like he was her personal teddy bear. He was scarred and scary and... adorable. "You're a keeper, Ander. I can see why Jessica loves you so much."

His already dark skin darkened three shades as I stared, fascinated. Jessica chose that moment to appear, laughing, wrapping her arms around my shoulders in a best friend hug. "Oh my God. What did you say to him? He's *blushing!*"

Her smile brighter than I'd ever seen it, she stepped into his arms and kissed him. Hard. "I love you, Ander."

He leaned back and glanced from Jessica to me, where I stood, fascinated, watching them—and the colors that had exploded around them, turning them into a couple of giant glowsticks. Whoa, that whole color explosion thing was crazy. One moment of his attention was all I got, and he was staring at Jessica like she was the only person in the room.

"You are dangerous, female," Ander growled at his mate.

Jessica turned her head and winked at me. "Earth girls are badass, right Trinity?"

It was my turn to laugh. "You know it."

We left Ander to suffer alone and dove back into preparing

me to impress a planet. When the ladies were finally done with me, I stood before a full-length mirror and saw a stranger staring back at me. My hair was an intricate explosion of twists and curls interwoven with sparkling diamonds as it cascaded in a central river of huge, golden curls halfway down my back. The dress was something straight out of a fairytale book, the fitted bodice a shade that matched my skin, but covered with elaborate curlicues and patterns that sparkled like holographic rainbows when the light hit them. And the skirt of the gown? Dark, vibrant red that hung straight down my body but flared in the back with a train long enough to trip any bride trying to make a grand entrance.

I didn't look like Trinity Jones, small-town girl.

I looked like a princess.

I looked like my mother.

I *looked* like a queen.

Jessica rested her hands on my shoulders and peered at me, her gaze solemn as we stared at one another in the mirror. She, too, wore a dress, but it wasn't like mine. Hers was simple but beautiful. A red that perfectly matched the mating collar around her neck. But that was all. No jewels. No glitter. No fuss.

I wasn't wearing just a dress. I was wearing a *statement*. And she hadn't been kidding about the glass slippers. They weren't glass, exactly, but they glittered like the bodice of my dress and were so comfortable I could stand in them for hours.

"Are you ready, Your Royal Highness?" She winked at me, but knew it was time for me to slip into the role I was born to. "It's time to address your people."

I lifted my chin. I was the princess of Alera, rightful ruler to the throne. I had a job to do. A planet to run. Peace to restore. And hopefully, I could hand it all off to my mother so I could go off with Leo and do some headboard banging. "Okay. Let's do this."

9

*T*rinity, *Planet Alera, City of Mytikas, The Palace*

A ROAR FILLED my ears the moment the freezing, twisting pain of transport left my body. I swayed, but Leo was there, his hand on my elbow—like a respectful guard and not my lover. My everything.

He was dressed in the traditional uniform worn by my mother's royal guard. He'd copied his father's uniform from memory, inputted the data into the S-Gen and it created it perfectly, even though the style had faded away when my mother disappeared all those years ago.

The tight-fitting black hugged every gorgeous muscle. The uniform was designed to show the guard's fitness, his strength. Unfortunately, it also showed Leo's bulging cock which only showed he'd been newly awakened. We'd both hoped the amount of fucking we'd done would have dimmed his need a bit, just like my Ardor had been soothed, but apparently not. With my sparkling dress and my very existence, we hoped people would ignore him. At least for now.

And that hope appeared to be coming true. I turned.

Blinked. We'd transported directly into the coordinates of the palace, but we weren't alone. Far from it. The roar grew in volume as more noticed we'd magically appeared and I stared out over a sea of people gathered in the courtyard of the Queen's Palace.

"And we thought this would be less crowded than the citadel," Leo whispered to me. "Princess," he added as a reminder of our roles.

I straightened my spine and lifted my chin, looking as composed and regal as I could manage after just having had days of sex, cross-galaxy travel, a murder attempt, falling in love with a stranger and transporting through thin air.

All in a day's work for a queen, or at least a princess. I waved and smiled. Posed as people took pictures and videos of me. Fortunately, they were all at a safe distance and Leo didn't have to keep himself from ripping their heads from their bodies. I was real. And I was here to stay. I hadn't gotten all dressed up for nothing.

"Trin-it-ee! Trin-it-ee!" The crowd was chanting my name, the name they'd only learned via the video pronouncement I'd recorded while on the Battleship Karter. They'd expected me, as we'd planned.

I was still waving, still smiling, as the giant double doors behind me swung open and an older couple came sweeping down the steps like they were welcoming an esteemed guest. Like the castle was theirs.

Maybe it was. But not for long.

"Cousin!" The woman stepped forward and took my hands in hers. Leo allowed it, but he held onto his weapon, watching every move the middle-aged couple made. "Welcome, Your Highness. I am your cousin, Radella, and this is my mate, Danoth." She bowed her head slightly in deference.

I nodded at her. "Pleased to meet you. You are my mother's second cousin by her Aunt Zetta."

The woman looked shocked, but quickly got past it. "Yes. Of course. And you are Queen Celene's daughter?"

"I am." I'd told everyone as much on the recording, but it wasn't surprising she would want confirmation. I mean, I appeared out of nowhere after twenty-seven years.

"No offense intended, Your Highness, but where is your mother?" She glanced about as if my mother were hiding behind me.

"And where are the royal gemstones? Your arrival here, alone, has caused quite a stir. No one is certain that you are who you say you are." Danoth, my cousin's mate, spoke. As he did so, the color around him changed. Darkened.

He was lying. I knew it as surely as I knew my heart beat in my chest. Now I knew my power, knew there was more than one color that gave people away.

"The citadel knows," I said plainly.

Perhaps it was my tone, but definitely the look in my eye, for Leo moved slightly closer.

My glare was full of outrage. Maybe I didn't need that stupid acting class after all. He'd only said one sentence and I didn't like him at all. "My mother will join us in her palace soon. We must prepare for her arrival."

"Of course. Of course." Radella bowed and swept her hand to the side. "Please, welcome to our home. Come in. Come in. We have had chambers prepared."

Our home? It was my mother's as far as I knew. But I didn't say as much.

"The queen's chambers?" I asked. I would not be a guest here. It was my mother's palace. Mine, with my spire lit. I wouldn't give any leeway to my cousin's mate after he lied to me. He knew exactly who I was.

We entered and I was led to a parlor—Leo closely following —that would rival any on Earth. The walls were lined with breathtaking works of art and gilded trim. Crystal chandeliers that glittered silver and white hung from thirty-foot ceilings.

The carpeting was so think and plush, I lost two inches in height the moment I stepped onto it, sinking down. Everything in the room, from the massive sofas to the carved writing desk screamed money. Lots and lots of freaking money.

Holy shit. Just how rich was my mother? We'd never lived above our means. Our house was average. Middle-class America. My sisters and I had had chores growing up. I'd scrubbed toilets and done laundry. Oh, we'd gotten a flat screen TV when they came out and a new washer and dryer when the old one flooded the basement, but we never splurged. It just wasn't the way we were. If I'd grown up here, my life would have been much, much different.

"Please, Your Highness, please, sit. Would you care for any refreshments?" Radella led the way to the center of a large gray sofa embroidered with silver outlines of Aleran flowers. It was so beautiful, I hesitated to sit down. But I did. The crowd outside continued to chant my name so loudly the rumble echoed through the palace.

I would endure their company for as long as I could, but I wished to be alone, to be with Leo. I sat on that couch with my back rigid and my hands in my lap. Leo stood behind the couch, close enough to touch, the strength and heat of him keeping me sane. My cousins rambled on, clearly uncomfortable.

Good, I wanted them unsettled. To them, I was a stranger. A stranger who might be taking their very livelihood away.

They first spoke of neutral things, like anyone would do on a bad blind date. Then they started probing, subtly trying to get information from me. I refused to answer any of their questions, Danoth becoming more and more agitated as minutes became an hour, then two. I'd had enough. When their assistant, or butler, or whatever the hell he was, came into the room stating that there were news groups requesting entry for interviews, I turned my head to look behind me and met Leo's gaze—a silent *get me the hell out of here* all over my face.

I turned to the butler person. Stood. "Not today, thank you. I am tired and would like to be shown to my rooms. Please tell the reporters that I will send personal invitations to them for interview times very soon."

Radella's mouth dropped open. "You're going to talk to *all* of them?"

She looked as if I offered to give them a belly dance.

"Yes. Why would I not?"

"It's not done," she replied. "The premiere teams are hand-selected and approved by the royal family. They always cover the royal events."

And this was where she lost her powers. Three. Two. One. "Radella, thank you for your counsel on that. As you can see, and so has everyone in Alera, I am the heir to my mother, the princess. It is my duty to rule now until her return. *I* am the royal family now."

"But—" she began, but I cut her off with the slice of my hand through the air.

"Is your spire lit?"

Her mouth fell open but no sound came out.

"Yes, I thought not."

I lifted my gaze from her stunned, insulted face to the butler. "You will report to me now. Please tell the reporters what I said. I do not wish to repeat myself."

He bowed so low I thought his nose was going to hit his knees. "Yes, Your Highness."

He left with haste and my cousins scrambled to their feet.

"I would like to rest. Is there a S-Gen available in my rooms?"

"Yes, Your Highness," my cousin's tone had changed tremendously.

"Good. I'll see you soon. I do not wish to be disturbed."

Radella cleared her throat. "Your Highness, my son returns to the palace tonight for dinner. Might you be inclined to meet him?"

I paused long enough to pretend I was considering her request. In reality, I was about to collapse. Between the sex, the dress-up, transport and spending two hours with my *family*, I was exhausted. "Perhaps tomorrow, cousin. I really am quite tired."

"Of course." She bowed and waved for one of the servants to come over. "Show the princess to the queen's suite, please."

"But, that's your—"

She interrupted the poor man, clearly afraid I'd scold her some more. "Is it clean? Prepared?"

"Of course."

"Then stop arguing and show her to her rooms."

"Thank you, cousin," I replied. "I look forward to speaking again in the morning."

I left them gaping at me as I walked slowly up the grand staircase behind the servant. Here I was, on another planet, and I felt like I was in a storybook castle, complete with winding staircases, wicked, pretend queens, and a huntsman after my heart. And following behind—thankfully.

The servant led me to a bedroom suite that was the size of a three-bedroom apartment. The bathing room was larger than the living room in the house I grew up in. And everywhere, gold. Silver. Handmade art. Paintings I assumed were priceless. And artifacts that were obviously alien and collected from all over the galaxy—as clearly indicated by the engraved, gold-leaf labels on the display cases.

My mother had lived in a fucking museum.

I dismissed the servant with less ice than I gave Radella and turned to find Leo standing in the doorway, staring. I stared back. There was nothing more I wanted in the world than to pull him into the room, strip naked, wrap his arms around me and go to sleep.

But we both knew that wasn't going to happen.

I followed him as he inspected every room, every door and window, every closet and potential hiding place. While it was his role as guard, even if he were known as my mate he'd have done the same. When satisfied, he walked to the door, opened it. "I'll be right outside your door, Your Highness," he said.

"Sleeping on the floor?" I asked.

His grin said he'd slept in worse places. "Yes. Until I can contact my father, yes."

I nodded. That, too, was part of the plan. Leo had shared that his father was royal guard, had served my mother. Never lost faith. Leo's father would know who we could trust, and who we couldn't. Which families were truly loyal, and which had fallen or had ambitions of their own. And a legion of fifty-year-old, experienced, loyal guards would be a gift I would gladly accept.

He bowed to me, both love and duty in his eyes. "My princess."

He closed the door with a soft click.

Yes, I was his princess, but it was a lonely role.

I twisted and cursed for twenty minutes trying to get myself out of the dress. Alone. No doubt Leo would have had it off me in two seconds. And up against the wall riding his cock. In the end, and with immense frustration and pent-up sexual need, I ripped it and let it fall to the floor. The S-Gen unit would reclaim it, use the energy in the material to make me something new to wear tomorrow. Or give me back a duplicate, none the worse for my rough treatment.

I didn't have pajamas, or a t-shirt, or anything remotely comfortable, and I didn't feel like wrestling with the S-Gen unit to get it, so I gave up, climbed into bed naked, and tried to sleep. Without Leo, it was... lonely. While I knew it wouldn't happen, I ached to have him decide to sneak in and sleep with me. Knowing it wasn't going to happen, I grabbed a pillow and hugged it to me. I fell asleep pretending it was my mate.

When I woke, the room was pitch black, the full darkness of night having descended. A dip in the bed let me know that Leo was crawling in next to me. Yes! He was as eager for me as I was for him. He couldn't hold off, his need for me so great to slip into my rooms. I loved that he was so bold and we'd have to be quiet, and quick, getting him back to his post before dawn.

"You aren't supposed to be here, but I love that you are." My words were husky with sleep, a smile playing about my lips, but no real reprimand. If I could steal even fifteen minutes in his arms, I'd take them.

"I saw you today, Trinity, and knew you were going to be mine."

I froze as a naked male body pressed to my back, a hand rising to cup my breast. The body. The voice. This wasn't Leo. This wasn't my mate.

It was all wrong.

All. Wrong.

⁂

Ready for more? Read Ascension Saga, book 3 next!

Although Trinity grew up on Earth, she's Aleran. She's been chosen by the artificial intelligence that bestows special gifts upon those deemed worthy. She's been chosen to rule. To lead the planet and avoid the rising tides of war.

Leo is hers. She feels the truth every time he touches her. But enemies hunt them, her sisters are off on dangerous missions of their own, the queen is still missing, and in the royal court, nothing is what is seems...

Click here to get Ascension Saga, book 3 now!

BOOK 3

PROLOGUE

ueen Celene Herakles, Location Unknown

I WASN'T FOOLED. Not by the feast laid out on the long table before me, nor the false smile on the face of the man stuffing his mouth with food as if he hadn't a care in the world. I knew the truth, and the warm clothing and slippers he'd provided a few hours before I'd been escorted to this dining room did not make me want to talk. Not to him. Not to anyone on this doomed space cruiser. They'd given me a ReGen wand and access to a bathing tube. I felt well... for now.

This was a test of patience, a test of wills. Who would endure? A test of faith. Trust. Patience, for it had been twenty-seven years since I'd been home, to Alera. I'd escaped their machinations all those years ago, but they'd finally found me.

I had no regrets. Back on Earth, I had no doubt that my beloved Adam was worried. But he knew me, knew our daughters. He had chosen to love me despite who I was and the future that we both knew would come for us.

I imagined him back on Earth, impatient. Trusting in his

daughters. It wouldn't be easy, but I knew it was only a matter of time before he came for all of us. He was a Marine who'd gone to college, then law school. He'd earned the respect of his peers and became a judge. He was rock solid. My anchor and my love. When he arrived, he would fight for our daughters with every ounce of his being – the soldier and the judge. These idiot kidnappers wouldn't have figured him into their equation. And they hadn't expected Trinity, Faith and Destiny. They doubted my strength, and they doubted my daughters as well. The attitude might be more typical of Earth, but for an Aleran male, it was quite surprising. Women ruled the world. Literally. And always had.

While these mercenaries—and their master—had captured the queen, they'd accomplished nothing. If my spire went dark, Trinity would ascend to the throne. My capture, the interrogations, this meal, were all for nothing. Twenty-seven years of waiting, twenty-seven years of planning, of organizing. Of preparing my daughters to take their rightful place, would not be ruined by one meat-head pawn and an enemy afraid to show his face.

While I was queen and held the highest power on Alera, three princesses shared it now. It would only be a matter of time before they realized that. And so, I continued to be patient. And endure. And have faith that my children would become the powerful rulers they were destined to be.

I lifted a piece of well-cooked meat to my lips. Not because I was hungry, but because I needed the strength to survive for my daughters. I didn't want to die. Of course not. But now I could die without the worry for my people. They were in good hands with Trinity, and with Faith and Destiny by her side. I hoped to live so I could see them rule, to see them seated beside me on the throne.

This idiot had no idea who he was messing with. As Destiny often said, no one fucked with the Jones women.

Including me. I taught my girls everything I knew. And so had their father.

I hid a smile at that thought and glanced at my captor. He was gorging himself and lifted a carafe of wine. He poured the dark liquid, filling my glass until it nearly ran over. He swallowed, then burped. "Drink. Eat. Then we will talk."

Talk? As my daughters would say—that was soooo not going to happen.

I ignored the wine and reached for water instead. I needed to keep a clear head. The food was quite good, a wide variety of delicious meats, cheeses and fruits. Some, I hadn't eaten since I was a girl, their flavors exploding on my tongue like a thousand memories long forgotten.

"Where are your daughters, Celene? I assume all three are yours?" He spoke while still chewing, his teeth ripping apart the meat, small chunks flying out of his mouth to land on the table. Gross.

"I thought we were going to eat first, then talk," I countered, then popped a berry into my mouth. I would not let him have the better of me, so I ignored him, closed my eyes and bit into the juicy flesh. I expected him to reach out, perhaps slap me for my backtalk, but the blow never came. Evidently, he wanted me whole, clean, content. For what, I didn't know.

For now, I savored the sweet fruit. I used to pick berries with my grandmother in the mountains, laughing and playing in the tall grasses, chasing butterflies as she followed behind with a basket of woven silver. The citadel had given her the gift of nature, of being able to nurture plants and make them grow, to heal black, burned soil. To save a tree with a touch of her hand.

Chewing slowly, I wondered what gifts the citadel had given my daughters. The spires were alight. My captors had revealed this to me, shown me the vids. My girls had been chosen—just as I knew they would—and blessed by the ancient intelligence housed in the citadel's walls. But blessed with what? I was desperately curious. When I'd first heard of their success, I'd hoped that my Destiny would be given a gift that would help her track me to my prison. I still held that hope, that they would find me and I could give this asshole a middle finger salute. I might have taught my daughters some things, but they'd taught me as well.

With a deep sigh, I opened my eyes and looked at the screen that filled most of the wall opposite me. If this were a dinner party, the view of Alera from where we orbited in space would be fantastic. Beautiful. I knew the planet looked much like Earth, but with more green hues in the atmosphere, less water. More mountains. Like my home. Mytikas. A home I might never see again. *Hope. Faith. Trust.* I clenched my hands together in my lap. I had to stay strong, but there was no ReGen wand for one's psyche.

"Where are the royal jewels, Celene?"

I shrugged, putting a few berries in my mouth. So much for *later.* "I'm sure my daughter has them by now."

"No!" He slammed his hand down on the table, making the silverware jump and land with a rattle. "Where. Are. They?"

My mouth was full of food and I took my time finishing. Just because he was a barbarian, didn't mean I had to act like one as well. I was a queen. He? Well, as best I could tell, he was just a mercenary. And not a very bright one. He scowled at me, his eyes shadowed by a long, tangled mess created by eyebrows that desperately needed trimming. I guessed his age to be near sixty, the lines around his eyes and mouth were deep and not pleasant. He was lean, not fat, but the lack of weight deepened the lines in his face, aging him as if he'd lived a hard life, half-starved and tired. His skin was burned a deep red, as if he'd started off a nice brown but been baked by the sun so many times his body have given up healing. But that burnt-on color was broken in a long, white, hooked scar that started at the left corner of his mouth and ended just below his jawline, as if he'd been caught by a fisherman's hook and torn his cheek to pieces breaking free. He wore a bland soldier's uniform with no insignia or markings to indicate his rank. But he was clearly in charge aboard this ship. The other, younger soldiers cowered in fear whenever he was near, as if readying themselves to be beaten.

"Tell your master that I haven't seen the jewels in almost thirty years," I told him.

"They could be anywhere."

"You are not a good liar."

"I am not lying."

His smile was wide, calculating, his eyes narrow as he scowled. "Trinity is making quite a spectacle of herself." He waved his hand and one of the guards who'd helped him beat me just hours ago touched a control pad, changing the scene on the large screen to that of my daughter. "As you can see, she is not wearing the jewels. Nor is she taking the crown, insisting that so long as you live, you are the rightful queen."

I watched as Trinity stood on the steps of my old family home, the palace in Mytikas. I recognized the stonework, the plantings, the grand entry. It had not changed. She had, though. Her usual jeans and t-shirt were replaced with a breathtaking gown, sparkling like white fire and diamonds on top, the long skirt a pool of dark red blood and power. She looked magnificent with her long blonde hair, makeup. Her chin was tilted up, shoulders back. She was Aleran through and through, nobility was in her DNA. She looked like a queen.

My chest squeezed tight as I watched the short recording play through again and again, obviously on some kind of loop. Pride and love filled me up until my eyes overflowed with the emotions clogging them. I could have held them back, but I didn't see any reason to. The asshole next to me wouldn't understand what the tears truly meant. He would assume I was upset. Sad.

The opposite was, in fact, the case. I had never been so fiercely proud, so confident in my daughters. They were warrior queens. Strong. Smart. Alera didn't need me. Not anymore. Not when they were so ready to lead. I drank more water, ate another berry, all as my captor watched me like a snake about to strike.

"The jewels will not help your master now. They are of no value, not with Trinity on the throne."

He laughed, dashing my mood. "So naive. You think the fact that you bred daughters will stop my masters? They eliminated the entire royal bloodline, every single one of you capable of carrying the gifts."

My head jerked up and my eyes were wide with shock before I could control my reaction to his words.

"Oh, yes, Celene. We know about the secret gifts bestowed upon you by the citadel itself."

My heart pounded, but I maintained the queen's reserve. "I don't know what you're talking about." Deny, deny, deny. "What gifts? The light of the spire is a gift to the people. That is the only gift."

Maybe he was bluffing. No one spoke of the psychic and telepathic gifts outside of the family. No one. It was forbidden, therefore, no one should know about them.

He leaned back in his chair, rubbing the matted remains of what once must have been a full head of hair. The greasy strands looked like they hadn't been washed in weeks. "I wonder what gift your daughter received," he replied, ignoring my words. Standing, he lifted his chin to the guard. "Take her back to her cell."

I stood; I wouldn't be yanked from my chair. The guard grabbed my elbow and I let him lead me away. I was unhurt at the moment. My stomach was full. Trinity was in the palace. Destiny and Faith were, as yet, unknown on the planet. Everything appeared to be going according to the plan my daughters and I had agreed upon years ago. *Patience. Faith. Trust.*

"And, Celene?"

I turned my head at my captor's voice. The guard stopped, allowing me to stand still to listen.

"It doesn't matter what gift she has. The gifts didn't save your parents. They didn't save your husband. You might have hidden for decades, but they didn't save you either. And they won't save your daughters."

1

I COULD SENSE ALMOST IMMEDIATELY that it wasn't Leo in bed with me. It took my brain an extra few seconds to catch up. The feel of his hand on my skin was different. Damp with sweat and none of the callouses I was now familiar with on Leo's palms. Leo had hair on his chest and the one pressed against my back was bare. Smooth. The cock nestled at the crease of my bottom was *definitely* not Leo's. It felt disturbing and... insufficient. It was the voice though, that kicked my brain into gear.

"I saw you today, Trinity, and knew you were going to be mine."

I was already Leo's and no one else's. My eyes popped open but I could barely see the outline of furniture because of the thick drapes. Before I could jump from the bed, he shifted and pulled me onto my back. A leg was thrown over mine, a knee nestled at the juncture of my thighs.

I knew he hovered over me, for his hot breath fanned my skin.

"Who... who are you?" I asked, pushing against his chest. It was too dark to do more than see a silhouette of him. I could tell he had dark hair, his skin was pale. While he wasn't as large as Leo, he wasn't small. I cringed at the feeling of his cock pressed against me.

"Do not panic, Princess. I am the Royal Consort. I will not hurt you." He gave a small laugh. "I know of your Ardor. I am here to help. I will bring you much pleasure."

Yeah, right. I didn't care that he was a fricking gigolo and it was his job to hop into bed with every single royal. I didn't want anything to do with him. While I didn't fear he would rape me, since I knew from Cassander that consorts had women willing and eager to fall onto their cocks, still, I didn't like this vulnerability.

"I'm all good on pleasure, so your services aren't needed," I countered. "Let me up."

"You should not have to please yourself," he practically scolded. "Your hand will not ease the Ardor I have been told plagues you."

Apparently, this jerk knew nothing about Leo, or that he'd taken very good care of my Ardor. But then, hadn't that been our plan? Leo was to pretend to be nothing to me. Nothing more than a guard. But how did this consort know about the Ardor at all?

"Look, Mr. Consort, you need to get out of my bed. Now."

"Shh," he crooned, his hand sliding over my hair as if pacifying a skittish female. "Relax. I know I am not Cassander, the one you were first promised. But I am eager to serve."

Fuck. His eagerness was growing more and more obvious against my leg. Yuck. Just. No. "No thank you. I told Cassander the same thing. Now get off me."

"I am very skilled, Princess. You'll enjoy my touch. I promise. Lord Jax sent word to me that you are in need."

"Lord Jax was misinformed." I tilted away from him and pushed, but he wouldn't let me move. I was slightly panicked because I'd never had a man I didn't want on top of me before. And we were naked. He hadn't touched me anywhere inappropriate. But still, we were naked. In bed. And he was on top of me. He seemed to actually want me to be *into it* before he did more.

But he wasn't taking no for an answer and that pissed me off.

I pushed again, but he was strong.

"Princess, it is my job to soothe your Ardor, to bring you satisfaction. Other royal females have been well-pleased." He lowered his head and pressed a wet kiss to my bare shoulder. I shuddered. Ugh. "Let me fill you up and ease your need. You can take my energy. Ride my cock. Be free of the hunger that plagues you."

Well, if I'd been in the condition I had been when I'd first met Cassander—what seemed like months ago, not a few days —I might have taken him up on the offer. But now I had Leo. And I wasn't in heat, I was in love.

God, I couldn't believe he was in bed with me and bragging about his other royal conquests. Just—no. I sighed, remembered a saying Destiny always told me. *If you can't get out of it, get into it.*

He was too strong and totally not getting that when a girl said no, she meant no, so I changed tactics. "You're right." I tried to relax, although it was pretty difficult when I wanted this guy off me pronto.

"That's better, Princess. I promise satisfaction."

"Oh yeah? Let me see what you're going to use to satisfy me," I practically purred. Good thing it was too dark for him to see me roll my eyes. My hand slid down his bare chest, over his abs and to his cock. I swallowed, trying not to vomit in my mouth. It was big and hard, but it wasn't Leo. I couldn't see it, thank god, but I could feel it.

He hissed at my touch. "It is I who should be touching you. And my hard cock shouldn't be in your hand, but in your royal pussy."

I slid my hand lower and cupped his balls. They were

swollen and full, as if he'd been saving up just for me. If he thought he had a case of *blue balls* before, he was about to get a whole new definition of the term.

"A wild one?" he asked.

"A woman who's not interested," I countered loudly so he finally got the point, tightening my grip on his balls until they were crushed in my fist.

He curled up as best he could since he was on top of me— and I wasn't letting go—and roared.

Right then, the door burst open and the room immediately brightened.

The consort hovered over me, his head turned toward the commotion. Now I could see him... and Leo, who stood big and brawny in the doorway. Leo took in the two of us in the bed, his gaze narrowed, his breathing making his broad chest rise and fall. His fists were clenched at his sides. And his cock was a thick telephone pole in his pants.

"What the fuck is going on here?" he shouted. He wasn't looking at my face, but at my hand on the consort's balls. No sheet covered us.

The consort's face—I could see it now—was red and he was in blatant pain. Good. He was a fairly attractive male, dark hair, a few years older than me. I had to assume that since he had a cock that worked, he'd found his mate. Either she was some-where else in the castle waiting for him to complete his duty, she had dumped his sorry ass, or she was dead. Which, I had no idea. Nor did I care. This consort needed to learn some manners.

I twisted and wiggled to his side—still not letting go. "You need to learn to listen." My voice was soft, but even I could hear the shiver of rage.

"Please let go!" the consort begged in the high-pitched tone of a thirteen-year-old girl.

Happily, I released him and he fell to his side in a fetal posi-tion. I hopped from the bed and Leo came over in two strides, tugged the sheet from the foot of the bed and wrapped it around me. As for the consort?

A gagging sound came from behind me. Followed by heaving as the contents of his stomach hit the bed. Asshole. I doubted he'd be *servicing* any other royal for a while.

"How dare you touch my mate!" Leo growled.

I put a hand to his chest, the one that I was familiar with and loved to kiss and stroke, even through the uniform shirt. "He was just doing his job."

"You had your hand on his cock," he countered through gritted teeth.

I looked up at Leo, saw the anger, the fury there. Dark eyes, flushed skin, tendons in his neck all but bulging, like the veins at his temples. This wasn't a warrior in battle, but a mate protecting his own.

"He's the Royal Consort. Lord Jax sent word to him that I was suffering from Aleran Ardor." It wasn't much of an excuse, but maybe it would keep Leo from killing the stupid fool. He was decades younger than Cassander had been. Perhaps even younger than me. If I'd been nineteen or twenty when my Ardor hit, I'd probably prefer him to an older man like Cassander. But being young didn't excuse not listening to the woman he was in bed with. He wouldn't live to the ripe old age of forty if he didn't change his ways.

"Like that makes a difference to me," Leo countered. "You had your hand on his cock," he repeated.

"Yes, I am well aware of that, and I really want to wash them now. Do you actually believe I'd be interested in someone else?" I asked. I stepped forward and leaned into my mate, breathed him in, because he was mine and I could. His arm came around me and he took a step away from the bed, pulling me with him.

Leo was breathing hard and eyeing the consort as if trying to figure out how to murder him. Whether it would be a quick neck snap or a dangle off the balcony before tossing him.

"You had your hand—"

"Stop saying that. He wouldn't let me up, so I had to make him think I was interested so I could get a hold of his balls. And not in a pleasant way."

"He didn't let you up?" Leo growled, his entire body tensing to beat the man to death.

"I can take care of myself," I countered.

He looked at me as if that were debatable, but then the consort dry-heaved and I smirked.

"I grabbed him in self-defense. Leo, after I cup your balls, do you look like that?" I pointed to the consort, who I now felt slightly sorry for. Just slightly.

He actually looked a little green beneath the profuse sweating. One hand cupped his injured balls as he curled up even tighter into himself. The vomit before him only added to his obvious misery.

The corner of Leo's mouth tipped up, but that was it.

"Why was he in your bed to begin with?" he asked.

I shrugged, tugging the sheet closer about me. "I told you. He said Lord Jax contacted him about my Ardor. As the royal consort, I guess he wanted to help. It's his job, I assume, to satisfy the royal women."

"Are you telling me because he came to your bed, you think he was simply doing his job, mate? No male can look at you and not want you." He pushed me behind him and took a step toward the bed. "Touch her again and I'll kill you, consort. Your bullshit excuse is not going to work with me."

I rolled my eyes. "Leo, I took care of him all on my own. See?"

He stared at the guy, although he didn't look the least bit sympathetic.

"How did you get in here, consort?" Leo called.

The younger man didn't answer, only lifted his arm and pointed. We turned to look at a door which was slightly open in one wall. Neither of us had noticed the hidden door before.

There was no handle or any indication that it was there. Leo stormed over to it, pushed it inward and stuck his head into the dark space.

"Secret passage," he said when he came back to me, hooking me into his side. "How many are there?"

"All over," the consort groaned. "So I can service the females at their convenience."

That explained a lot. Leo had been guarding my bedroom door, all the while there were other ways to access me. So much for keeping me safe. The assassin could have slipped in at any time and finished me off if he knew of the secret passageways' existence, which was certainly possible. I shivered at that thought.

"This is why I didn't want to pretend to be just a guard. Things like this happen and you are unprotected. Mate, you were naked with a male on top of you."

"I do see your point of view," I offered, knowing he was right in this. "Perhaps it's time to adjust the plan."

"The plan changed when that fucker climbed in your bed." Leo eyed me heatedly as he pointed at the moaning consort.

I nodded. "All right, mate." At my agreement, some of the tension faded from my mate's shoulders and I realized just how difficult it had been for him to pretend I was nothing more than a job to him. To stand at my side while I pretended he meant nothing to me. But he'd done it because I'd asked him to. Because he'd trusted my judgment.

Maybe it was time for me to trust his. Maybe I should tell him about the plan. About what my sisters and I had agreed upon. Either he was mine, or he wasn't. And every cell in my body said he was. *Mine. Mine. Mine.* It was like a chant on a microscopic level.

"Do any of the secret passages lead to the guard quarters?" Leo asked the consort.

All he could do was nod, then throw up some more.

I cringed. Now I *did* feel sorry for him. What if I'd neutered him?

Then again, he should have listened.

"Know this, consort" Leo began, his voice loud and very clear. "Share this with all who will listen. Princess Trinity is my mate. The only cock she'll touch, the only balls she'll fondle, are mine. Having yours practically ripped off will be nothing compared to what I'll do if someone even breathes near her again."

The guy fell back onto the pillows and just lifted his hand by way of response.

Leo took my hand and tugged me toward the hidden doorway, then pulled me into the darkness.

This time, surrounded once again in pitch black, I knew I was with the one person I could trust, the one person I wanted close to me while I was naked.

2

$\mathcal{L}$*eo*

"I'm sorry, Leo. I should have listened to you back on the Karter." Trinity's soft admission soothed me as I closed and locked the door to my quarters. I knew for a fact there were no secret passageways in or out of this room. There was no exit or entrance other than the thick door I'd just bolted. And the bolt was heavy. Meant to withstand an assault. A last resort should the guards' quarters ever be attacked.

Or the next cock-swollen consort who decided he needed to seduce the future queen.

"I know." I had no doubt the consort was told by Lord Jax to attend to the new princess. But I also knew that many consorts conspired to seduce the matron of his household. Many held more power than all but the head of the house, herself. Rulers were female here, and being welcome in a wealthy patron's bed was not without additional rewards for the right male. Getting Her Royal Highness, Princess Trinity, to accept him into her bed? It would have been a major boon for the fucking bastard.

Even for the royal consort, Trinity was *more* than just a job. She always would be. And that was why she needed me. I didn't care if she wore a crown or a sack. She was mine, and I was in love with her. She'd transported across the galaxy to save her mother and fight for her planet. She'd survived an assassin's attack, the Ardor, and made it to the citadel. She'd held her head high, walked into her mother's palace, and faced her cousins who most likely wanted her dead. And she'd done it all without raising her voice or losing her head. She was fearless, strong, in a quiet way. A rock, not the storm.

The labyrinth of dark passageways behind the walls of the main rooms did lead to the guard sleeping area, just as the consort had said. I hadn't doubted his word, since he knew I was ready to rip off his already bruised balls and shove them down his throat.

When I turned my head and glanced at her, I realized I'd never seen anything so beautiful. My mate with just a sheet wrapped around her, a hand at her breasts holding the ample fabric closed. Her pale shoulders were bare, her blonde hair long and tangled. She looked fuckable, and worried. Her straight teeth bit down into her plump lower lip and her chin was down. Not the regal bearing she usually had. Only with me did she show her true feelings. A princess. And she's just apologized to the poor son of a soldier.

"Are you mad at me?" Her eyes were round, worried. I'd dragged her the length of the palace wearing nothing but a sheet.

Worse, I'd made her doubt my devotion. My anger at seeing her naked with another male had made her seek to comfort *me*. It was my job to fix this, to make her happy and whole. She should never doubt my feelings for her. She was my mate. A miracle, if I were being honest with myself. More precious and perfect than I deserved. I had blood on my hands. A lot of blood. Years of war and killing had stained them permanently in my mind.

But she allowed me to touch her anyway, with these scarred, bloody hands. I was the monster guarding the gate, a trained killer, but I was her monster. I served Mytikas. I served the citadel and Queen Celene. But above all, I served Trinity now.

"Mad? Yes. But mate, not with you."

She sighed and offered me a small smile.

"I admit, I want to go back and rip that consort's head from his body. Clearly you are irresistible to all males on Alera, and not just me."

She laughed at that. "He was just doing his job."

"You are not a *job*." I tugged my shirt, lifted it up and over my head. I would not pretend to be the guard sleeping at the door. No. We would now sleep. Together. Where we should have been all fucking along. "Please explain to me why you had your hand on his balls."

She rolled her eyes. "You're not going to forget that, are you?"

I arched a brow as I settled my hands on my hips. "Would you like to find me naked and in bed with a woman with my fingers buried in her pussy?"

Her lips thinned and her eyes narrowed. I had no interest in another female, she had to know that, especially since she'd brought about my awakening. My cock was hers. She ruled it.

"You have a point." She spun on her bare foot, glanced around the room, picked up a glass of water and took a drink. "Destiny said—"

"Ah, I can't wait to hear this one," I murmured, thinking of the fearless and half-mad female. I'd never met a female more aggressive. If Trinity was solid and steady as a rock, Destiny was the storm that raged against it.

Trinity rolled her eyes again. "Destiny said that when fighting someone, or in self-defense, sometimes you have to recognize you won't be able to get out of a situation."

She went to the bed and sat on the edge. This room wasn't

opulent like her chambers, but the bed was large. Large, but simple. Basic. Plain. I didn't give a shit if it were a cave as long as Trinity was with me.

"That is true," I offered. I'd fought enemies before, hand to hand and in more firefights than I could remember.

"So if you can't get *out* of a situation, you need to get *into* it," she finished.

I saw red and rage simmered. "Are you telling me the consort was forcing himself on you?" My voice was little more than a whisper, but one word from my female would send me back to end him.

Her blue eyes widened. "He wasn't forcing me. He was just surprised I wasn't... eager. I decided, instead of fighting him to try to get out from underneath him, I'd get into it. To let him think I'd stopped resisting. So, I pretended to check out the goods."

I didn't exactly understand *check out the goods* but I had a mental picture of what that meant. Pretend to like his cock and balls so she could get a hold of them and squeeze them like little berries.

"I'm sorry you had to see that. I am." She stood, tucked the length of sheet into itself at her breasts so it remained closed and came over to me, put her hand on my bare chest. I went instantly rock hard. Just her scent, her touch and I was done. No wonder the consort was so eager to taste her. She was so fucking alluring just breathing.

"The only balls I want to touch are yours. The only cock I want to stroke is yours."

Her hands were on my uniform pants, opening them.

"You stroked his cock?" I growled. Balls were one thing, but his cock?

"Shh," she replied soothingly, then she gripped my length.

She was trying to distract me, and it was working. I groaned, all thought of the consort, of Alera, of anything but Trinity was gone.

Her hand was on me. Stroking me, her thumb sliding over my slit, catching the pre-cum that slipped from me. I couldn't help it.

Thank fuck, her hand was on my cock. Mine.

Fuck, yes.

I reached up, tugged the sheet from her, let it fall to the floor at our feet. She was gloriously naked and all mine.

"You can work the cum from my balls, mate," I said, glancing down at her, staring at every perfect, bare inch of her. "But it's going in your pussy. You have ten seconds to play."

She glanced up at me, a sly smile on her lips as her hand continued to expertly move up and down my length. She might be a princess and rule a fucking planet, but right now, she ruled my cock. And she reveled in that power.

"No more," I said as I grabbed her by the waist, scooped her up and tossed her on the bed. I stood in just my pants and boots, my cock out, hard and long and aiming right for her. And if a bead of pre-cum just dropped to the floor, I wasn't paying much attention. "We talked about this, mate." I angled my head toward the locked door. "You're in charge out there. In here, you're mine."

She bent her knees, spread them wide so I could see every glorious inch of her pussy. Oh, fuck. The power of that sweet pussy.

Determined, I grabbed an ankle and tugged her across the soft bed toward me, which made her laugh. And then she gasped, when I flipped her onto her belly. The gasp turned to a moan when I hooked an arm about her waist and pulled her back so she was on her hands and knees.

She looked over her shoulder at me with a mixture of surprise and arousal.

When my hand came down on her upturned ass, a bright pink replica instantly appearing, she gasped, then wiggled her hips.

"That's for being naked and in bed with another male."

I pushed my pants lower on my hips and crawled up behind her. Spanked her again. "That's for touching another man's cock and balls."

I lined up my cock at her entrance and slid in with one long, hard thrust. "And that, mate, is your reward for being such a good girl. Using your brain." I fucked her as I talked, gripped her hip. She felt so good. Wet, tight. Hot. How had I lived without this? Without her? "Being so smart, so beautiful. Perfect. Fuck, this pussy is perfect."

Her hands clenched the bedding as she pushed back into my thrusts, taking me as deep as I could go. She was panting, crying out, clenching me. This was going to be fast. Hard. Intense.

I leaned over her, covering her body with mine. Skin on skin. I wanted her to feel me. Smell like me. Surrender. Give me everything.

I lowered one hand to the bed to brace my weight and used the other to wrap beneath her, looking for her center, the swollen clit I knew begged for attention.

She arched beneath me when I found it, her soft cries making my cock jump where it was buried deeply inside her. I stroked her without mercy, sliding in and out of her wet heat in a slow grind I knew would make her scream. I wanted to feel the walls of her pussy shudder and clench my cock in hot waves. "Come for me, mate. Come all over my cock. Remember, who rules you."

She did come then, a scream ripping from her as her inner walls spasmed, milked me, pulled me in deeper, all but begging for my cum.

I couldn't hold back, the hot sizzle of need too great. The hottest burst of pleasure dissolved my bones, temporarily blinded me. My balls tightened and then emptied, filling her with spurt after spurt of my seed.

When it was over, my body shook. I couldn't hold myself up

any longer and to keep from falling on her, I scooped Trinity into my hold as I fell to my side, tucking her in against my chest, my cock still deep inside her.

I might have come, but we weren't done. Not yet. I was going to be inside her sweet body all night.

"Your cock rules me?" she asked, her tone a little caustic when she finally got her voice.

I chuckled and kissed the top of her head. "Based on the way you screamed just now, I'd say so."

She put a hand on my arm where it rested over the curve of her waist, slid her fingers over the skin absentmindedly. "I guess you could be right."

"You doubt, mate?"

"Maybe you'll have to try again to make sure."

I pulled out, tugged her so she was on her back and I was looming over her. Her eyes sparkled and she smiled brilliantly.

"It might take more than once," I shared.

"It might," she agreed, reaching up and cupping my jaw. "We have all night."

"And in the morning, there will be no doubt by anyone who sees you—even that fucking consort—that you are my mate. Well-fucked and at my side."

She just grinned and pulled my lips to hers. But I wasn't finished. "We will have a formal mating ceremony."

"Are you asking me to marry you?" She stilled beneath me, as if listening with her entire being.

"You are already mine, love. But yes. I want our mating recognized by the entire planet. I want your name linked with mine in the clerics' archives. You're mine, mate, and I want the whole fucking planet to know it."

"You're mine, too, you know." She ran her hands through my hair, gently. A lover's caress, and my entire body shuddered with need at her simple touch.

"I am yours. Always."

"Yes, Leo," she said so sweetly.

I dropped my head and took in one plump nipple. Sucked.

"Yes, Leo," she said again, this time with a completely different tone.

3

Trinity, Two Days Later, The Royal Reception

THIS WAS A ZOO, and I was the most popular attraction. When my cousin, Radella, had said she'd hastily arranged a reception for my arrival, I hadn't expected this. Perhaps a small dinner, maybe even a drinks and hor d'oeuvres event with dignitaries and political people. But this...

Leo had tried to tell me what to expect—that everyone wanted to celebrate with me, be with me, see me... but I still hadn't understood. I did now. Hundreds of people milled about a grand ballroom. One wall was completely open to the outside, which was good because it would have been stifling otherwise. I just had no idea how they'd gotten rid of one whole wall of the room. Alerans of all ages were dancing, drinking and eating. Coalition uniforms mixed with Aleran guard attire as well as formal garb for those not in service. Everyone had pulled out their finest from the backs of their closets and were partying like it hadn't been done in a while.

Perhaps it hadn't, since my mother had been gone for almost thirty years. She'd married my father a year before she fled to Earth, and I had to assume there had been some kind of ascension ceremony.

Out of everything she'd shared, of everything we'd planned, she'd never told me about that, so I asked Leo, who was practically glued to my side. "Yes, she had an ascension ceremony when your grandmother passed on and she became queen."

He looked so handsome in his Aleran guard finest—all black with a Batman utility belt full of weapons and... stuff— and even more so now that everyone knew he was all mine. All that big, broad male belonged to me.

"Thank you for helping me explain to cousin Radella that I didn't want to claim the throne. I can't believe she argued with us for so long."

I wasn't queen. My mother's spire was still lit, which meant she was alive. Somewhere. That she was still the queen. Therefore, an ascension ceremony would be disrespectful and wrong.

But Radella and her husband saw things differently. They said Alera had been without a rightful ruler for too long. That further delay would destabilize the great houses.

I had to disagree. And, I later admitted to Leo, I needed the *great houses* to be running scared. One of them had kidnapped my mother. I was sure of it. And fat, contented bears didn't leave their dens. I needed them to be worried. Scared about what I might do next. Afraid I would take what was theirs.

"I think your cousin wanted a reason to have a party," Leo commented, as he looked out over the crowd. We were standing on a raised area that circled the entire central dancing floor. Music from a small orchestra guided revelers through the steps of—what I assumed—were Aleran dances. It reminded me of Scottish reels and even a little like square dancing, although without the caller.

"I'm not too excited about her since she was obviously the one who sent the Royal Consort to my bed," I grumbled. Most Aleran women would find her gesture thoughtful... seeing to my *every* need, but me? No way. I spared a glanced at Leo. I didn't even feel him stiffen beside me at the mention of the Royal Consort, but I had a feeling that was because everyone knew—and could clearly see—that we were mates. No more naked men in my bed except Leo. "But I have to give her credit. She'd make an amazing wedding planner on Earth."

Leo turned my face so I looked at him, and I almost got lost in his dark eyes, forgot there was an entire ballroom full of people watching us. "You are not upset that this isn't a wedding reception?"

I swallowed, thought of my family. Shook my head. "I accept you as my mate. I do, Leo. But I can't have a wedding or celebrate with my mother... somewhere. And my sisters. Faith and Destiny can't come out of hiding, and risk what they're doing just to be my bridesmaids. They're safe because they're anonymous. And my dad should be here. Well, my step-dad, but he raised me as his own. I don't want a wedding without my family there. I would rather wait."

"This formal ceremony or wedding, as you call it, makes no difference to me. You are mine. A ritual of this sort or even grander reception won't change what's between us," he said, leaning down to kiss me. "All of Alera knows you are mine. I am content to wait until you are ready."

He kissed me. And just that fast, I was lost. No one else mattered. No one but Leo. We were alone in the middle of a crowded ballroom—

A roar broke out across the room and we broke apart to look. Everyone was clapping and cheering our kiss. I couldn't help but smile, and I felt my cheeks heat. Caught lusting after Leo by half of Mytikas.

Leo wrapped an arm around me. "No going back now," he murmured as he pressed his lips to my cheek with a satisfied, very male, grin.

I felt like Cinderella at the ball. I already had my Prince Charming—and everyone knew it—but there was no pumpkin hour and I wasn't in disguise. I was in a frou-frou, pale blue dress and my hair was pulled up in a fancy complicated twist. I looked like some Disney princess at a southern beauty pageant.

The Alerans who had waited faithfully for their queen's return seemed to be happy. Thrilled, even, that while Queen Celene wasn't here, her daughter was. I gave them hope, a happiness that had been missing. The cousins who frowned, or worried what my appearance meant to their status, I ignored. For now.

Smiling, I waved to everyone and was just glad Leo was at my side instead of across the room pretending to be just a guard.

"You are mine, Trinity." His gruff voice was a blast of heat in my ear. "We must dance."

I wasn't sure if we must dance, but I wasn't going to stop him from holding me in his arms. Even with his size, he led me around the dance floor with a grace that only came from practice. He moved slowly, the dress I wore even more elaborate than the one I'd first appeared in on the palace steps after transporting from Battleship Karter. Definitely Cinderella.

"You are mine, Leo. Forever." I smiled up at him because I could and laid my cheek to his chest, holding him close. I had no doubts. Not about his love for me. Not when this strange gift I'd been given made his love shine around him like a halo. So easy to see. The ability had grown stronger the last two days. The energy around people so bright and easy to read, it felt like cheating.

The dancing couples who swirled and moved past us laughed and nodded to us. Cheerful and happy. Others though, I could see the envious, mud-colored auras of several men and women around the edges of the dancing area. Either they didn't have enough to drink or were just party poopers. I ignored them, closed my eyes, and breathed Leo into my lungs. He smelled familiar and warm. So perfect. Sexy. I could stay here all night.

But that was not the plan. First, Leo and I would make a

complete circuit, then, one by one, we would be required to dance with other guests. "I must hand you off to others now. While I wish to keep you in my arms all night, it would be rude and ill-formed of you to neglect your subjects."

Leo sounded grim, like he was going to hand me off to the Royal Consort, not Aleran citizens who wanted their turn to dance with the princess.

"I wish I had an ion blaster strapped to my thigh," I told him. "Destiny's mad self-defense ideas would work great with a dress this... poufy."

I glanced down at the big skirt of my blue dress. I could hide a football team beneath it and no one would notice. A small ion pistol in a thigh holster would be nothing.

I was sure each and every guest would want to question me about my mother, the other women who had entered the citadel, the light of the spires, how I'd found Leo and all about our mating. They'd ask—but I wouldn't answer. I had no idea where my mother was. I had no intention of telling them where to find my dad, back on Earth. My sisters were anonymous, and I intended to keep it that way. And Leo? Well, Leo was mine. All mine. They saw us kiss. That was more than enough.

There was no divorce on Alera. It didn't exist. Leo, Radella, and even Danoth, had told me that if two people decided they no longer wanted to be together, they simply set up separate bedrooms—or, if they were wealthy, wings of the house—and went about their lives. But their children—those born of their union—inherited everything together. There was no his, hers and ours here. The society was very formal but had gone on this way for centuries. Bastard children inherited nothing unless there were no heirs born of the marriage. From what I'd been told, most of the children born out of wedlock volunteered to join the Interstellar Fleet, either as a warrior, or as a bride.

Aliens. They were so advanced in some ways, and so

behind the times in others. Maybe, once I was queen, I'd change some things...

"An ion pistol? Not happening, mate," Leo replied. "This is our only dance. I'm going as slowly as I can, but all too soon I will be forced to give you up. Whatever you are thinking about or plotting, it can wait." His hand tightened on my hip, his strength tempting me to melt into him and let my brain turn to mush. I loved what he did when he made my mind shut off; it always involved very naughty things. But I couldn't let that happen. No, I had to have a clear head now. Focused.

Leo and I would be in bed together tonight when this was all done, but we couldn't have a honeymoon, or be selfish and think of nothing but ourselves, of having sex for days on end. Not until my mother had been found and my sisters were safe. Then, I'd take Leo to bed and not let him put clothes on for a week. We'd have that honeymoon. A real honeymoon where I didn't have to wonder after my mother, worry about my dad on Earth, imagine what Faith and Destiny had gotten into. Not this tangled mess of politics and assassin hunting.

"I wish my mother were here." Mother. She should be here. My sisters. My dad should be pestering Leo with a thousand questions, getting ready to walk me down the aisle, not hiding from some stupid Top-Secret alien hunters back on Earth.

"I am sorry, love. I know this situation is not ideal, but I am not sorry that I claim you as my own. You are mine, and I want every male, every consort and warrior on every planet to know that."

I thought of the Royal Consort. He knew and I was sure he was spreading the word... if he'd gotten his balls untangled from his tonsils.

"I love you, Leo." I wanted to marry him—the human way. Maybe it was silly, but I wanted an ivory dress made of the softest silk, embroidered with a waterfall of delicate pink and lilac roses on the skirt and sleeves. Like the one I'd imagined when Faith, Destiny and I played pretend wedding when we were little.

I wanted Leo, but he was already mine. I was in love with him. I trusted him. I couldn't imagine my life without him. But this royal reception? This party for the nobles? My introduction to society? This was a show. This was me luring a killer into making his move. Thus, why I'd wanted a thigh holster and ion pistol. Oh well.

"Let's go then. Get this show over with. I know he's here. He has to be here. The sooner we find him, we'll be one step closer to finding my mother."

Leo scowled and forced my body a few inches from his, lifted his hand from my hip to tip up my chin. "This dance is real. We are real. This is not for show. Not for the assassin or your cousins, most of whom are probably plotting ways to kill you. This is for us. Me and you. They watch us like we are performers on a stage, but this is real. You are in my arms. Your taste is on my lips. I claim you in front of everyone here, in front of the world. I'm not letting you go."

"I look like a big blue blob of cotton candy." The dress really was huge. A bit much, to be honest. But damn. I had to admit. Black on black on my man? Oh, a guy in uniform made my ovaries jump for joy. Everything about him made my heart race. And as ridiculous as I looked, he was the opposite. Muscles. Mystery. Sexy lips. Hard shoulders. Hard... other places.

"What is cotton candy? If it is beautiful, then I will agree with you."

I burst out laughing. I couldn't help it. Not with the sincere expression in his eyes. He loved me. He saw past my title, my bloodline, the masses of people around us, the ridiculously fluffy dress... and saw me. Truly thought I was beautiful. I could see the truth of his words in the light that surrounded him, that strange light I'd been seeing since I'd connected my life force to the citadel.

I kissed him, full tongue. No, I ravished him. Claimed him. Right there, in front of everyone. Royal decorum be damned. I was an Earth girl, and I didn't really care if the uptight nobles approved or not. I was the princess here, and if I wanted my mate's tongue down my throat, then that was what I was going to get.

Leo didn't resist. In fact, when I finally came back to myself, we'd stopped moving completely and stood on the threshold of the place where we'd begun our dance. We stood still, looking at one another as silence stretched in the room before breaking into a roar of applause. Again. I tried to love him with my eyes. His lips were pink. Bright pink. Smile growing wider, I forgot all about our audience and lifted my thumb to his lips to wipe off the remnants of my lipstick.

"You've had her long enough, young man. As father of the groom, I claim the next dance with the lovely princess." The voice was deep, kind, and sounded very much like Leo's.

Turning away from me, Leo bowed to the older man and pulled me the last few steps to stand before him.

"Father, may I present my mate, Trinity Jones Herakles, Princess of Alera." He turned to me. "Trinity, this is my father, Captain Travin Turaya, former leader of the Royal Guard and lifelong defender of Mytikas and your mother's rightful place on the throne."

Leo took my hand and placed it in his father's wizened grip as if I were made of glass and would break. Leo wrapped his arm around my waist and I beamed at the older gentleman, truly honored to meet him. "It's an honor, sir."

"The honor is mine." It was obvious he and Leo were related. Same dark hair, although his father's was mixed with some gray. Same wide jaw, dark eyes. They even had the same soldier's bearing. "I have waited, faithfully, many long years for Queen Celene's return."

His words were kind, but the reminder that my mother was out there somewhere still stung. But his aura—as I'd started to think of the strange color and light I could now see around people—was full of sincerity, and healthy doses of both love and pride for his son. I liked him immediately.

"Yes, we all are," I replied.

"She will be found, Princess," he vowed. "In the meantime, you have Leo to keep you safe. And I will offer my personal assurance that he and I have spoken about your safety. I have hand-selected every guard here tonight. Every guard in the palace."

I was surprised by his vehemence, but impressed with his allegiance. Leo looked to his father and they shared one of those silent conversations. It finished with a nod from Leo's dad.

I cleared my throat. "Thank you," I replied. "Shall we dance?" I held out my hand.

His smile deepened the lines on his face and, as he pulled me into the dance, I had a flash of what my future with Leo would be. Thirty years from now, Leo would look just like him. Fit. Strong. Still good-looking.

I was very glad Leo had a good example to follow, as I'd begun to be plagued with thoughts of having children. I suspected it was part of the Ardor, but I had to admit that wasn't all it was. It was Leo. I wanted to give him everything. I wanted to love him and make babies with him and make him blissfully happy. I was greedy. I wanted the dream. Husband. House. A few perfect kids. I'd take a palace, didn't need a white picket fence.

I wondered if I could get a Golden Retriever or a Staffordshire Terrier out here. One with a big black spot around its eye, and big, dopey paws. I was being ridiculous, not even knowing Leo just a short time ago.

"I've never seen my son this happy. Thank you, Your Highness."

No. That was not how I was going to roll. "Call me Trinity, or daughter, or kiddo, honey. Whatever you would call your own daughter, please. I love your son. He is an unexpected gift."

The older man teared up and I felt bad for a moment, until he pulled me into a tight hug. "Goddess bless you, child. He loves you. I can see it in him. You are the gift."

His hold lasted only a moment, but I felt the hard line of some kind of weapon under his tunic. He was Leo's family, and his aura was good. I didn't know how he'd gotten the weapon past the other royal guards, but Leo said his father used to be their captain. They probably hadn't even searched him. I knew Leo was armed as well. So I let it go.

He was family.

He cleared his throat and stood tall, whirling me around the room at record speed. Leo was a few steps behind us, dancing with Radella. A line had formed along both sides of the dance floor, one of women who wanted to dance with Leo. And one for me. While this was a reception celebrating the princess's arrival, Leo was part of the insanity. He would never be a prince, but as my mate, it seemed he was desired as well. As long as the women kept their clothes on, then I was good.

My line was three times as long. My feet were going to fall off by the time I danced around the room with all of them.

Travin led me across a silver line on the dance floor I hadn't noticed before. A gong sounded and Danoth took my hand. Around and around I went. Cousins. Soldiers. Nobles. Clerics. So, I danced with all of them. Leo's cousins. Mine. Tradition stated that neither Leo nor I could refuse a dance with anyone who wished to claim one of us and take us around the room. Dance. Make small talk. Try not to shudder at a few of them. Dance. Dance. Dance. One at a time in a procession.

 rinity

"Princess, I am Thordis Jax." A man bowed before me when it was his turn to lead me around the dance floor. The name sounded familiar, but I'd met so many people, the names were a blur. "I would like to wish you welcome, but also my apologies for the... dangerous welcome you received upon your return to Alera."

"Oh!" I replied. "Lord Jax, yes. I remember that name now," I replied. What did one say to someone who had planned for our protection but provided anything but? What did I say to the alien who ruled the house that my sister, Faith, was probably snooping around in at this very moment? But then again, Prime Nial had trusted him. So I wasn't sure what to think. Luckily, I didn't have to come up with anything to say because he smiled at me—a gigawatt smile—and twirled me around so fast it made me dizzy.

"Thor, please. Lord Jax is my father." Thor was charming. I had to give him credit. His hair was golden blond, he appeared to be close to my age, but his eyes looked calculating. Old eyes in such a young man. They were blue, a dark gray-blue that reminded me of stain-washed denim. He was tall and handsome, and I didn't fail to notice the amount of attention he got from the rest of the ladies in the room. Throw some tights on the guy and I'd be talking to Captain America.

I glanced down. I couldn't help it. Umm, yeah. One problem with that—no female Aleran had woken him up yet. There was no tenting in his pants. Not like Leo, and a few of the others here. He'd told me that his constant erection would go away after a few months, waiting for one glance or one touch from me to come roaring back to life, hard and ready.

Leo. Where was my mate now? I lifted my head and craned my neck to see around blondie's shoulders.

"You look like you're done with dancing for now." Thor glanced behind him, saw that there was no one there. There was, however, a large area set with tables and on those tables? Food. Drinks. I was both hungry and thirsty. "May I escort you to the refreshments?"

He held out his bent arm like Mr. Darcy from *Pride and Prejudice*. His aura looked warm, friendly. Not the intense passion and devotion I saw when I looked at Leo, but Thor appeared to be safe enough. And besides, we were only going to the buffet table on the other side of the ballroom, not the dungeon. So I said, "Thank you," and took his arm.

Faith was in the Jax household, so I had to wonder if she'd met one Thordis Jax. Because wow, he was gorgeous. I had my hottie, but still. I had sisters. Single sisters...

I caught a glimpse of Leo, who was dancing with some Aleran woman in a pale yellow dress. There was stomping and clapping and twirling in the dance, a quadrille or a jig or something complicated. Yeah, Thor was hot, but my man was hotter.

"I don't think I would be able to handle that one," I said as we skirted around the dancers. "The steps look too complicated."

"It is complicated, but we are raised learning them, so they are not difficult for us."

Leo caught my eye and he was able to follow the intricate moves while watching me. I hand signed that I was getting a drink and he nodded, drawn back into the dance.

Thor led me to a table covered in pre-filled wine glasses. The crystal and ruby liquid looked brilliant in the lights. He handed me a glass and I took a sip, then another. Delicious, yet I could taste the alcohol and it no doubt packed a serious punch, especially to a lightweight like me. Thor didn't say anything, just let me take a moment to myself as we watched the dancers.

"Thank you," I said finally.

He arched a brow.

"For the break. I needed this. And, of course, for the group of guards who met us at the transport."

"They failed miserably," he murmured, glancing down at the polished floor. "I had Prime Nial to answer to for that one."

"You?" I asked. "But I thought your father was Lord Jax. Wasn't he in charge of the men?"

Thor chuckled, but there was no humor in the sound. "Officially, yes. And he did select the lead guard, told that man to select his own soldiers to accompany him to transport to meet you." He took a sip of his wine but didn't look at me. "But when it was time to face the consequences of our failure, he was conveniently unavailable to take Prime Nial's comm."

Damn. Would have been nice to be a fly on the wall when that was going on. But then again, maybe not. It wasn't Thor's fault we were attacked. I sensed no subterfuge in his aura. Only regret. And I knew Nial and how nice he was. And how intimidating. I could only imagine what it had been like to be reprimanded by the leader of all of Prillon Prime, and then some. And Ander, his second, was even scarier. I would not want to be on the receiving end of a smack down from either of them. "I am sorry so many of your soldiers died. I'm sure they were good men."

He nodded. "Not good enough. And one of them had to have betrayed us. Someone who knew about the guards, that they were to protect you. Somewhere in the chain, there is a rat."

I wasn't touching that one, not with Faith sneaking around under his nose. In his house. "And I'm sorry for the loss of your consort. I understand they are very difficult to replace." It was all I could think to say. What was there to talk about regarding a man paid to have sex with noble women? He excelled at his job? He seemed eager to advance his career? He was a good sport when I told him I wasn't going to let him touch me? Ugh. It all sounded bad in my head.

Thor's mouth tipped up in a smile. "Cassander is none the worse for wear. In fact, he's said that it was quite an experience."

I turned my head to him, the dancers ignored. "He's not dead?"

Thor shook his head. "No. Stunned, shot in the head. The medical team found him alive. It must have looked like he bled to death, but the wound was not much more than a surface injury."

I remembered seeing him fall, the blood. The consort unconscious. I'd never gone back to check on him because a guy in all black had just crashed through the window and shot the person next to me. Hell, I'd just assumed... Stupid. I'd learned my lesson. Never assume. "Well, that's good to hear. Please tell him... no hard feelings."

"I don't know that term, but it seems that you have found someone to ease your body's needs on a more permanent basis."

I watched Leo circle by, the dance still going, the music mixing in with the lively conversations all around us. It was a long set. He lifted his gaze to mine, and I felt like I'd been punched in the gut. Just like that, the air was locked in my lungs. God, he was so freaking hot. Sexy. I wanted to— "Yes, well..." That was a thread of conversation I wasn't going to continue. "Who are they, the group in capes?" I asked, tipping my head toward several men and one woman in black capes on the edge of the room. It was definitely time to change the subject off of consorts, mates and my needy vagina.

Their uniforms were interesting. If I were being honest, they looked like high school cheerleaders—skipping the tiny pleated skirts. Black, white and silver, the zig-zag geometric designs on their shirts were distinct. Different from everyone else in the room. Black shoulders. White chest. Silver darts at the side and a black triangle pointing up toward the heart. The upper arms were white beneath the shoulder, but from the elbow down, the uniforms were shimmering, metallic silver. Their pants and boots were black. There were both men and a woman wearing the strange outfits, like they were the only ones who thought they were coming to a Cos-Play and no one else got the memo. Their capes were thick, black on the back, a soft, shimmering silver on the inside. It looked like sparkling silver mink.

Weird. Did that come from a bizarre Aleran animal? And if it did, how could they kill something so damn beautiful?

At the top of the black peak on their shirts, just under the sternum, each of them had a distinct symbol. What was that? Their rank? And what was with the swords hanging from every one of their hips. They weren't decorative. They were simple. Slim. And they looked very well used—and sharp.

"Clerics," Thor commented.

"Priests? Monks?" I asked. Okay. Weird outfits for a priest, but I was on a different planet.

"Not exactly." He cleared his throat and took his time, as if working out how to explain. "I apologize, Princess. It is hard to remember that while your mother is Queen Celene, you have only been on Alera a short time. The clerics... they are spiritual leaders, but not of the type I believe you are suggesting. Those present here are of the highest order. The leaders. But the Clerical Order has existed for as long as your royal bloodline. They are sworn protectors of the crown, and of the citadel. There are thousands of them serving all over Alera. Their lower ranking members train to serve the people in a spiritual sense, counseling others in times of stress or grief. Officiating at births and deaths. Marriages. Matters of finance. But they do not hold court, or preach from a book, as I understand your religious leaders do."

Finances? Right. So, not so different from the churches back home. Maybe like higher-ups in the Catholic church at the Vatican. "What are the symbols below their chests?"

"That is their family crest. They are all volunteers, called to serve in the order. Some are born without legacy or inheritance, and it is a way to keep a roof over their head. Others are healers. But all keep their family crest on their uniform. If they have no family name, they take the sign of the order."

That was depressing. I'd have to find out more about that system once my mother was back on the throne. "What about the old man talking to them? Is he a cleric too?" The man I asked about looked like he was in his seventies, but quick-witted. Not dull. His hands moved in an animated fashion as he spoke and the others bent close to listen, as if what he said mattered.

"That is Lord Wyse on the left, and no, he is not a cleric. He is the head of the Royal Guards' Optimus unit, his title being Inspector Optimi. It's a fancy title for being in charge of the group who mete justice. They investigate crimes, examine evidence and prosecute and try the guilty in court."

He sounded impressive and looked a little... daunting.

"Actually, he is one of your cousins, Princess," Thor continued. "He is very, very rich, and I have no doubt that his many children and grandchildren will not be pleased about your return." His grin was contagious, so I gave in and grinned back at him, for I knew what family was like. You couldn't choose them and you were stuck with them, no matter what.

"Running away with the family money, am I?" I asked, joking.

Thor cleared his throat. "Oh, yes. Starting with his eldest daughter, your cousin Radella. I'm sure she is already wondering when you will force her out of her home."

I didn't see a resemblance between Lord Wyse and Radella, but I didn't doubt their father/daughter connection. He looked like he swallowed a lemon, a look I saw frequently on Radella's face. "It's my home," I countered, clarifying that Radella had settled in too well to a home that didn't belong to her. "It's my mother's."

He raised his hands, palms out. "I accuse you of nothing. It is your rightful home. But Radella and her family have lived there for more than twenty years, ruled the roost, so to speak. They will not be happy to leave the house—or the status —behind."

I squinted, trying to get a better look at this Lord Wyse. My cousin? Radella's father? Ugh. "Who is the scary looking guy behind Lord Wyse?" He looked like he'd just ridden in from the desert. Perma-sunburn. His face was thin and he looked... mean. And he had a large scar on the side of his face, from the corner of his mouth down to his jaw. Like someone had put a jagged knife in his mouth and not cut... but ripped through his flesh. Gah, that must have been horribly painful, especially since there were ReGen wands and pods to heal wounds.

I looked closer, trying to see the color of their energy. Strangely, I saw nothing.

Confused, I turned my attention to a group standing closer to me. Perhaps Lord Wyse and the clerics were too far away.

Nope. Nothing.

What the hell? What happened to my superpower?

I turned my head too quickly and the room spun, just for a moment. I was tipsy. Off one glass of wine.

5

Damn. So, alcohol was going to kill my secret ability to see people's energy? That totally sucked. I'd have to be a lot more careful at these kinds of events in the future. I needed every advantage I could get. Lord Wyse might just be a shrewd businessman. Or he could be a serial killer. One glass of wine and I couldn't tell the difference.

Thor frowned, his gaze following mine as I returned my attention to Lord Wyse, the clerics, and the man with the scar. "I do not know the male with the scarred face standing behind him. He looks like a hired bodyguard. The practice is not uncommon among the nobility."

"Do we need bodyguards?" I asked. I had Leo, but he couldn't be with me twenty-four seven. It just wasn't practical. He wanted to try, though. Regardless, I wanted Leo with me, not constantly scanning the crowd for potential threats everywhere we went. He felt it was his job to protect me, and I was fine with that, to a point. If I needed additional security, then so be it.

"Prior to the attack that killed your father, it was unheard of. Now? Well, unless you are a trained warrior, I do believe guards will be a necessity." He took my empty glass from my hand. "Another glass of wine, Princess?"

"No, thank you. One is probably enough for now." I didn't want to tell him it was going to be impossible to figure out how to pee in a dress this fluffy. And I refused to ask Leo to hold it up out of the way. No. Freaking. Way. But that wasn't the only reason. I realized just how much I'd come to depend on that secret weapon—reading auras—knowing a person's true intention or mood.

Thordis Jax's aura had been powerful but not overly friendly. Not hostile either, so I liked to think he was simply withholding judgment about me. But the envious, sickly green I'd seen around some of the women when they looked at me after gazing at Leo? The cloudy gray and sickly brown resentment I'd seen around my cousin, Radella, and her husband, Danoth? Gone. They looked like everyone else.

One drink and I was flying blind. I didn't like it. Not at all.

Someone in the crowd caught me eye. "Hey! That's your injured guard." I pointed. "He made it."

Thor turned about, looking for the person. "Where is this guard? My father interviewed him after the attack, but I have yet to catch up to him."

"In the Aleran uniform. Light hair. He was one of the guards who escorted us from the transport. He was shot by one of the assassins and he was still alive when it was over. We helped him, although it was more like Boy Scout skills than anything. I'd never even seen a ReGen wand before, but I guess it helped."

"Yes, I'd heard one of our men had survived the attack, thanks to your intervention."

It was my sister, Faith, who had tried to save him. But since no one knew much about Faith or Destiny, I couldn't correct him. I would have helped, but I'd been too caught up with my first glimpse of Leo and my stupid Ardor to give the dying guy too much attention. At least one of us Jones sisters had their wits about them.

Leave it to the most scatter-brained of the three of us. But then, Faith was sneaky like that. Half the time I believed she said the most outrageous thing possible just to make people think she was clueless. In reality, she was wicked smart. And she didn't miss things. Not like Destiny, who would rather strike first and ask questions later. If Destiny was a bull in a china shop, Faith was a black-widow spider—hunting at night. And what did that make me?

The main attraction, apparently. Or distraction. All of these people were here, trying to talk to me. Learn about me. Figure out what I had planned and where I'd come from. Where my mother was. That left my sisters free to move around anonymously, which was exactly what mother had wanted. So far, it was working, for I was the shiny—or pale blue object—everyone was staring at while my sisters sneaked about to learn more. We couldn't find out the truth if people only told us what they thought we wanted to hear. Or what they wanted us to know, and I had a feeling I was solely in that camp.

Smiling, I waved at the guard in question. He saw me and lifted his glass in a salute. Surrounded by a group of other guards, his friends laughed and slapped him on the back as he made his way to me, then bowed to first me, then Thordis Jax. The poor man seemed thrilled to be close to me, but wary of Thor. The guard kept his face averted from his master, never raising his chin or straightening to his full height.

Not a lord, my ass.

"Your Highness. My Lord, good to see you."

Thordis bowed his head. "It has been a long time, my old friend." The two clasped forearms before the guard returned his gaze to me.

"I am Guard Zel, a humble warrior serving the Jax family."

"I know who you are." Glad, now, that I didn't have the

drink glass in my hand, I stepped forward and hugged the man. Bear hug. I didn't care who was watching, or if this was acceptable royal decorum. I just had to hope Leo didn't come over to clobber the guy. I was going Earth-girl on this one. I couldn't see his aura, but I didn't need to. "You saved all of us. You almost died. Thank you."

He stood completely frozen, his arms locked to his sides. Probably afraid Leo would cut them off if he dared put his hands on me to hug me back, but I didn't care. I squeezed him as tightly as I could, then stepped back. He was stiff as a board, his cheeks a dark red with obvious embarrassment. Otherwise, he looked perfectly fine. Not like he'd been shot by an alien blaster. He'd have to deal. I wasn't taking it back. "You saved my sisters. Thank you."

"Sisters, you say?" Lord Jax was suddenly very interested in the conversation. "At long last, the speculation has been confirmed."

Oh shit. One glass of wine, one friendly face, and I was spilling secrets. Damn it. I turned on my megawatt smile and played dumb. "Excuse me? What did you say?"

Lord Jax's smile was devilishly handsome, and I blinked at the laughter I saw in his blue eyes. It was a good thing I was totally and completely in love with Leo, because damn. He was a hottie. And he knew it. "I would not repeat such gossip for unknowing ears."

My smile was real. "You keep the juicy gossip to yourself?"

"Knowledge is power, Princess. The sooner you learn that, the better. You are in good hands, Princess. I shall take my leave." He inclined his chin to me, patted Zel on the shoulder and walked away to mingle. No doubt, he'd know every bit of juicy gossip in the room by the end of the night. I watched his retreating back for a moment, studying the difference in culture here. He was gorgeous. Rich. But his cock lay dormant. Well, I assumed it did since there wasn't a mate clinging to his side. Because of this, I assumed that was why the young ladies left him alone. Rather than young, attractive women pursuing him around the room, it was older men and women both. Not after sex, but after his wealth. Power. Influence.

The dynamic was completely different than what I'd seen on Earth, and I knew I would need to study the subtle variance. Adapt.

"May I have a dance, Your Highness?" The guard's blush was fading, but he still looked very young. Like a hopeful puppy.

"Of course." I had no reason not to dance with him. I'd danced a complete circuit with everyone of note, apparently. Except Thordis Jax.

Zel took my hand and led me to the dancing area as the last bit of the prior song ended. Another group dance began, but as I stumbled with the complicated—and unknown—steps, someone directed the musicians to play something slower. Something their poor, ungraceful princess could actually dance to.

"Do not worry about the steps. I will lead you," he murmured, one hand holding mine, the other on my waist. A respectable distance was between us, like a seventh grade dance.

"Thank you. I'm sorry. I just don't know these dances yet," I murmured, glancing down at his feet.

Radella had tried to teach me a few. I had no doubt Destiny would have moved like water across the floor in a matter of minutes. Faith would have done the wrong steps, thrown back her hair and laughed as she stepped on toes. Seemed I was cursed with the desire to make sure everything was perfect.

I let him lead. His touch was light. Respectful. He made sure to twirl me past his friends, who all cheered and clapped as we passed. We danced closer and closer to the open wall and the large, outdoor area. I was too busy watching feet instead of figuring out how they'd engineered an entire side of the ballroom to be gone. The fresh air felt wonderful, and I took a deep breath to clear my lungs, and my head. The effects of the wine were fading. Thank god. I hated not knowing whether or not I could trust people. I knew this "gift" the citadel had given me was a form of cheating, but I wasn't giving it back. Hell, I didn't know how, even if I wanted to. Which I definitely did not. A girl needed all the help she could get.

"The fresh air is wonderful. Thank you." The music ended and Zel held out his arm, facing a stone terrace that overlooked a large garden. I took his elbow and followed him to the railing, looking out over the labyrinth of pathways and tall hedges. It reminded me of an elaborate maze, something I'd seen in a movie. "I had no idea they actually made gardens like this. It's like Versailles, I think, but I've only seen those gardens in pictures."

He nodded as if understanding that I spoke of somewhere on Earth. "There are many places to conduct business within the gardens. Every large estate has one."

"Really? Every single one?"

He nodded. "Yes. The plants chosen are designed to muffle noise. Business deals. Secrets. And—" He cleared his throat, cutting himself off mid-thought. "Other things."

I could imagine what those other things might be. In fact, now that I had the idea in my head, I wanted to take Leo out there. Tonight. Find a hidden corner and make love under the stars. To get lost for a few hours and just be alone. Away from all these people. The noise. I wasn't an extrovert by nature. The party had lasted a few hours and I was already exhausted.

A couple walked arm-in-arm toward one of the tall entrances, flanked on either side by dense foliage twice their height. I felt my shoulders relax a bit when their glow came back. Golden. Pink. With flashes of red. They were in love, whoever they were. And they were sneaking away to do what I wanted to do with Leo.

Be alone. And have some sexy times.

But that was not my destiny this night. I had to play dress-up for a while longer. Smile and shake hands and kiss babies. Well—there weren't any babies here—but it was a thing. Political. I had to be political.

"Thank you for the dance, Zel, but I really have to get back —" Shit. My gift had returned.

His aura was dark. Not grumpy dark, or greedy dark. Not envious or angry.

Evil.

He must have seen the knowledge in my eyes, because he grabbed my arm in a vise with one hand, and placed the tip of a dagger just under my ribs with the other. Right below my heart. It hurt, cutting through the fabric just enough to nip my skin. One thrust, and I'd be dead.

"What are you doing?" I hissed.

"I'm taking you to your mother," he murmured, deep and deadly. "Be quiet and come with me. One word, one scream, and you're dead. Understand?"

"Yes." I understood all right. He was a liar. He was evil. The one guy we'd saved in battle turned out to be a killer.

But he knew where my mother was, or at least who had her. That flash of truth had sparked through his aura as he spoke. I'd cooperate, for now. The chance to find her was worth the risk. I'd go with him, find out where my mother had been taken, and trust Leo to find me. I winced at the nick of the knife and allowed him to pull me down the stairs and out into the dark night.

I didn't really have any choice.

6

Leo

I WAS SO DONE DANCING with other females. It was as if custom intentionally kept mates apart. I breathed in the perfume of the dozen or more dance partners that clung to me. Goddess, I needed a bathing tube before I even got near Trinity. The same probably went for her as well. The idea of another man's scent clinging to her—even passing it to her as innocently as a public dance—made me see red, but even that was better than the vision of a naked consort in her fucking bed.

The final song came to an end and I bowed to my partner. As soon as it was acceptable to leave her, I spun on my heel and searched out my mate. She'd been speaking with someone by the wine table and I'd seen her walking with a guard. A guard who I barely recognized from the ambush the evening of the three sisters' arrival on Alera. He was whole and healthy, quite an improvement from that night.

He would have to get on his knees and thank Faith for saving his life.

Trinity had been relaxed and smiling at him. Knowing my soft-hearted mate, she wanted to offer her thanks for his bravery. That was all well and good, but I wanted all those smiles, all that attention, on me. Yes, I sounded like a sullen little boy, but where Trinity was concerned, I was greedy. Flaunting what was mine in front of the other males was not something I enjoyed. The dormant males would not understand what they were missing. The mated males had no reason to envy me. The consorts and the rest? They would be made to understand that if they hurt one hair on my mate's head, I would make them suffer ten-fold before I killed them.

Trinity was a princess, but I didn't care about politics. I was a soldier, plain and simple. Rich. Poor. None of them mattered to me unless they were willing to stand next to me on the field of battle. Pretty words meant nothing if one wasn't willing to bleed for them.

I had no doubt Trinity would stand next to me against an entire horde of Hive Soldiers, if I asked. Hell, even more likely, she'd refuse to leave a fight even if I ordered her out of danger. Not as a battle-hardened soldier wanting to fight hand-to-hand like Destiny—she was too tenderhearted for that—but leading, organizing, planning.

She was magnificent. And mine. I had nothing to prove to anyone but her.

My instincts were screaming at me to find her, but I shook the nerves away. I hated large crowds of pretty people. I would have to learn to deal with events like this, I knew, so I could stand at Trinity's side and be what she needed. I'd seen images of the events that her mother had hosted. Grand balls. Parties. Events that required smiling, dancing and worst of all... sharing Trinity.

She deserved a partner. An ally.

And, when the need arose, her enforcer. Queen Celene's bloodline was back on the throne, where it belonged. Not officially, since Trinity had refused to take part in an ascension ceremony. But four spires lit the sky.

The days of noble houses battling over the queen's table scraps were over.

After one pass of the room, and no sight of my mate, my instincts kicked up another notch, from the vague feeling that something wasn't right to full-out alarm. On the exterior terrace, there was less than a handful of guests milling about. The evening was late and many partygoers, especially the elders, had already gone home to seek their beds. The young and ambitious, or just bored, would stay until the dawn, dancing and drinking.

The consorts in attendance would be busy tonight.

For myself, I only wanted Trinity. I paced the length of the wall, looking down to see if she'd gone toward the gardens. I didn't think she'd go there with anyone, for she knew the risk to her life. There was luring out the assassin and then there was being stupid. Trinity was anything but stupid.

I knew that the music and laughter would not die until the light of dawn rose over the garden. In the past, I'd been one of the silent protectors on the edges of the room, never anyone of note. But I'd watched them all. Learned who could be trusted and who played foul.

The nobles spoke freely in front of the servants, as if they were nothing more than an inanimate object to be ignored. I knew just how far from the truth that assumption truly was. And I knew exactly who I needed to talk to now.

A dozen royal guard lined the walls, watching everything. Seeing everything.

If they were good at their jobs, they would know where I could find my mate.

I strode to the guard nearest the refreshment table where I'd last seen Trinity with Lord Jax and the guard who'd nearly died in the initial attack. True to form, he looked straight ahead, ignoring me, as if he really were a statue. I had to give my father credit. He had hand-selected every guard watching tonight. I'd told him upon our return from Battleship Karter there had already been an attempt on Trinity's life. Trapped in that opulent palace, I'd used what resources I could to keep my mate safe. And my father was one of the best resources I had. He'd been a royal guard for decades. Knew every guard by name. Knew their histories. Their families. He'd promised me that every man guarding my mate tonight could be trusted.

"Stop pretending you don't see me, soldier, and tell me where to find my mate."

He blinked, hard, his gaze darting to me for the briefest moment before returning his attention to his job. But he did answer me. "The princess was escorted onto the terrace by the guard from Jax's house ten minutes ago."

The terrace? I'd already looked out upon the people there. She was not among them. "Are you sure?"

This did get his attention, and he tilted his head up in a challenging manner. "I belong to the queen's guard, sir. It is my job to be sure."

Fuck. My heart began to pound out in silent alarm. I grabbed the guard by the shoulder and shook him gently until he looked up at me. "What is the queen's guard?"

He looked straight ahead at the dancers, once more ignoring my physical presence. "That is a question for your father, my lord."

"Listen, your job right now is to keep your head down and find my father as quickly as possible. Do not speak of this to anyone else, do you understand me? Bring my father to me on the terrace. Immediately."

"Yes, my lord." Thank the goddess he didn't question me or my order, but took off at once across the room, as if he knew exactly where my father might be. Grateful, I watched him for a second and thanked fate that my father's hand-selected guard had been paying attention.

Fuck me. I'd failed my mate, because I had been dancing

and talking politics like an idiot while Trinity disappeared. Two things I hated.

I never should have left her side. Appearances be damned. She had insisted we act as if nothing was wrong, that if her first public appearance was as a fearful weakling, it would affect her reputation for years to come. Take her power and respect. I'd respected her wishes. Even Prime Nial had agreed with her. He knew a lot more about ruling than I did. So, too, did my mate, with her mother teaching her what she would need to know since she was born.

I'd listened. Considered. Gone against my instincts and allowed Trinity to place herself in danger.

Fuck.

At least she had a guard with her. I would keep faith in knowing he would protect her with his life.

If I found the guard dead? Well, that would change things.

Moving quickly now, I went out to the terrace and responded to the greetings of the few guests, not because I cared, but because I needed information.

"Have you seen the princess? She was escorted onto the terrace by a guard and she owes me a dance."

The two ladies shook their heads. The two males with them looked at one another for confirmation before the elder of what looked like two brothers turned to me. "We have not seen Her Highness, my lord. Apologies."

Biting back a growl, I rotated on my heel, looking for something, anything. A flash of blue in the gardens below. A hint of her sweet scent. A glimpse of moonlight on her golden hair in the darkness.

A sparkle of blue on one of the stairs...

I stilled as I caught sight of one pale blue shoe. A female's shoe with sparkles and gems I'd seen before. On Trinity. I grabbed it up, held it. Why the fuck wasn't it on Trinity's foot? If it had fallen off, surely she would have paused to put it back on. It was dainty and had a heel that was pointed and unstable—

how females moved in such tools of torture I had no idea—so it would be awkward for her to walk in just one.

Unless… I whipped my head around, frantic. I wanted to shout her name, to make the music stop and everyone to stand still so the space could be searched. She wasn't here. I knew it. I felt it. She wouldn't have left a fucking shoe otherwise.

Was the assassin here? Had he made a move at last?

Trinity *knew* she was not supposed to leave the ballroom unattended. The only reason I had agreed to bring her back to Alera and attempt her mad scheme of acting as bait for the assassin was because she had given me her word she would be careful. Take no unnecessary risks.

The gardens. Would she have been taken that way? Into the maze where it was easy to get lost? No, they would be caught within the shrubbery. They needed an escape, perhaps around the sides of the garden to a vehicle? Or out in the city?

As I headed to the nearest garden entry, I heard commotion. Not from the ballroom, but from a side hallway situated on the lower floor of the palace. The structure was large, with a host of hallways, tunnels and covered drives that led into various areas of the palace. I stormed through the open door and into the hall.

A gathering of well-dressed servants was murmuring together, no merriment or laughter on their faces, despite the music playing behind them and the array of food and beverage scattered throughout the smaller hall. Seemed the nobles weren't the only ones celebrating the return of the royal family.

"The princess," I said, stopping hastily in front of them.

"Captain—my lord—apologies, I don't know how to address you."

"Leo will do."

"Yes, my lord… Leo," he bowed slightly and I shifted on my feet. I didn't give a fuck about titles or status. I just needed to find my mate. Thankfully, he continued before I had to beat the information from him. "The princess was with another guard.

She didn't say anything beyond a simple greeting, but she looked unhappy."

An older female spoke. "She was walking strangely, with a large limp, and being pulled along by a very tight grip on her elbow."

I held the only clue I had in my hand, the sparkling blue shoe, and they stared at it.

Another in the group stepped forward and held out his hand. "After she was gone, we found this by the door." In his grip was the matching shoe.

I took it from him. My mate was leaving a trail for me to follow, although I didn't know what she could remove next. "Did she ask for help, or say anything to you as she passed?"

The first man shook his head. "No, my lord."

"Another guard?" I asked. "You're sure?"

All of them nodded. There was no doubt among them. But the assassin, Vennix, wasn't a guard, unless he had used one of the royal uniforms as a disguise to gain entry, to gain Trinity's trust.

But that would not work either. She'd seen his face in the initial attack. He'd been standing over her, ready to kill her. As much as the thought pained me, I was quite sure that male's face would be branded in her memory forever. So who had taken her?

"Which way did they go?"

"Farther into the palace, up the grand stairway."

I looked in that direction. Up those stairs were the hallways that led to the royal family's private chambers. Why would anyone take Trinity farther *inside* the palace?

Unless...

I left them and found several guards stationed outside the ballroom. These two I knew by sight. "The princess has been taken." The words were like acid on my tongue. I'd failed my mate, allowed danger to come to her. "Where is my father?"

My father stepped forward immediately. "I'm right here. I heard the news. What do you need?"

"I need that fucking consort who tried to seduce my mate. And I need him right now."

My father frowned, clearly confused. Out of all the possible things I could request, a consort was not high on the list.

"The consort? For what purpose?" That voice was deep. Curt. All too fucking familiar. And evil.

I dropped to my knees, rolled across the floor and burst forward, weapon out, before he'd finished the question, and looked up into the eyes of a killer.

Vennix. The assassin was here, and he was inches away from murdering my father.

rinity

"WHAT DO you think you're doing?" The tip of the knife was still shoved painfully against my ribs, but now the blade was at my back. Still inches away from my heart, so not much of an improvement.

"Following orders. Which is what you should be doing. And I told you to stop talking," Zel hissed in my ear as he twirled the tip of blade just enough to cut through the fine fabric of my dress and break my skin. It stung, but I refused to give him the satisfaction of a reaction.

"Where is my mother?" I asked. He had to know where she was.

"I said, stop talking." His free hand squeezed my shoulder, directing my steps through the winding maze of hallways and rooms in the palace. The place was too quiet. Deserted. Apparently, no one had wanted to miss the party.

Lucky me.

But I never was good at following orders from a bully. Destiny had taught me well. "You said you were going to take me to my mother, which is the only reason I didn't scream bloody murder on the terrace and have all of Alera come running. So, where is she?"

"Alive. For now. If you give my master what he wants." He laughed, and the sound was like listening to a hyena. Twisted, coming from a human being. But then, not exactly a human. An Aleran. At least, I assumed he was Aleran. He could have been some other species I didn't know about. I heard the Everians looked just like humans as well. Or so close it was very difficult to tell them apart. But he was crazy. Insane. Perhaps he was losing his mind slowly, or struggling with orders. I hadn't been alone on Alera until the ball. His patience was wearing thin, or his *master's* was.

"And what is it you want from me?" I shouldn't have asked, but since his grip was so freaking painful it felt like he was slowly cracking my collarbone in half, it was either talk or scream. Screaming would give me a knife up and between my ribs.

I'd ditched one shoe, then the other, hoping people would see it for what it was, a *Hansel and Gretel* breadcrumb trail.

"The jewels, Princess. Where are the royal jewels?"

I put my hands up to my ears, felt the large tear-drop gems, tugged them off.

What? No, he wasn't talking about my stupid earrings. Oh shit. "*That's* why you idiots kidnapped my mother? For some stupid black rocks?"

He howled in delight, as if he'd gone just a bit mad in the last few minutes. We continued to walk as we spoke and I dropped one of the earrings on the floor as we went. "Black? So you have seen them! Tell me where they are and I won't kill you."

Shit. I could use the pain in my shoulder and the knife at my back as an excuse for my stupid, loose tongue, but I wasn't one to lie to myself. I'd just made a dumb mistake. Damn it. "I don't know."

"Oh, you do. And if you don't tell me, you'll tell *him*. When he's done with you, you'll beg him to take them from wherever you've hidden them."

Great. Threats of death and torture. Completely irrational, based on Zel's heavy breathing and overall excitement level. Faith would say something sarcastic. Destiny would have probably tossed him against the wall and smashed his throat with her boot by now.

Why did I have to be the cool-headed analyst?

And as I pondered that question, the thought that had been tickling the back of my mind since this hostile turn of events blurted out of my mouth. "Why did you try to save our lives when we arrived, but threaten to kill me now? Why are you dragging me off with a fucking knife in my side?"

"Oh, you royals really are just as stupid as my master said you were." He shoved me into a room I'd never seen before. Based on the musty smell and the light coating of dust on the desk and shelves next to the huge, canopied bed, I guessed this room hadn't been used in quite some time. At least the knife wasn't jabbing me now.

"Stupid, stupid princess."

He laughed again as he shut the door behind him, but this time I didn't find it at all entertaining.

\|/

Leo

"Leo, no!" My father stepped in front of the deadliest assassin I'd ever known and blocked my kill shot with his own body.

"Get out of the way, Father!" Standing behind him with a condescending grin on his face, Vennix—or Nix when we'd been on friendlier terms—used my father as a shield, and fucking *smiled* at me as he did it. He didn't blink. Didn't even flinch that he was about to die. I could take the head shot. I had a few inches of leeway. But it was my father's brains I'd blow all over the fucking ground if I missed.

Fuck.

"Move, Father," I growled. Thinking of what Vennix had done, how he'd almost killed Trinity in that suite made me see red, made my finger twitch on the trigger. "He's a stone-cold killer."

"So are you." Cold words. Hard. Intent. The words of a commander and I tore my gaze from the assassin, Nix, the male I'd served with on several missions, the male I'd once respected as a warrior, and looked my father in the eye.

"What the fuck is going on? Trinity has been taken, and you are protecting the man who tried to kill her?"

Vennix stepped out from behind my father, and I adjusted my aim. One blistering shot through the heart would do the job just fine. But his hands were up in the air, and my father was waving me off. "Don't you dare, Leo. Put it down. That's an order."

"I wasn't trying to kill your mate, you love-sick idiot. I was trying to save her. Which I did." Vennix had the gall to bow slightly at the waist. "I had to climb down a rope and break through a fucking window. The fight cost me two good men, asshole. You're welcome."

What. The. Fuck?

My father cleared his throat. "Nix isn't the bad guy. He wasn't at the suite when the princesses arrived and he's not one now. There is a traitor inside the Jax household. One of my informants caught wind of the plan when Cassander was invited to ease Trinity's Ardor upon the sisters' arrival on Alera."

"How do you know the females who went into the citadel with her are her sisters?" I asked my father. "They covered their heads to remain anonymous and no one has mentioned their relation."

"I told him," Nix said.

Traitor.

Maybe I should shoot him just for fun.

My father continued. "Put the ion pistol down, Leo, before you shoot someone. Or at a minimum cause a scene. The fewer guests who know of the princess's disappearance, the better."

I sighed, pushed off the ground and stood before my father, but my focus was squarely on Nix. My pistol was aimed at the floor, but that didn't mean I wasn't prepared to use it.

"Cassander was innocent in the plot," my father continued. "He truly believed he was simply doing his job. But one of the guards sent to escort the females told a friend that as soon as her Ardor was eased, they were to murder the consort and frame him for the females' deaths. The three sisters would have disappeared and no one on Alera would have been the wiser. Or even know of their existence."

"Except Lord Jax." So, I needed to kill the man as well. I needed to start a line, just like for the dancing.

"No. This runs deeper than that," Nix added. "Lord Jax is a pompous old man with too much money and too much time on his hands. He doesn't have the patience to plan something like this."

"His son does." Thordis Jax. I could kill him just as easily. And he'd been speaking with Trinity earlier.

"Listen," my father said, settling his hands on his hips. He had an ion pistol on his belt, but didn't make any attempt to use it. As if he didn't think Nix was a threat. As if he were one of his own. "I will tell you more when Trinity is safe. We don't know if Thordis was involved. We don't know who is behind the queen's kidnapping. When we learned of the princesses' arrival on Alera from Earth, of the threat on their lives from those who had met them at transport and vowed to keep them safe, Nix and two queen's guards went to the safe house to save them. They hadn't been harmed... yet, thank the goddess. But they *did* save them."

"I stormed through the window before the guards could get to Trinity and Cassander in the bedroom. I had to get Cassander out of the way, but I did not kill him. Trinity ran to the other room to escape, assuming I was the enemy and afraid I was going to harm her as well. But the other two guards with me were already in direct combat with the Jax guards when I followed her. Then you stormed in and let one of the bastards live," Nix accused.

I paused, thought about the cluster fuck that was that bloody confrontation. Blaster fire, dead bodies. Fighting. Innocent females.

Fuck. Nix was right. One of Jax's guards had survived. I'd even given Faith my ReGen wand to save him. And now Trinity's life was in danger because of it. But I'd had no fucking idea the Jax guards were actually the enemy. Neither had the princesses.

"You should have told me."

"Before or after you blew my head off?" Nix asked. "Would you have believed me? Would the princesses? I was the one who came through the suite's window, remember? I was the one who they'd thought killed the consort in the bedroom. I left them in your hands, Leo. You've lost two of them and now your mate is missing as well."

"They aren't lost." I glared at my father. Now wasn't the time to let him know about Faith and Destiny's plans to infiltrate and learn about their missing mother. "And *you* should have told me the truth."

"Just as you told me about your conversation with Prime Nial? Told me about the mission he gave you?"

Score one for the old man. Shit. He was right. And not done rubbing it in.

"I only discovered the truth when Prime Nial contacted me himself, looking for information on an assassin he intended to hunt down and eliminate—on information he'd received from you, son."

I'd told Prime Nial and Ander about Nix on board Battle-ship Karter, when we'd all agreed to allow my mate to use herself as bait to draw the assassin out of hiding. The *assassin* being Nix. But now...

Leave it to the protective Prillon leader to try to help me protect my mate, without her knowing of his additional inter-ference. Calling my father in for reinforcements only made me respect my friend even more. Also, thankful it was my father he'd contacted, who'd been helping. I was grateful, not angry.

Without his help, Trinity would have died before I ever met her—and I would have killed Nix, an innocent male. An honor-able warrior. He'd sacrificed and killed during the Hive war, just as I had. Now that I knew he was not trying to murder my mate, I found I had a deep and abiding respect for him. "This is a mess. And my mate is in danger. Is there anything else I need to know? Tell me now. Right now."

"I ordered Nix to back off when I learned of your mating," my father said. "I knew you would stay at your mate's side. And I needed him to help me root out the informant inside the Jax household while you kept Trinity safe."

Slowly, I put my weapon back in the holster knowing I wouldn't use it on Nix. The guard I'd spoken to inside the ball-room ran up behind my father, the consort—who'd slipped naked into Trinity's bed—right behind him.

The consort took one look at me and came to a sudden stop. He swallowed hard, glanced at my father, the weapon at my side, and Nix's frozen features and stumbled back, hands going to protect his groin. All color drained from his face. "My apologies, my lord. I think I'll just—"

"Don't fucking move or I'll shoot you in the back." I sounded like a psychotic killer, but I didn't have time to argue with him. The consort froze in place.

"There is one more thing you should know, Leo," my father said as I stared down the consort. I'd threatened to cut off his balls so he had to wonder why I'd specifically requested him.

"Explain," I said, not glancing away.

"I was with Queen Celene on the night of her escape."

One sentence stopped me cold and I did ignore the consort now. "What?" Even the consort stopped fidgeting and stood, riveted.

"I was a young man then," he said. "The captain and I helped her sneak through the streets to the citadel because of the attack. She was covered in blood. Her mate had been killed right in front of her. But she was strong, Leo. So strong. Before she entered the citadel and disappeared, I vowed to her that I would remain and protect her kingdom and her throne until her return. And I kept my word."

"The queen's guard?" I asked. "That's what he was talking about?"

The young guard—the one who'd first mentioned the term —stood next to my father and nodded fervently.

I pointed at him. "There is no queen's guard. Never has been."

Nix tilted his head, his arms crossed. "On the contrary, I've been in the queen's guard for most of my life. As has every guard on duty tonight."

A feeling of confusion, or betrayal, burst through my chest as I looked at my father in a new light. "You? You're their captain?" He was retired. An older man. Not the leader of an elite unit of guards that didn't exist.

"Yes, son. For twenty years. Since the death of the former captain, Balkan. He and I alone escorted the queen to the citadel, knew of the child she carried. Trinity."

"Why? Why didn't you tell me?" What I wanted to ask was why he'd left me out, why he hadn't made me a queen's guard. But that would reveal too much pain. Still he seemed to know what I was truly asking, because he answered the question.

"You came back from the Hive wars changed, son. You lost faith. Even with the queen's spire lighting the sky, you gave up hope of her return." My father glanced off into the night, toward the citadel where, even from this distance, the bright light of four spires could be seen clearly, like glowing white needles on a black canvas. "The queen's guard is a secret. Always has been. It requires total devotion. And faith."

"And before Trinity, I had none." I took a step back. My father was right not to have tried to convince me to serve in his secret queen's guard. Before my mate, I'd been existing day to day, with no hope or faith that anything would change. The night of Prime Nial's call for help, I'd been contemplating the fall of the great, mythical city of Mytikas itself, a city that had been home to the ancients, and then the royal bloodline for thousands of years. "I was a fool, Father."

"Now he understands." Nix lifted an arm in an impatient gesture, swinging it around. "Save the male bonding for later. We must find the princess."

"I don't know where she is exactly. But I know who is going to help us find her." I turned my glare to the consort, who'd remained as still as a statue the entire conversation. Perhaps hoping against hope that I would forget he was present, that his balls would remain intact.

"Me?" He took a step back, but the young guard I'd spoken to in the hall pressed an ion blaster to his back with a grin.

I was really starting to like that young male.

"Yes. You." I took a step toward him. "You know every secret passage in this fortress, or so you claimed when you used them to climb into my mate's bed to fuck her."

He had the decency to flush and look at the floor.

"The princess was seen being led up the grand staircase," I continued. "*Into* the palace. It would be stupid of her attacker to take himself deeper into a place with no escape. Do you know of any passages that lead to the outside? Escape routes?"

He blinked, confused for a heartbeat, but his eyes cleared and filled with purpose. He stood straighter with understanding. "Yes. There are three."

"Do any of them lead to the private chambers upstairs?"

He nodded. "Yes."

"And where is the exit?"

The consort looked around, unsure. "It's secret, my lord."

I looked at my father. "Jax's guard took her to the private quarters. I have no idea what his intention is, but whatever they want from Queen Celene, they obviously didn't get it. They are either getting desperate or thinking Trinity knows something."

My father stepped forward and placed a calming hand on the younger consort's shoulder. "The princess has been kidnapped and taken to the private quarters. We suspect the traitor is going to try to sneak her out of the palace. They might kill her. We need your help."

He swallowed hard.

"That tunnel exits inside the clerics' healing temple two blocks north of here." He nodded. "I can show you the way, but the tunnels inside the palace are too complicated for me to simply offer directions."

"All right," I replied, nodding. "Father, you and your guards split up. Send some to cover the exit he spoke of. Send some to go upstairs and make sure they can't escape through the palace interior. I'll go with the consort and search through the hidden passageways."

"I'll go with you." That was Nix, and it wasn't a request.

I didn't want to waste another moment arguing. I could use his help, for while the consort knew where he was going, his skill was in fucking, not fighting. The very idea hardened my resolve. I wanted to beat the shit out of him all over again, but vowed to save it for the Jax guard who truly deserved it. And that was right before I shot him dead.

"Let's go." I turned to the consort. "Lead the way. And make it fast."

My father and a handful of guards ran off, moving silently, like shadows. One guard peeled from the group, heading to the party, no doubt to round up others to cover the exit in the clerics' healing temple. Nix and I stared at the consort.

"Ahh—um... Maybe we should start in the library? There is an intersection nearby that leads to the royal bedrooms."

Nix and I both drew our weapons.

The consort jumped, then realized we weren't going to shoot him and ran off in the direction of the library—a room I had yet to discover—with the two of us right behind him.

rinity

I HAD no idea where we were in the palace. If I ever got out of this, I would get someone to take me on a tour. This room hadn't been used in a long time, perhaps since my mother had been around. I dropped my earring behind me, thankful my big skirt hid the action. I had nothing left to take off. My dress wasn't coming undone without help. The only good thing was that we were moving the dust all around, our footprints and weird swirls from the hem of my dress now marred the floor. Someone would easily see someone had been here, and recently. Hopefully, in time.

The guard reached out, grabbed my wrist and tugged me toward a corner. There was no escape, no way out. "If you're going to kill me, just do it."

He laughed. "I told you, Princess, you're wanted by my master."

His hand pressed against the wall and a doorway was revealed. Crap. A hidden passage. Now no one would ever find me, especially since I had no idea where the passages led. Out, I assumed.

He tugged me down the narrow corridor parallel to the abandoned room's wall, then we turned. It was dark within, but I could see my feet, Zel before me. When Leo had led me through from my bedchamber to his, it had been exciting. Romantic even —except for the consort and his balls—but now I felt getting farther and farther away from anyone who might be able to help.

When I heard the pounding of heavy footsteps—not ours —I quickly changed my mind. Zel stopped, listened. Yes, someone was in the passageway.

"We're here!" I shouted, the sound echoing off the narrow walls.

"You bitch," Zel hissed, spinning around and backhanding me. I fell into the wall and I put my hand to my cheek. The metallic tang of blood filled my mouth and stars floated in front of my eyes, but I was fine. I could do this. I could survive until whomever was in the corridor got help.

He shoved me back the way we came and I stumbled. A tight grab on my elbow kept me from falling, then I was shoved again. We came back out into the abandoned room. Without letting go of his hold, he stormed toward the exit—the way we'd originally come in—but the door flung open.

Two guards burst through, pistols raised. With a harsh yank, Zel pulled me into his side, his arm banding about my waist. The knife was back, this time at my neck.

It was Leo's father who stood before us, along with a second guard in a matching uniform.

"Put the weapons down!" Zel shouted.

Travin and the other guard held their arms out away from their sides but didn't drop their ion pistols.

The footfall we'd heard in the passageway was loud behind us. Zel spun partially so he could see who came in behind us.

Leo!

A thrill shot through me at the sight of him, but I frowned as I recognized the assassin from the suite. The one who'd killed the consort, Cassander and tried to kill me and my sisters.

Was Zel and the assassin in on it together? Was he Zel's master?

But the assassin—Vennix, I remembered—held his ion pistol steady. And it wasn't aimed at Leo or even his father, but at Zel.

I didn't understand, but with the knife at my neck, I wasn't going to try and figure it out now.

Leo eyed me, raked his gaze over me from head to toe. I was whole, but I was sure I had a swollen cheek and would probably get a black eye. And I knew I had stained the dress red with a bit of blood where Zel had poked and twisted the blade under my ribs.

"It's over, Zel," Travin said.

"Put the weapons down or she's dead," he shouted.

I felt his ragged breathing against my back, the shaking of his muscles.

"You're dead. You just haven't realized it yet," Leo countered.

We were at a standoff. When the knife pricked my neck, I hissed.

I could tell Leo wanted to jump him, rip the knife from his hand and kill him, but I'd be dead first. No ReGen wand in the universe could heal a jugular from being severed.

"I will go with you," I said, glancing at Travin, then Leo, although my words were for Zel. "Leo, tell the guards to stand down. Spread word to let us pass through the palace."

"No fucking way," he vowed.

I wasn't Destiny. I couldn't fight my way out of this. I wasn't Faith. I couldn't humor my way out of a knife at my throat. But I was Princess Trinity, and I could think my way out.

"Remember the saying, mate. If you can't get out of it..."

Leo's eyes flickered with awareness before he finished. "Get into it." He slowly squatted down, put his weapon on the floor. Told the others to do the same.

They didn't look thrilled with the idea, but they followed Leo's order.

"You got what you wanted, Zel. The weapons are down." I tried to keep my voice calm, my tone even. Diplomatic, although it was totally fake and coated with lies.

"They'll let us pass, but I can't walk with a knife in my neck."

Leo took a half step back and the others did as well.

After a few seconds, Zel moved the knife away and nudged me toward the door. I moved forward about two feet, then did what I'd been waiting for. I stepped back, my leg going between Zel's. Since my hands were at my sides, it was easy for me to grab his crotch. Yeah, I could easily feel his cock and balls beneath my palm. This wasn't a lover's caress. No, it was a *get the fuck off of me* grip just like with the Royal Consort.

I grabbed, squeezed and tugged as I dropped my weight. Zel's hold loosened and I could see out of the corner of my eye Leo grabbing his weapon and firing.

One shot. That was all it took. Zel's head was gone, his body falling to the ground with a hard thud. His groin slipped from my tight hold as he went. It was only then that my brain stalled, that I couldn't even think of what to do next.

But that didn't matter. Leo had me in his arms and was carrying me across the room before I had a chance to blink. The feel of him, god. He felt so good. Big, strong. His steady heartbeat beneath my ear. He was safe. Whole. Alive.

So was I.

I started to shake as Leo looked down at me, studied my face, my neck. Setting me on my feet, he grabbed the ReGen wand from his belt and waved it over my face. I closed my eyes to the blue glow, but felt the sting in my busted lip disappear, the nick in my neck no longer throb. He ran it over the small cut under the bodice of my dress, then twirled me around, must have seen something similar in my back, and used the wand there as well before spinning me back around to face him.

I heard voices behind me, but ignored them. Others had come into the room, but Leo didn't move, didn't even talk to anyone else, just tended to me.

"Better, mate?"

I opened my eyes, saw that the ReGen wand was gone and so was all my pain. I nodded and that was all Leo needed before he lowered his mouth to mine. Kissed me with all the fervor and need we both felt from the incident. His hands cupped my face gently, but his lips told the truth. He'd been scared. Worried.

Yeah, I had too.

"Excuse me, Princess."

A voice from behind me had Leo lifting his head. He wasn't ashamed though. No, he looked annoyed at being interrupted.

Leo pulled me into his side, just as Zel had, although this time I wanted to be there. I wanted to feel his hand on my waist, the heat of his strong body along my side.

The assassin bowed. "I wish to introduce myself properly. I am Vennix of the queen's guards. I apologize for deceiving you since your arrival."

Travin moved to stand beside him, blocking out the four or five other guards who were dealing with Zel's dead body. "You are well?" he asked.

I nodded.

"That was an interesting... move," he commented. "I apologize for not protecting you better."

I reached out and touched his arm. "None of us knew he was a traitor."

"I did," Nix commented. "And yet he still got to you."

"I am fine and he is... dead."

"I should have kept him alive to get him to talk," Leo said.

When I glanced up at him over my shoulder, I saw he was

mad at himself. "He talked to me. Told me he had a *master*. That he wanted the queen's jewels."

Nix and Travin looked to each other.

"We will talk with you more later," Nix said, then bowed. "I am sure your mate wishes to see to your wellbeing."

He said *wellbeing* in a way that meant *naked body*.

Another guard came over, handed my shoes to Travin, who turned to me. "I believe these are yours. We followed them, along with one of your earrings, to find you."

"Yes, an Earth children's tale had a good lesson in creating a trail." I held up my hands in surrender. "The other earring is on the floor somewhere. As for the shoes, they're lovely, but I never wish to see them again."

Travin and Nix bowed, then departed.

"Come, mate. You've been getting your hands on too many males' balls. I feel neglected."

Instead of taking my hand and leading me from the room, he swept me up in his arms again, and carried me out into the hallway.

I'd left a glass slipper for Leo to find, just like Cinderella. He was my hero.

But I didn't remember the part of the movie where the princess gets ravaged by her prince.

eo

SEEING a knife at Trinity's neck was the scariest thing I'd ever seen. Not a trio of Hive with weapons beyond our technology. Not being on a shuttle that had been hit by Hive fire and the planet's surface looming too fast. Nothing compared to seeing my mate in mortal danger.

I should have kept Zel alive. Should have kept him breathing so we could interrogate him. Learn what he knew. Trinity had said he hadn't acted alone. He was a mere pawn. I had to wonder even if we'd ripped his fingernails off if he'd say the name of his *master*. I had to wonder if he even knew who it really was. He was a pawn and had been used.

Discarded.

But that didn't matter. Not now. Only Trinity mattered. She might think otherwise, worry for her mother's life—wherever the fuck she was—and the safety of her sisters. The queen knew she had enemies, that was why she'd had to flee the planet in the first place. She'd known they were still around, that they'd come for her eventually. That was why she'd prepared her three daughters. Trinity was skilled enough in protocol and leadership to take over the throne from her mother. Queen Celene knew this and was prepared for her spire light to be extinguished.

It was my duty to the queen to keep Trinity alive. Safe.

And I'd almost failed tonight.

That would not happen again. I'd be at her side all the time. Hell, I'd be *inside* her all the time. At least for the next few days. My father—who hadn't even told me about his band of special-ized mercenaries—could deal with the aftermath of Trinity's kidnapping. He didn't need me for that. He had Nix. My job wasn't with the queen's guards. My job was as Trinity's mate.

And I would show her how dedicated I was to the role. I kicked the door closed to my quarters, locked it. Tossed Trinity on the bed with a solid bounce.

Even if someone knocked on the door, I wasn't answering. The only way someone could communicate with me or the princess was through my NPU. And it damned well better only be Nial and then only if it were life or fucking death.

I turned, stared down at my mate in all the frothy pale blue fabric.

"The dress has to go."

I stalked to her, tugged her so she stood on the bed, then spun her about so she faced away from me. The fastenings down her back were plentiful and tedious, almost impossible for my big fingers. So I ripped the back of the dress, rent the fabric so it split in two, then carefully worked the straps from her shoulders.

Fuck, she had on nothing beneath. For when the dress pooled on the bed around her ankles, she was bare. Her perfect heart-shaped ass was right before me.

She turned around and now her breasts were right. Fuck-ing. There.

If she were offering, I would take, so I sucked one pert tip into my mouth, felt it harden against my tongue. Her hands went to my hair and tangled, held me in place.

"Leo," she breathed.

My cock, which I discovered would flag when my mate had a knife at her throat, was hard as a rock, pulsing to break free of my uniform pants.

I didn't release her nipple from my mouth as I worked my pants loose, toed off my boots, removed my belt and holster. I had to pull back long enough to tug off my jacket and remove my shirt.

"You're so gorgeous," she breathed, running her hands over my chest. "Hurry."

"You want fast, mate? Works for me. This time."

I lifted her up so I could yank her dress away, let it fall to the floor. I lowered her to the bed and I settled on top of her.

"Yes," she breathed, letting the word go long. "God, you feel so good."

She parted her legs, bent her knees so I could settle at the juncture of her thighs, let my cock nestle against her wet heat.

"Now, Leo. Please, now."

I looked down at her, saw the dark desperation in her eyes, felt her anxiousness in the way she moved, trying to get closer. The only way to do that was to shift my hips and slide into her. Deep. Deeper still.

She cried out as I filled her. Stretched her. "It's like coming home," I murmured against her neck. I rested on my forearms as I held my weight off her, even with my cock bottoming out inside her.

"Yes. God, it's perfect."

I moved then, gave her what she needed. Me. Us. To feel alive. Together. To know she was safe beneath me, that she was whole with me filling her up.

"You want to come, mate?"

Her hips lifted to meet my hard thrusts.

"Yes!" she cried.

With a hand behind her, I rolled us so she was on top. Her legs moved so she straddled me, keeping me deep inside.

"Ride me. I want to watch. I want to see you come. To watch those gorgeous breasts bounce as you take your pleasure. To feel your pussy milk the cum from my balls. To see you come apart."

I settled my hands on her hips as she began to move. Her hands settled on my chest for balance as she lifted and lowered, circled and rubbed her clit against my lower belly. "Leo," she said once, then again. Like a chant as her eyes fluttered closed, her head fell back.

Her neatly styled hair hung wild and tangled down her back, her nipples hard and upturned. Her pussy was dripping and slick, my cock sliding in and out of her without any resistance.

I knew the second she was going to come. Her inner walls clenched down and there was no way I could hold back my own release a second longer. I was done for.

The building could collapse. The queen's guard could burst through the doors. I would know none of it for I was lost in Trinity. In what we created. In the pleasure we wrung from each other's bodies.

She was mine. Whatever the future brought, we'd tackle it together. And we'd get through it, one orgasm at a time.

∗∗∗

Ready for more? Read Faith's story in Faith: Ascension Saga - Volume 2 next!

Faith Jones is an Earth girl...and she's not.
She's half Aleran. And not just any half – a royal half.

Her mother is the queen, her sister is the heir, and her twin is determined to kill every alien on the planet if that's what it takes to find their kidnapped mother. Faith's job? Infiltrate the Jax household and spy on one of the most powerful families on the planet. There is a traitor in that house, and Faith is determined to find him, no matter the cost.

Thordis Jax always gets what he wants. He's rich. He's gorgeous. He's the heir to one of the most powerful families on the planet. But when his body comes alive at the sight of Faith Jones, it will take every ounce of seduction and skill he possesses to get into her bed—and to earn her trust.

Faith thinks she's got it all under control, until she meets Lord Jax's oldest son, Thordis. He's sexy. He's hot as hell. And the first time he sees her, he tells her the one thing she absolutely does not want to hear...Mine!

A real Romeo and Juliet scenario. Which just stinks. Because as Faith discovers, it's tough to hunt down a traitor when the only thing her heart wants is to give everything to an enemy.

Click here to get Faith: Ascension Saga - Volume 2 now!

THE ASCENSION SAGA

Thank you for joining me on this exciting journey in the Interstellar Brides® universe. The adventure continues...

www.AscensionSaga.com

FIND YOUR INTERSTELLAR MATCH!

YOUR mate is out there. Take the test today and discover your perfect match. Are you ready for a sexy alien mate (or two)?

VOLUNTEER NOW!

interstellarbridesprogram.com

DO YOU LOVE AUDIOBOOKS?

Grace Goodwin's books are now available as
audiobooks...everywhere.

LET'S TALK SPOILER ROOM!

Interested in joining my **Sci-Fi Squad**? Meet new like-minded sci-fi romance fanatics and chat with Grace! Get excerpts, cover reveals and sneak peeks before anyone else. Be part of a private Facebook group that shares pictures and fun news! Join here:

https://www.facebook.com/groups/scifisquad/

***

Want to talk about Grace Goodwin books with others? Join the **SPOILER ROOM** and spoil away! Your GG BFFs are waiting! (And so is Grace)

Join here:

https://www.facebook.com/groups/ggspoilerroom/

GET A FREE BOOK!

JOIN MY MAILING LIST TO BE THE FIRST TO KNOW OF NEW RELEASES, FREE BOOKS, SPECIAL PRICES AND OTHER AUTHOR GIVEAWAYS.

http://freescifiromance.com

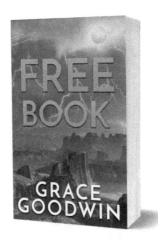

ALSO BY GRACE GOODWIN

Her Cyborg Beast

Cyborg Fever

Rogue Cyborg

Cyborg's Secret Baby

Her Cyborg Warriors

Interstellar Brides® Program: The Virgins

The Alien's Mate

His Virgin Mate

Claiming His Virgin

His Virgin Bride

His Virgin Princess

Interstellar Brides® Program: Ascension Saga

Ascension Saga, book 1

Ascension Saga, book 2

Ascension Saga, book 3

Trinity: Ascension Saga - Volume 1

Ascension Saga, book 4

Ascension Saga, book 5

Ascension Saga, book 6

Faith: Ascension Saga - Volume 2

Ascension Saga, book 7

Ascension Saga, book 8

Ascension Saga, book 9

Destiny: Ascension Saga - Volume 3

Other Books

Their Conquered Bride   .

Wild Wolf Claiming: A Howl's Romance

ABOUT GRACE

Grace Goodwin is a USA Today and international bestselling author of Sci-Fi and Paranormal romance with more than one million books sold. Grace's titles are available worldwide in multiple languages in ebook, print and audio formats. Two best friends, one left-brained, the other right-brained, make up the award-winning writing duo that is Grace Goodwin.

They are both mothers, escape room enthusiasts, avid readers and intrepid defenders of their preferred beverages. (There may or may not be an ongoing tea vs. coffee war occurring during their daily communications.) Grace loves to hear from readers!

All of Grace's books can be read as sexy, stand-alone adventures. But be careful, she likes her heroes hot and her love scenes hotter. You have been warned...

www.gracegoodwin.com
gracegoodwinauthor@gmail.com

ABOUT GRACE

Grace Goodwin is a USA Today and international bestselling author of Sci-Fi and Paranormal romance with more than one million books sold. Grace's titles are available worldwide in multiple languages in ebook, print and audio formats. Two best friends, one left-brained, the other right-brained, make up the award-winning writing duo that is Grace Goodwin.

They are both mothers, escape room enthusiasts, avid readers and intrepid defenders of their preferred beverages. (There may or may not be an ongoing tea vs. coffee war occurring during their daily communications.) Grace loves to hear from readers!

All of Grace's books can be read as sexy, stand-alone adventures. But be careful, she likes her heroes hot and her love scenes hotter. You have been warned...

www.gracegoodwin.com
gracegoodwinauthor@gmail.com